FORGOTTEN DESIRE

THE DESIRE SERIES BOOK 6

BARBARA DONLON BRADLEY

FORGOTTEN DESIRE
Copyright © 2024 by Barbara Donlon Bradley

ISBN: 979-8-88653-221-0

Published by Satin Romance
An Imprint of Melange Books, LLC
White Bear Lake, MN 55110
www.satinromance.com

Published in the United States of America.

Cover Design by Ashley Redbird Designs

ONE

S torm held Heather close as she continued to sleep. His fingers brushed against her soft skin. As busy as their schedule was, it was nice to have a little of the morning to themselves. Heather still wasn't getting enough rest dealing with the twins and he did his best to let her nap when he had the chance, even though he could think of other things they could be doing right now.

"You do have a one-track mind." Heather opened her eyes and looked at him.

"You are supposed to be sleeping." He ran his knuckles along her jawline.

"It's hard to sleep when you keep thinking of our intimacy. Were those memories or fantasies?"

He gave her one of his bone-melting smiles as he pressed her back into the bed. "Yes."

"Yes?" She smiled up at him.

"Because somewhere along the way my fantasies become reality and then memories." He nuzzled her throat.

"Is the door locked?" She tilted her head so he could have better access.

"No. Why?" His lips caressed her mark, sending little frissons of heat through her blood.

"Because your son has figured out how to open the door."

"He's not tall enough to reach the panel to open the door." Storm stopped long enough to lift his head and looked at her. "But it doesn't surprise me he figured out another way. He is our son."

"I sure don't want him tottering in here at the wrong time." She touched his face.

"Then he won't." Storm surged into her. Tendrils of excitement filled her as he entered her. She wrapped her legs around his waist.

"What?" She shifted so she could accept him in deeper.

"Haven't you noticed that they are never looking for us when we're arguing, amorous, or intimate?" He pulled out and drove back in. "You have a mental connection with them that tells the children when it is safe to come in."

She brushed her fingers against his mark and was greeted by him sucking in his breath. "Too much talking."

He chuckled as he pressed his lips to her mark. "I have created a monster."

"One you are very proud of."

"Oh yes." He pulled her into a sitting position, bracing his arm along her spine to give her support as she slid up and down his length. Her muscles rippled against him as she moved. They shared everything, including their intimacy. He could feel her desire as it swirled through her, filling her with excitement.

Storm leaned her away from him a little so he could hit the spot that brought her more powerful orgasms. Each time he brushed the spot, her need blossomed to a point where she felt her body shake with each stroke. One particular stroke drew a moan out of her. She was close, so close.

Muscles tightened against Storm, and her blood hummed. Slowly the heat built in her stomach. The flames licked along her insides until it enveloped her, sending her out to the stars.

Storm eased her back onto the bed as he continued to rock into her. Another moan escaped. Everything tightened again. The heat of his mouth latched onto her mark as his release started to unfurl. Feeling his orgasm brought her to the brink again. She soared through it with him.

"Beautiful." He brushed a few strands of hair from her face. "My heart."

"A great way to start the day." She smiled up at him. Her smile widened when she sensed her son opening the door. *Someone has come to visit.*

"Papa?" Terrik, their son, toddled over to the bed.

"Yes, son?" He touched her face once more before rolling off her and looked down at his son. One of the biggest joys in his life was their children. Terrik was brilliant like his mother yet had the ability to strategize like him. A sharp wit and a smile that reminded him of his own gave Storm a hint at what his mother went through with him before he mated with Heather. His daughter rivaled her brother in intelligence and her mother in beauty. Shyer than her brother, she would look at people with her big violet eyes and melt any male's heart who saw her. He knew he would have his hands full when his children started coming of age, but he welcomed the challenge.

"Mama wake yet?" He looked up at Storm with gold eyes surrounded by a violet ring and a bright smile.

"Yes, she is." Storm offered his arm to his son who grabbed it just above his wrist so his father could lift him to the bed. Something they had started when Terrik had been old enough to crawl to the side of their bed. He held his son until Heather could move. She always needed a few moments to regain her mobility after they were intimate. "You're awake a little early today."

The boy snuggled against his father as Heather watched him. "Heart."

"I know, she's my heart, too." He pulled his son close and pressed a kiss to his head. Storm smiled at how fast the twins picked up on key phrases and words.

Heather smiled when he crawled to her side. He was careful to not disturb her too much as he snuggled against her.

"Heart, mama."

"You're my heart too, sweetheart." She touched his face. "Just like your sisters and your father. Where is your sister? She's normally right behind you."

"Sleeping."

"Perhaps we should go check and see if she is awake now." Heather sat up with the cover wrapped around her.

"Do you need some time, my heart?" Storm looked at his son curled up against her. She normally spent a little time with the children when they first woke but had promised to be ready quickly. They had hoped to be back before the children would wake up. This changed things. "We need to travel to Bert's compound this morning. I told him we would be there as soon as we got up. He is expecting us, but I'm sure we can take a little time if you need it."

"We can go as soon as I get dressed. It won't take me long to get ready. Kuarto and Tiko have promised to take care of the twins while we're gone." She stretched, careful to keep the cover up to shield her nakedness. Nudity wasn't something Vespians found embarrassing, but being raised on Earth she still was a bit shy showing her body to her children.

"Not the great spoiler?" Storm picked up his son and placed him on his chest.

"Your mother has council meetings today and the last time your son was in council chambers he was a bit too active. He disrupted several disputes, forcing Kuarto to go and get him. She had to promise to take time off when she watched the children after that." Heather didn't keep the laughter out of her voice. "I promised her it would be her turn next time. Bert said we could bring them with us, but Kuarto has been pestering to spend time with them."

"You have come to trust Bert," Storm commented as he entertained their son while Heather got out of bed and dressed.

"He has been honest with us so far and has taught us a lot about our abilities. I feel he can be trusted." She closed the seals on her gown then reached for the boy. She touched his nose as she turned from the bed. "And how is my little protector this morning?"

He pressed his hand against her heart the way he had seen his parents do so many times. "Hungry."

She laughed, hugged him and headed to the twin's room. "Then let's get your sister and feed you two."

Storm climbed out of bed and dressed while she fed the children. He came into the main room once he sealed his uniform and picked up the cup of coffee Heather had waiting for him. "Do you think Terrik knows what the gesture means?"

"He knows that gesture is one of the ways we show affection for each other." Heather leaned against her mate with her cup when he came up behind her and wrapped his arms around her. "The fact he wants to do it too is just so sweet."

"You still have trouble leaving them behind, don't you?" He hugged her close when he heard her voice fill with such emotion.

"You have the same problem." Careful of their coffee, she

turned in his arms and touched his face. "Besides it will only be for a few hours."

"And we need to get going." He took her cup and placed his and hers on the table. "The transport is ready. Is your brother coming here or are we bringing the children to him?"

"I'm coming here," said Kuarto as he walked in.

"You don't knock?" Storm growled when he realized the man was behind him.

"I was told I didn't have to." He walked up to Heather and kissed her on the cheek. "Being family has its perks."

"The children are almost finished with their breakfast." Heather started running through her list of things to do for the children. "I have their clothes laid out on their beds. Um, they do dress themselves, but you might need to help Terrik. He has a little trouble getting the seals closed properly."

"They'll be fine, Heather. Stop worrying." He sat with the children as they finished their meals. "Now go. We're going to have fun today."

"Mama?" asked their daughter, Zunarka. "You leave us?"

"You get to be with Kuarto and Toki for a little while today." She touched her daughter's cheek. "We'll be back soon."

"Can we go to garden?" asked their son. He had already dismissed them and was ready to play.

Storm put an arm around Heather's waist and escorted her out of the room. "Your soft heart would keep us there another hour if I didn't pull you away."

"I'm not that bad." She looked up at him. "Am I?"

"It's one of the reasons why you are my heart."

———

It didn't take them long to get to Bert's compound. Once the elders had a chance to question Bert, they gave him permission to stay on some land in a remote area of Vespia so he could do his research on what happened to the rest of the ancients. They felt it was better not to alert the entire race that they had a living, breathing ancient among them. If the planet was aware of his presence, they would never leave Bert alone.

Heather and Storm walked into his main computer room and found him working on assembling a large piece of equipment. He had parts floating in the air as he used a three-dimensional image to move them around until they were ready to be put into place. There were small clamps on the pieces floating that allowed them to defy gravity.

"You have been busy." Storm looked around at all the different components Bert now had up and running, not sure if he was happy with the elders' decision. The only other ancient they had been involved with had a fixation on his mate and he feared the same thing would happen again over time, but Heather trusted the man so he kept his opinions to himself.

So far Bert had been the exact opposite of Ialog, but how long would that last? Would he develop that strange overpowering desire to have Heather the way that Ialog had? She was part of his visions. He had told them she was important to the future of their races. Would he try to take matters into his own hands like Ialog did? Storm knew he had to be leery, or they could be caught unawares.

"A lot of the equipment I need for my search was already in my ship so it was easy to transfer it. Others I brought from my other compound, plus I have been working on a few more to make sure I have everything I need to begin my search." He looked at Storm. "I know you have no reason to trust me. Ialog did ruin that, but I promise I have no ulterior motive. I just want to find my people. It is hard knowing I am alone."

Did the man just read his mind?

Heather touched Storm's arm. He could see that she understood. She had lived with being unique all her life. He placed his hand on top of hers. He trusted her. If she felt Bert was safe, then he would too. For now.

The simple gesture had him wanting her again. She started smiling at him so he knew his eyes had started glowing once more. Good thing they had the ship with their favorite chair in it. He just might get a scream from her on their way back.

Storm walked around, looking at the different pieces of equipment. All types of machines covered the walls along with several large screens. "Fridon would love this place."

"Then bring him next time." Bert grinned as he worked on connecting a board to one of the screens. "I enjoy his sharp mind."

Storm nodded as he rested his hip on one of the consoles.

"Oh, Storm don't lean there—" Bert frowned as Storm winked out of sight. "Oh, dear."

———

Bert sprinted to where Storm had stood only seconds ago. This wasn't good. Storm wasn't supposed to disappear this soon. Was he? The information he knew about Storm's time travel gave him the impression it wouldn't happen for a few months. How did the timeline get off? How was he going to fix it? Using a handheld device, he scanned the area then started pulling up data.

"Oh dear?" Heather grabbed him by the shoulder, turning him to face her. "What do you mean by 'oh dear?' Where did he go?"

"It's not the where I'm that worried about, it's the when." The data he looked through on his handheld also filled one of the screens. Heather watched in awe as he flipped through thousands of images in seconds. It didn't take him long to find him, but he knew where to look.

"The when?" Heather rubbed her forehead.

"I know this doesn't make sense." He needed to explain instead of just ignoring her and trying to fix what happened. "The thing Storm rested against is a time machine. I have used it as a viewing apparatus to watch and learn about people I had to deal with as well as travel to times and places I wanted to learn more about. I assembled it here so I can travel where and when I need to gather clues on what happened to my people. Not knowing where to start I wanted to start in the past, from where I last saw them.

"It was on because I was finishing the installation. But it wasn't set properly. Normally I have a timeline and location set, along with how long I plan on being there. It also has the DNA sequence of the person going back so they don't get harmed by the transfer. Storm set it off without any of that being done so although I now know the where and when he went, I doubt he remembers anything. Extracting him is going to be complicated and we have to be careful on how we do that."

"Wait. A time machine? No one has been able to control time travel yet." Heather moved close to the machine, but Bert blocked her way. If she touched it the same thing would happen to her, and he didn't need two of them lost in time.

He hoped he was right about where and when Storm landed, but he needed to check history to make sure the timeline was still intact. If Storm was supposed to go back now, then he was safe, and the next step would be to send Heather after her mate.

"None of the races you're familiar with have the technology yet, but we have been able to successfully control it." He moved to another computer to get historical data before going back to the time machine.

"Great. So my mate is trapped back in time somewhere? Bert, we have to bring him home."

Bert watched her as she looked at the machine. He knew she was thinking if she did what her mate did would it send her back to the same point in time? Heather instinctively moved toward the machine to find her way blocked by Bert again.

"Please don't touch anything. Without it being prepared properly you don't know when or where it will send you and your mind will be wiped. You could end up on another planet and in another timeline if I don't do this right. That won't do Storm any good. Once I verify a few things we'll work on bringing him back. It shouldn't take too long. I promise."

Bert laid his handheld on the surface. The equipment he sat it on hummed as it worked.

"Why didn't your machine send that little handheld off to who knows when?" Heather asked when the device didn't disappear.

"Safety protocols because of my DNA." He gestured to it. "It's on the handheld."

Heather gave him an exasperated look.

"Dealing with a time machine is tricky work. In order for me to touch it over and over without being sent all over time uncontrollably I set protocols in that remote. The machine reads the remote which tells it to remain idle. I have to have that handheld on the machine to control it while I program the machine. Normally I have it set not to send anything without permission, but because I was still installing it and never expected Storm to touch it, I hadn't quite gotten to that. It's hard to install the protocol when the machine isn't fully installed and calibrated." Although he should have. He knew Storm time traveled; he just didn't know when until now. He had thought it happened a little too early, but the timeline hadn't changed so he was feeling more optimistic. Bert pressed a few buttons. "Storm is on Earth. Looks like the western section of the…oh dear."

"Again with the 'oh dear?' What now?"

"He's in the early twenty-first century. Looks like Washington State of the United States." He turned to look at Heather. Storm was where he was supposed to be. He didn't see the connection with the location until now. "Isn't that where Ialog kept you when he kidnapped you on Earth?"

"Yes. It is also where I was found as a child and where I left Sam after I wiped her memories. Wonder why that area seems to be a focal point." Heather pointed to the machine. "Have you calibrated it?"

"Yes."

"So retrieve him."

'It's not that easy." He picked up his handheld and looked at the data on the screen. "Because the machine hasn't been configured for his DNA it can't read him properly. Retrieving him won't work. Someone will have to go after him."

"I'll go." She took a step toward the machine.

"Heather, slow down."

———

"Slow down? Bert, I want my mate back." Now she knew how Storm felt when she disappeared. The thought of him not being here for her had her stomach in knots. A feeling she didn't like.

"His mind was overloaded by the transport. According to the records I'm finding in history, he's been in that timeline for about two years. There have been no ripples in our timeline so he was supposed to go back there to have the universe we know. I can't change that, or we could find ourselves in a different timeline. And what is going to be a problem is your mate has been diagnosed with amnesia." He looked at Heather. "He won't know who you are."

"But I can still go back and get him, right?"

"Yes, but I'll need a little time before you leave. You can't go back and just drag him forward. You need to make him remember before you can bring him forward and I don't know how long that will take. I'll need to create a life for you in that timeline. A history that withstands scrutiny. Although their computers were still in the beginning stages, their security systems were great at ferreting out false information. You need to have an iron-clad identity. I also need to give you the proper supplies to survive then as well."

Survive? How long was this going to take? "Why are you going through all this? I just want to go in, make him remember, and then bring him home?"

"I'll explain as we go." Bert crossed to another screen and worked on a keyboard near it. "It shouldn't take too long to get everything ready."

Heather didn't like the fact that her mate had been on Earth with no memory of her for two years. He had a libido that would cripple the normal human. How many women had he slept with since he had been gone? And how many had he put in the hospital?

The sooner she went back and found him the happier she would be.

"I need to make a manual upload to your insert." He stepped up to Heather and made adjustments to her device. "There. You should have all the details of the life I have made for you. I have also given you timeline events that need to take place while you're there. That green color will run along the edge of your sight the whole time. If you see it turn red you need to let me know."

"How am I to do that?" Images and information flooded her mind. "Wow."

"I'm working on that as well. Now I won't be able to talk to you directly, so making sure those things that downloaded happen will allow me to follow you as you move through the timeline properly. If something goes off, I'm going to set an alarm to go off here, so I'll know." He stepped back and went to the console that sent Storm away. "I know you're anxious to get going, but I have a few more things to do before I can send you back. My job right now is to make sure you have everything you need to bring him home."

"Just hurry, Bert. I want my mate back." Heather crossed her arms over her chest while she waited. She knew she looked like Storm but didn't care. Not knowing what she was going to find when she found him made her nervous.

———

"Bert." This was taking too long.

"I know you're anxious." He finished what he was working on. "For you."

Heather walked around the motorcycle Bert showed her. She liked the sleek design. This was going to be her mode of transportation back in time? It made her smile.

"This vehicle has two functions. One is for you to use in the timeline you are going to. I have created it so it will fit in with the vehicles they use. The other is it is your time-traveling device. It will take you there and bring you both back." He patted the seat. "I thought the design fit you."

It reminded her of the air bikes on Vespia. The two tires were where the resemblance ended. "Tires, really?"

"Yes. They still used personal vehicles instead of transports. Everything traveled on roads instead of in the air like you're used to." Excitement danced in his eyes. "When you are going still rely on fossil fuel to run their transportation. They have started to work with alternative fuels but so far only solar and electric were popular when it came to transportation. This will store the fossil fuel they use, and I have programmed the bike to use it, so you won't draw attention to yourself by running a machine that never needs gas, but it will take a lot longer to disappear than any of the vehicles there and it will burn the gas cleanly. No pollution. If someone asks you about what kind of mileage you get there are three key words to use. One is new, the second is prototype, and the third is hybrid. The mileage you will actually get won't be believed. If you have to come up with a number for someone who is a little too curious take the average mileage for a motorcycle and double it. That data should be in the information I have downloaded already."

She nodded. There was a lot of data in her mind for her to go through so she could fit into the timeline. She hoped it would be easy to sort it out when she needed it. Heather touched the handlebars. "I do like the design."

"Good. I did my best to mimic the designs of the timeline. It does have a few perks from our timeline that will work there. In order to make sure it can travel back and forth the energy source is protected against EM pulses and time fluctuations." He pulled up the computer system. "I have included a shield that will protect you if you were to have a spill as well."

"I'm a good rider, Bert."

"I'm not questioning your abilities, but during this timeline there are accidents because people aren't paying attention. Although they have GPS and cell phones, the computer systems in their vehicles haven't been designed to drive the car yet. You could get bumped by a car switching lanes because they didn't see you. The bike also has a holographic program that will hide the fact that you can't damage the machine. If you get into something where the bike should be damaged the system will create a false image that can be seen and touched from any angle." He turned on the hologram so she could see what he was talking about and grinned at her. "I'm quite proud of that."

Heather walked up to the bike which now looked like it had slid across concrete and touched the damage. It felt real to her. "That is wonderful."

"All you need to do to get the original look is rearrange the crystals here." He opened a panel and moved a couple of the crystals, then the bike went back to normal. "Even damaged the bike will still work so you do have to be careful if you do end up in some sort of fender bender as the locals call it. Make sure the bike working seems believable if you do get in an accident."

"Wow." She loved this.

"There are a few other things I'll go over before you leave but I want to focus on this garment first." He moved to her suit and held it up for her to see. "This is designed to withstand the temporal change. There is a second one for Storm that I have put in the bottom of the saddle bags."

"And the suit will protect us?"

"Yes. A spare helmet, boots, and gloves are built into the frame of the bike for Storm when he's ready to come back. The suit will also double as a regular garment while you're there. If you don't close all the seals, you can wear it in units, and it will look like a biker outfit." He separated the seals so she could see what he was talking about. "This will keep you protected while you're riding so please use it when you should."

"Why is that important?"

"Because I think you're going to be there a while. According to history, Storm was a bit of a recluse, only leaving a mountain hideaway to do photoshoots. You might not find him right away."

"He's a photographer?" Heather shook her head. "I would have thought he'd be in the military. I can see him as a drill sergeant."

"He probably doesn't know how to control his shifting so keeps to himself as much as possible." Bert handed her a small pile of clothing. "This should be up to the fashion there. You can pick up more once you arrive."

"What type of bartering system are they using?" She didn't like the sinking feeling she was getting. How hard was this going to be? "Cash?"

"Yes, and I have that for you as well. They also use plastic."

"Plastic?"

"I'll explain that in a few minutes."

Heather nodded. This was a lot to absorb.

"I can get you to the area he has shown up the most, but there is no record of his address in any of the files. Any money he received for his work was done with direct deposit, and he had a post box as a mailing address. There's no record of a physical address. If he needed something delivered, he used a local diner. That is where I would start."

"Post box?"

"It was a small box one could rent from the postal service where your mail could be delivered. The area I'm sending you to is remote. It is possible he doesn't live in a location where they could deliver mail to him." He touched her collarbone. "I won't be able to communicate with you. The delay will be too great." He handed her a small communication device. "But with this, we will be able to get messages to each other in case of an emergency. Like I said earlier, cell phones are prevalent when you're going so I created this handheld to mimic the standard smartphones most have there. You can also use it to fill in the gaps as you interact with the local people. You hear something you never heard of this will tell you what you need to know so you don't raise flags. The people then were into texting so that is how a lot of the data you might need will appear. All you need to do is glance at the screen. Since so many do the same thing, you won't look out of place."

"Anything else?" She wanted to get there and find her mate.

"Yes. I'm going to try to drop you into a secluded area, but you might be seen. Your landing will cause an EM pulse and knock out all the power there. I'm hoping there won't be anyone around, but you need to hide the bike and the suit as quickly as possible if you find there are too many who might see you and you can't ride away immediately."

Heather removed her dress and climbed into the suit, snapping her gloves and helmet on, but left the visor open. Sealed, it resembled the Vespian security uniform.

"I'll need to cover your mark."

"Why?" She placed her hand against where it was hidden by the suit. Her mark was something she wore with pride. It proved she was Storm's mate.

"Storm has the same mark. You could frighten him by having the same tattoo he does. That is what most people will think it is. Not having his memory he's not going to know that it shows his bond to you."

She hadn't thought of it that way. "Do we have to?"

"I think it's best."

Heather nodded. Not something she wanted but she did see the logic in it. She removed her helmet and bared her neck.

"I promise it will still be there. It will be like Skye's. Unseen, but still there."

Bert had a few more last-minute things that kept cropping up. She just wanted to go.

"If you're ready I'll send you back. Once you arrive, I'm going to continue to stream data to you so you have as much info I can give you to function there." He handed her a thin card.

"What is this?" She flipped it over.

"A credit card. That is what most of the people use there to store their money."

"And how did you get money into this timeline?"

"We have been traveling through time for a while. This is the generic account for any ancient to use. As long as you don't use too much of the money in one place you shouldn't draw any attention to you."

"And what is too much?"

"During this timeline? Ten thousand or more."

"Good to know."

"I have also made you money from that timeline. It should be enough to afford hotels and food for about a month." He handed her a thick wad of bills.

"That sure seems like a lot."

"I didn't go any higher than a hundred-dollar bill and those will raise eyebrows if you use too many at the same time."

"I'll try to be careful." She slipped the money inside her suit.

"You've never dealt with money like this. Try to stick to the smaller bills and only use the bigger ones when your total is high enough to warrant it. Cash can't be traced, but people in this timeline worry about people who flash too much cash. Try to give exact change whenever you can. Once you get there and start breaking bills, you'll be getting coins as well."

"Change. Right. The coins are less than the bills."

"Just remember this timeline is when homeland security had just started. It is what Earth security blossomed from. But when it first started, they were a bit overzealous because of what had happened." He went to the time machine. "To us it is ancient history but to the people you'll meet it was only twenty-three years ago."

"What are you talking about?"

"September eleventh, two thousand and one."

"Oh." There were many things in history that changed the shape of the world. The attack on the Twin Towers and the Pentagon was one of them. That one day started a series of events that led the planet to the world she knew. "Right. I'll be careful of what I say."

"The colloquial language is a lot different there too. Be prepared for that download. There is a lot." He tapped a few keys on the small pad he held. "Ready?"

She nodded. How bad could it be? Her mind was flooded with so much so quickly. She said the first thing that popped into her head. "Holy shit!"

"The download worked." He grinned. "The language of the time will flow naturally from you although you might mentally question your choice of words."

"This is crazy. Can I go now?" She grinned back. That was strange to her.

"Almost." Bert held out his hand. "You need to leave your rings behind. I know they mean a lot, but they might cause more trouble than you want with Storm."

"He's still going to see the marks they left behind." She sighed as she pulled them off and dropped them into his open hand.

"I know but it is easier to explain the lack of rings than why you'd be willing to break your vows with a stranger.

And that is how Storm will see you and any relationship you might try to start with him."

"What aren't you telling me?"

"There is a button on the bike that will bring you home when you're ready." He pointed to the button in question. He looked at her before answering her question. "Storm must remember before you can bring him back. If he fights the memory, then you need to stay with him and wait for him to remember."

"Okay. Why?"

"He'll never believe he's from another timeline or another planet. Forcing him to come back without knowing the truth could cause more trouble than you realize."

"But my brother has the ability to unlock the mind. Why can't I just go and bring him home? It doesn't make sense."

"I'm trying to keep the timeline intact. The handheld will also guide you to do the same thing. Any tiny changes could create a world you don't recognize when you come back so please understand that I ask you to listen to me without question. I can't explain everything because I'm afraid of changing things back there as well as here. I promise it will all make more sense when you're back there."

He was asking for a lot, but she needed to get to Storm and bring him home. She had to trust him. Heather nodded.

Bert smiled and continued explaining everything he could. "You also can use the button if you get into a situation that could cause bodily harm. But if you come back early, I might not be able to send you again so use it wisely."

She nodded again. The sooner she got going the sooner she could find her mate. She closed the helmet so she was sealed in.

"One last thing. If everything goes right no time will pass here while you're gone. You should return within a minute after you leave." He tapped a few more keys then looked at her. "Go stand by the bike and I'll send you on your way."

Heather did as he asked. The scene in front of her started to soften and then stretch as it broke into a thousand pieces. It felt like her body was being squeezed then pulled as she flew across the galaxy and time. Landing on Earth stunned her. She just stood there until Bert's comment about getting going as fast as she could filled her mind. She looked around and saw no one, jumped on the bike and took off.

Tires crunched against the rock-filled road she zipped along. Then she hit asphalt. The bike weaved a little as she adjusted to the new surface. It didn't take her long before she had control and was eating up the miles between her and her mate.

"Heather, you're going too fast. Speed limit here is sixty-five and they will stop you and give you a ticket if you're too far above that limit. You don't need to get yourself into any of the databases here."

She heard the computer's voice in her ear. She grinned as she slowed to the proper speed and continued. "I didn't know you were coming with me, Cim."

"Bert felt you might need me to assist you in this time-line. A friendly voice so to speak. I'm also tied into the phone Bert created for you."

"Ah. My handheld. Did he also alter the way you talked to fit into this timeline?"

"Yes, and the proper word is cell phone. They will merge with the handhelds but right now they are two different devices. In this timeline, handhelds are also known as tablets. The most famous one is the iPad. It watches movies, plays music, stores pictures, surfs the web, reads electronic books that can be downloaded into the device. There's more but you should realize that it's like a computer in many aspects."

"Pretty basic stuff then."

"But to these people, they are the cutting edge of technology." Her visor showed a truck stop that started to blink. "What is that?"

"A restaurant that Storm has been known for frequenting. It is also where he has packages delivered."

"Then I think we should go in for some coffee." Heather steered the bike into the parking lot. The place was busy. She turned her machine off and climbed off the bike. She felt nervous. Would he be here?

A little bell dinged when she entered the restaurant. The place was packed. The only empty spot was at the counter. Walking up to it, she felt lots of people watching her. Perhaps she should have removed her helmet outside.

"I believe it is the way you look in the suit," said Cim. "Heartbeats in most of the men have increased as they spotted you. They are aroused by your outfit."

"Great. Just what I need." She sat on the stool before releasing the seals on her gloves. Then she released the seals on her helmet. "Are you also part of my insert?"

"You want to know what happens when they see your face? I'll send you a text."

Heather pulled off her helmet and put her gloves inside. Her almost white hair now fell more than halfway down her back. Having it short for most of her life she was never one to spend a lot of time on it. A quick brush and she was done. Storm didn't mind, he loved her hair. One of the reasons it was so long now.

She heard a beep and looked at the phone. Cim's data on the men watching made her want to laugh. No matter where she was, she always got the same reaction.

A very pregnant woman stepped up to her. "What a ya' have?"

"Coffee for starters." Heather smiled at her. "When are you due?"

"About a month from now." She rubbed her belly absently. "Cream?"

"Please?" Heather picked up the menu that the woman handed her. There was a wide variety of food on the pages. So many she found it hard to pick something. Most of the people had gone back to what they were doing, giving her a chance to see what they were eating around her. A lot had breakfast in front of them. She looked up at the clock. The digital face said ten a.m.

The young woman came back with her cup and a few small white containers that she sat next to it. Heather picked one up. Okay. What was she supposed to do with them?

"Hey Patti, can I have the usual to go?" A man in jeans and a flannel shirt stepped up beside Heather.

"Where you off to now?" She pulled a pad out of the pocket of the apron she wore, jotted down some things and slapped it on the sill of a small window. "Order to go!"

"Florida. Got me going from one end of the country to the other. Have four days to get there."

"Four?" She poured coffee in a tall white foam holder then set the same small containers on the counter. He peeled the top back and poured the contents into the cup. He gave it a quick stir and the coffee lightened. Next, he grabbed a few packets in a small dish and poured them in as well. He took a sip and grimaced. He grabbed a few more packets. "Who made this? It takes like mud."

"Princess. Who else?" She pulled the empty packets off the counter. "Four days is pushing it, isn't it?"

"Yeah, but if I can do it in four days, I'll get a bonus. Got mouths to feed."

"You be safe." A bell rang behind her and a large brown

bag filled the small window. Patti picked up the bag and handed it to him.

"See you in two weeks." He lifted his cup to someone in the kitchen and headed back out.

Heather would love to ask a ton of questions, but at least she now knew what to do with the little white containers.

"Have you decided what you want?" Patti had turned her attention back to her.

"Um, yeah. Eggs, bacon and toast." She closed the menu.

"Bobby's favorite?"

"Huh?"

She opened the menu and pointed to the title of the dish. "Bobby's favorite."

"Oh." She felt like an idiot. "Sorry. Sure."

"You get grits or gravy with it."

"Don't really need either."

"I'll bring you gravy. It is the best. How you want your eggs?"

"Scrambled. Hard."

"You got it." Patti turned and gave her order to a cook. A tall good-looking man with dark hair and a well-kept beard filled the little window as he read over the order. They resembled each other. Heather would bet they were related somehow.

Heather picked up the creamer container, opened it, and poured it into her coffee. Since the computer always gave her a perfect cup, she didn't know how strong or how weak this cup would be. Her first sip wasn't bad, but she could still taste a touch of the bitterness she didn't care for. She looked at the small container that held the sugar packets. There were white ones, brown ones, pink ones, blue ones, and yellow ones. The white one said sugar so she went with that one. The packet tore open easily and she watched as the crystals fell into the dark liquid.

"A real sugar user, huh?"

Heather looked up at Patti. She looked tired.

"I love real sugar but turned diabetic with this bundle of joy. Found the yellow stuff closest to the real thing in coffee, even though I have to drink decaf." She rubbed her stomach. "Once the baby is born, I'm hoping for my first real cup of coffee in months. Decaf just isn't the same when you want high test."

"Don't they taste the same?"

"Not to me." Patti frowned for a moment.

"You okay?"

"Sure, sure." Patti smiled at her. "I'll bring your food to you as soon as it's ready."

Heather nodded as she watched the waitress move to one of her other tables. Another waitress passed her to drop off an order before heading to another group of tables Heather hadn't noticed right away. This place was a lot bigger than she first thought.

She watched her waitress. Patti wasn't moving right. Then it dawned on her. The baby had just dropped, making her waddle more than walk.

The cook came out of the kitchen with Heather's meal. After setting it on the counter in front of her he watched Patti as well.

"When did she say she was due?" Heather asked.

"Six weeks."

"You sure?" Heather looked at him. "She looks like she's going into labor now."

"What makes you say that?"

"The fact that the baby has dropped since I got here. Her walk too. The baby is getting in the way of her movements. It looks like her little bundle of joy is getting ready to come out."

"Hmm. Excuse me for a moment, will you?" He stepped away.

Heather took a bite of her eggs. Patti came up beside her and stopped moving for a moment, gripping the counter as she stood there.

"Sure wish you'd stop acting up." She spoke to her baby as she rubbed her stomach again. "It's really starting to annoy me."

Heather looked at the large clock on the wall in front of her, noting the time.

"You want some more coffee?" Patti asked her.

"Sure." Heather watched her as she continued to move slowly.

Patti brought over the coffee pot and freshened up her cup. "Oh, you already have your meal?"

"Your cook brought it to me while you were at a table."

"Mike didn't need to do that."

"I didn't want her food to get cold." He stepped out of the kitchen at that point. "And I had nothing left on the stove."

"Ha. You wanted to get a better look at the pretty biker chick."

"Patti!" He glanced at Heather, embarrassed by her comment.

"What? She is pretty and does ride a bike." Patti grabbed the counter again and frowned as she stopped moving for a minute.

"You're in labor," commented Heather as she took another sip of coffee.

"Don't be silly. I'm not due for six weeks." Patti let go of the counter but hadn't moved.

"Right. And babies know how to read a calendar. You grabbed this counter five minutes ago. That was when you complained that the baby was acting up. And you're doing it again five minutes later. You're sweating and I'm guessing it's from the pressure the baby is causing." Heather put down her coffee. "Shall I go on?"

"I'm not in labor!" Patti stomped her foot. Her face showed fear when her water broke and gushed to the floor.

"Yeah. I tend to disagree." Heather stood and took her to a chair near an empty table. "Sit."

"I can't be in labor yet." She lowered herself to the chair. "Mike needs me for four more weeks. This is his busy season. And Bo won't be back for three weeks."

"Don't worry about the restaurant and I'll call Bo." Mike pulled his cell phone out of his pocket.

"But you'll be short of help." She looked at him.

"Patti, I can help him out if that will stop you from worrying." Heather crouched down beside her and placed her hand on the woman's stomach, wishing her brother or Micali was there. They knew a lot more than she did about birth.

"That will work, won't it, sis?" Mike spoke to her in between answering the person he spoke to on the other end of his call.

"I guess." She didn't look happy.

Sirens grew louder as a large white vehicle pulled into the parking lot. A well-fit man walked in first, pulling a bed. Heather's mind translated it to stretcher. Another man came in with him steering the bed from the other end.

"Good thing we were on our way here for lunch or Patti might have had the baby in this diner. How far apart are her contractions?"

"Five minutes," said Mike. He stepped out of the way so they could get her ready to go.

"No problem." They did what they needed before securing her to the stretcher. "See you at the hospital, big brother."

"Thanks, Bob. I'll be there as soon as I can." While the paramedics moved Patti out of the building, Mike got on the phone and started making more calls.

Heather was worried that one of the other waitresses would slip on the fluid on the floor. She stepped behind the counter and looked for towels.

Mike spotted her behind the counter and put his hand over part of his phone. "What are you doing?"

"Looking for towels." She pointed to the floor.

"Oh. In the back, there. All I have are small ones, but there are paper towels back there, too. If the roll under the counter isn't enough." Then he went back to the call.

She saw the roll under the counter and pulled it out. Unraveling a big wad, she dropped it to the floor to mark the spot. At least the other two women would see the paper on the floor. All this man needed was to lose another waitress because she slipped on amniotic fluid.

She found the small towels as well as a few more rolls of the paper ones. Looking around she also saw chemicals. Another thing she needed to finish cleaning up the mess. What should she use? Heather decided to just get the fluid up off the floor then she found a spray bottle of multipurpose cleaner. That would work.

It didn't take too long before she had all the liquid picked up and the floor cleaned. Mike was still on the phone. Sitting back on her stool, she picked up her cup of coffee and took a sip.

"What are we going to do about Patti's tables? I've been slammed today and can barely keep up with my own," asked one of the waitresses as she walked behind the counter.

"It's okay, Princess," replied the one who was following her. "The rest of us peasant girls will pick up the slack."

The one who spoke first flicked her ponytail and walked

to the window in front of the kitchen. "Where's Mike? I have an order."

"He's busy right now, but you walked right past him," commented Heather. The young girl acted like Patti's baby was an inconvenience to her. One word popped into her head. Spoiled. "What do you do when he's busy in the kitchen?"

The second woman snatched the ticket from Princess and slipped it up in a silver round thing hanging in the window. "We normally put it here so the cook on duty can see it and she knows that. But Princess doesn't like to be put out."

Heather was right. She was spoiled. The place was packed, and more people were waiting for tables. Heather knew by the way Princess was acting she didn't want to have anything to do with Patti's tables and the other woman would end up doing all of it. She needed help. "If you show me what to do, I can at least get Patti's tables cleaned."

"You don't mind?" The second woman looked over at Mike who had now walked outside, still talking on the phone. "We have been busy. There's a gray bus tray you can use. They're stacked over near the sink. Just put the plates in them and bring them to the dishwasher. If you put her tips in a glass or cup, we'll make sure she gets it."

Heather nodded and got up. She found the trays and headed to the first table. She stared at the plates for a moment. Was she supposed to leave the food on the plates? The waitress she had been talking to came over.

"Never cleaned a table before?"

"Sorry. No."

"It's easy." She picked up the plates, scraping the food from different plates all onto one then sat the stack in the grey bin. She took the cups and glasses next and stacked two or three—the ones that didn't have a lot of liquid in them before putting one that did on top. The stacking allowed her to put more into the container. Heather had brought a clean glass which the woman put the bills and coins in. Then she sprayed the table with a bottle she had brought and wiped it with a cloth. "Got it?"

"Yep." That was easy. She cleared the rest of the tables in Patti's section first and lifted the heavy bin. Now what was she supposed to do with it? She carried it back behind the counter. Mike had come back in and saw her. He hooked a thumb behind him. Once again, she found herself back in the place where she found the towels. A loud clang and several swear words made her walk past that area and into a hot little room.

"Who the hell are you?"

"Um, helping out for Patti?"

"Patti?" He arched a brow at her. "She finally dropped that bundle of joy?"

Heather nodded.

"'Bout damn time. She's been whinin' since Tuesday." The man washing the dishes spotted the tray in her arms. "Put that there. Can you take the other one back with you?"

Heather picked up the tray filled with clean dishes.

"Thanks."

Mike stopped her before she made it back to the counter. "I only agreed with you to get my sister out of here. You don't have to do this."

"I figured that, but your waitresses are slammed, and I offered to help them so they can get caught up. I like busy work, keeps me from thinking about things."

"Problems at home or something?" He reached for the bin she was carrying.

"No, I just got back from overseas." Heather gave him the container. "Saw things I wished I hadn't."

"Military discharge?" He walked to the counter and set it down.

"Medical leave."

"You're not going to go postal on us, are you?" He looked at her.

"No." Heather laughed. "I got into a sticky situation and the doctors suggested I take some time off to see if I really want to stay in the service."

"Officer or enlisted?"

"Lieutenant." She climbed back on her stool. "This might just be what the doctor ordered."

"Okay, but I have rules. One, you need a uniform. That outfit might get you more tips, but I ask the girls to wear a pair of black shorts and a white t-shirt so everyone looks the same. For now, I think there is a spare set around here somewhere. The girls always leave clothes in case they get called in and don't have their uniform with them, but you'll have to go and get your own somewhere along the line."

"Okay." Heather couldn't believe her luck. He was going to hire her. Now she had the perfect excuse to hang around long enough to see if Storm would come in.

"Two. Everyone but Princess is a relative and all of them only work for tips."

"Oh, no problem. I can do the same thing." Heather smiled. "I guess I need to find a place to stay though."

"You haven't checked in anywhere?"

"I stopped for a cup of coffee." She shrugged. "I was going to see if there was a hotel nearby, but never passed one before I got here."

"Now I feel really bad. My sister is right, this is my busy time, and I could really use the help, but if you want to continue on, please don't feel obligated to stay. We'll work it out. If you stay, I can help with a room. There's a small efficiency above the restaurant. I lived there before I built the house around back. But I must warn you that will put you on call all the time. If one of the other girls calls in sick, you'll be the first one I go to."

"I don't have a problem with that." It might work in her favor. Cim told her Storm came here a lot and he could drop in anytime. The more she worked the better chance she had of running into him. She had tried to reach out to him, but his mind was blocked off somehow.

Mike disappeared for a moment. When he came back, he held the outfit for her. "You have a different pair of shoes?"

"In the saddles of my bike. Sneakers okay?"

"They'll do. You don't want anything too thin. You could burn yourself if a pan slips or could hurt yourself if you drop a tray of food. And you want shoes that don't slip."

Heather went out to her bike and pulled the shoes out. Bert had included the shoes with the pile of clothes he had handed her, but she hadn't tried them on yet. She also grabbed a pair of socks. A soft piece of lace peeked up at her. She needed undergarments here, didn't she? Better to be safe than sorry. The more delicate items she stuffed into her suit.

Hoping she didn't forget anything, Heather walked into the bathroom and changed. Her biker suit was soft and pliable, allowing her to fold it up small enough to fit in the saddle bags easily. Heather checked out her outfit in the mirror once she had finished changing. The course material felt strange on her. After having perfectly fitting clothing all the time to have something on this loose was weird, but the waistband was stopped by her hips so she didn't have to worry about it falling off her.

She stepped out to find Mike waiting for her.

"Sorry it's a little big." He handed her a large rubber band and pointed to her hair. "Needs to be up."

"No problem." She pulled her hair up into a ponytail

and wrapped the band around it. Not having a mirror made it a little difficult, but she got it back and off her face.

"Okay. Get to work."

"Let me stick this in my bike and I'll be ready." She held up her bike outfit.

Mike nodded.

When she came back in he explained how the sections were broken down so she would know what tables she was responsible for. He also explained how the workload was broken down so they always had silverware rolled in napkins, coffee and tea ready. Once he felt she knew what to do, he let her get to work.

TWO

Heather had been there about a week. She had picked up the job pretty quickly. Mike seemed happy with her work, he kept smiling at her and had called her in for an extra shift on more than one occasion. She hadn't been able to make it to a store to buy her own uniform because of that but was able to continue to use the one she was loaned.

"I think he's in love."

"What?" Heather looked at the waitress standing next to her as they stacked the dishes on the shelves. There was a lull in the traffic so they were playing catch up.

"Mike. You're cute, efficient, don't talk back to him the way the rest of us do and haven't dropped a damn thing since you started." The woman elbowed her. "You're making us look bad."

"Do I need to drop a dish or two, Susan?" Heather looked at the woman talking to her. "Make me more human?"

"It might make the rest of us feel better, Heather, but I

don't think you can do anything wrong in his eyes." She nodded toward Mike.

Not what she wanted to hear. Storm was her mate and the only man for her. What if Mike tried to be amorous with her? She wanted to stay here to see if Storm would show up, but not if another man could cause her trouble.

"Hey. I didn't mean to upset you." She touched Heather's arm. "Besides, he's not over his wife yet."

"Wife? He was married?"

"Widowed."

"Oh." Heather put a few more dishes on the shelf. "What happened?"

"Leukemia." She was quiet for a moment. When she started talking again there was a warble in her voice. "They were high school sweethearts. Married right after gradua-tion. They worked during the day and went to college at night. Then Nancy started complaining about headaches and dropped a lot of weight. At first, the doctors blamed stress. They had just opened this truck stop and had sunk a lot of money into the place. There were days when they weren't sure if they'd have food for the diners."

Susan wiped her eyes.

"Hey, you don't need to bring up something that hurts this much."

"It's actually a little cathartic. I haven't had a chance to talk about this with anyone because we all knew her and had our own stories." She smiled as she rested a hand on Heather's arm. "Then she came up with more symptoms. By the time they figured out what was really going on she was too far gone. Mike watched her die."

Heather handed Susan a cloth as her tears rolled down her cheeks.

"He loved her so much. We feared he'd never find another woman. You're actually a ray of hope. And we've seen some beautiful women come here because of Mountain Man. If you can stir his blood, then when the right woman comes along, he can fall in love again."

"Mountain Man?"

"Yeah. Really big guy, over seven feet, golden eyes. Very handsome, but a little scary. He and Mike are friends. Helped Mike build his house."

Storm. It had to be.

———

It took three more days before he entered the restaurant. She knew he was there before she saw him. Something deep inside told her he was there. A familiarity filled her. Made her aware. He filled the doorway as he walked in. She was used to his size, but here, in this timeline, he was so much larger than anyone else. Now she understood the title of mountain man by everyone around him.

Storm sat at the bar in the same seat she had occupied when she first arrived. Now what? Heather didn't know what to expect. Being introduced to Storm by Mike was one of them.

"Come here, I want you to meet one of our regular customers. His name is Heath Storm, but we all call him Mountain Man." He turned to his friend. "Mountain Man, this is Patti's fill-in, Heather."

"She have her baby?" He took her hand and shook it, but she could tell by the look in his eyes he didn't recognize her.

Heather tried to reach his mind but found her way blocked again. The heat of his hand had her desire climbing. His touch always did this to her. Yet she had to act like she didn't know him when she wanted to throw herself at him.

"Yes." Mike grinned. "A boy, eleven pounds about twenty-one inches long."

"That's a big one, proud uncle."

She wanted to recommend they give birth to Vespian twins before they comment about how big the baby was. Their twins were larger.

"Heather here is going to fill in while she plays mommy."

Now she was the focus again. She wasn't quite sure what to do. "Coffee?"

"Yes." He looked at her.

She wanted to throw her arms around him and beg him to remember, but instead, she nodded, brought him a cup, and poured the black brew into it. One of her tables called her over, giving her a chance to gather her thoughts. She was grateful they were ready to order.

———

The moment he walked into the restaurant he sensed something different. A scent he had never noticed before caught his nose. It was different, yet right. Mike talked to him, but he couldn't get the scent out of his hypersensitive nose. Then the new waitress came out of the back area. The moment he saw her his body hardened.

He had photographed some of the prettiest women in the world but none of them moved him like this one did. Bright violet eyes, straight white blonde hair that hung halfway down her back, thin athletic body, fair flawless skin, she was beautiful. She smiled at him, and he felt his heart stop for a moment.

Storm didn't really hear the introductions as an image of her at the height of a climax flashed in his head. Head back, eyes half closed, she whispering his name as her muscles tightened against him in an exquisite vice.

"Coffee?"

"What?" He needed to focus, or someone might notice. "Sure."

She nodded and grabbed a cup for him. After pouring the hot brew she set a few creamers out for him then moved to a table that had signaled for her. He couldn't stop watching her.

"She's something, huh?" asked Mike.

Storm didn't respond as he turned so he could continue watching her.

"Speechless, Mountain Man?" Mike teased him.

"What? No." He turned back to find Mike grinning at him. "You know I don't date the models."

"She's pretty enough to be one, but she's not one of your models. You have no excuse with this one."

Heather came back with her order and handed it to Mike. He went back to the kitchen, leaving them alone.

Now what should he do? Normally he just ignored the girls who worked for Mike, but this one was too hard to ignore. One of the other girls came back behind the counter, giving him a break.

"Princess is at it again," said Susan.

"What did she do now?"

He found he liked the sound of her voice.

"Told a customer to move to my station because she knew they wouldn't tip well. One of these days I'm going to stick my foot out and trip her when she has a full tray. The funny thing is the people she insulted tip me just fine."

"Susan." Heather laughed. Beautiful. It was like music to his ears. "Been wanting to ask you why you call her Princess anyway."

"She comes from a rich family. Spoiled rotten. Got caught driving daddy's new car while under the influence and landed her ass in jail. Then had a hissy fit when daddy and mommy didn't bail her out." Susan kept her voice low so no one would hear her, except Heather and Storm. "She was underage so when she was pulled over, she also got in trouble for being a minor. Spiked the breathalyzer to about a three-point-five."

"Bet her father wasn't happy."

"You kidding? He was pissed. Mom had caught her drinking before, but let it go. He knew if he let her continue the way she was she'd end up dead or in jail so he gave her a choice. Either work to earn her own money to pay for what she did, or he'd let the police lock her up for six months. He hoped if she got her hands a little dirty, she'd clean up her act."

"Doesn't seem to be working."

"I also think she has to make a certain amount of money each day. That's why she doesn't want the people who don't tip her well. What she doesn't understand is that they don't tip her because she has such an attitude. Her little friends come in each day, and she'll spend hours talking to them instead of taking care of her tables, but they always leave a wad of cash for her. I have a feeling she told them how much money she needed to make every day so she can spend time with them instead of taking care of her other tables. Mike has to get after her a lot because when they walk in the door, she forgets about the people she's serving."

"He has a big heart, doesn't he?" Heather looked over her shoulder to where Mike had gone to.

Storm found he didn't like her attention on his friend. What was wrong with him? She could be interested in anyone she wanted. It wasn't like she belonged to him.

"Not always to his favor either." Susan looked at one of her tables. "Got to go. Looks like table five is ready for their check."

Heather nodded.

Now they were alone again. Storm wasn't sure what to do.

"Want that refreshed?" Heather pointed to his cup.

"Sure."

When she poured more coffee into his cup, he noticed the indentation of a wedding ring. It figured. "Married?"

Heather looked at him, confusion on her face.

"Saw the ring marks."

"Oh." She rubbed the spot where they used to be. "Yes, but he disappeared several years ago. He either doesn't want to come home or can't. My family talked me into taking them off."

"You love him?"

"He is my heart." The words she used struck a chord in him.

"Yet you've given up on him?"

"No, but it's like he disappeared off the face of the planet. The government even went as far as to bury an empty coffin." She didn't look at him as she told her story. Must have hurt her to reveal something so personal to a stranger.

"Didn't mean to dig into your past."

"It's okay." She grabbed a cloth and wiped the counter down. Then she grabbed her pad and looked at him. He saw sadness in her eyes. "Have you decided what you want to eat?"

"Ah." She had him so flabbergasted he hadn't looked at the menu. Then it dawned on him he ate the same thing every time, yet she had made him forget that as well. All he could think of was the image of her in his arms as she climaxed. "Tell Mike my usual."

She nodded as she wrote something on her pad. He watched as she ripped it off the pad and stuffed it up in the small ring hanging from Mike's window. Then she touched his hand. "Do you need anything else right now?"

He shook his head. Her touch sent a jolt of desire racing through his blood. It took all his concentration to not grab her and pull her into his arms. What was wrong with him?

"Okay." She headed to one of her tables when several people sat down.

Storm couldn't help but watch her walk to the table. She was like a magnet to him. Heather had a nice swing to her hips. He could watch that all day long.

At the table though was a group of young men who kept trying to prove their manhood. They all had jobs in the area according to Mike, but they always seemed to have a little too much time to themselves. They were loud, rude, and loved harassing Mike and his staff. So far Mike had been able to keep them in line, but the new girl might not be able to handle them.

Mike walked out of the kitchen when he saw Heather walk to the table.

"Well, hello, darlin'. Heard you were hot, but nobody told me how smokin' you were." The young man at the table was loud enough for everyone to hear.

Heather laughed. "Never been called smokin' before. Ready to order drinks?"

"I know what I want." He looked her up and down. "But I don't think it is on the menu."

"Sorry, no special orders." Her voice sounded pleasant, but Storm noticed her spine straightened. Heather had her pad in her hand, waiting. "So what will it be, boys?"

"Oh honey, I ain't no boy. I'm all man. And the man for you."

"Really?" Heather put her hand on her hip. "You think you can handle all of this?" She gestured at her body with the other one. "Because I don't think so."

Storm planted his feet on the ground. He would pound the imbecile into the ground if need be but found Mike stopping him by placing a hand on his arm.

"She seems to have this under control. Give her a chance."

As much as he wanted to stop this before it got out of hand, Storm listened to his friend.

"Come on, baby." He slid his right hand up the inside of her shorts. "Give me a chance. I can rock your world."

———

Heather had put up with his attitude long enough. It was time for him to know who was boss. She grabbed the thumb of the hand on her thigh and applied a little pressure. Not enough to hurt but she got his attention. "You right-handed or left."

"Right. Why?" Her question caught him off guard.

"Because if you don't take your hand off my thigh, I will break your thumb. It's hard to eat and write without it."

"You?" He grinned, not believing she could do any harm.

"Yes." She smiled back as she pushed his finger more. This time he felt the pain. Sweat broke out on his brow. "And if you don't think I'm capable of that I'll snap your wrist to prove a little slip of a woman like me can beat your ass."

He pulled his hand out. "I didn't mean any harm."

"Didn't think you did, lamb chop, don't forget to tip your waitress well. You never know what she can slip into your food if she learns you're a bad tipper." She put a smile on her face and asked once again. "What would you like to drink?"

———

Mike turned his back to the people at the table and started to laugh. It was the first time Storm had heard him laugh in a long time. "Oh, yeah, she'll do fine."

"You attracted to her, Mike?" He wouldn't think of interfering if Mike had designs on his new waitress. No matter how much he found her attractive.

"Maybe a little, but not sure if I'm ready to start looking yet." Mike got his laughter under control and turned back around to look at Storm. "Why? Are you?"

Storm shrugged. He wasn't ready to commit yet either. He didn't know what he felt about her, but he knew she had his undivided attention.

"I do feel for the man who lands that one." Mike leaned a hip on the counter as he watched her walk toward him. "She sure is going to be a handful."

———

Heather didn't like the attention she was getting from all these different men. They all acted like they were on a deserted island, and she was the last woman. This never happened in her own timeline, why was it happening here?

She went back into the little alcove where the cleaning supplies were kept to calm herself down. That boy had his hand pretty far up her shorts. If Storm had been his normal self the poor guy would have found his feet dangling and his neck in a death grip.

Instead, she worried that she had what Storm had when they first met. Her soul could be calling for her mate, sending out vibrations or some sort of pheromone that was dragging all these men toward her. She'd have to ask Cim if that was possible, and if he didn't know then ask Bert. If she did, it was going to complicate things.

Mike walked back into the small space when she didn't come back out right away. "You okay?"

"Fine. Just wish they'd behave themselves." She straightened her shoulders and smiled. She walked back into the dining room with Mike right behind her.

"Maybe we should get you to the mall your next day off. Get those shorts tailored a little so no one else will try to be so bold."

Heather nodded, stopping in front of the counter where Storm sat. "It would save me from breaking too many hands."

"Could you really do that?"

"I worked in security." She smiled. "If you'd like I can show you what I can do, and I won't leave a mark."

"Nope, I believe you." He held up his hands in submission. "Can't afford any broken bones either."

"Where is this mall? I have a few hours this evening."

"Down the mountain, but you don't want to take your bike. You won't be able to carry too much in it." Mike looked around the dining room. "It isn't too busy. I can take you when Bill comes in."

"You don't have to, Mike. I can have anything I can't carry shipped."

"Are you out of your mind? It will cost you a small fortune. I'll take you." Mike's phone rang at that point. "It's Bill. I need to take this."

Heather found herself alone with her mate once again. He kept looking at her, yet there was no recognition in his eyes. The desire to shake him when he looked at her like she was a stranger was overpowering. Why didn't he remember? Why couldn't she connect with his mind? Something was wrong and she didn't know what to do about it.

It was near the end of her shift. All she had to do was take care of this last table, as long as the grabby man kept his hands to himself, and she'd be done. The first thing she wanted to do was shower to wash the smell of food off her body. The men at her last table were all very polite to her when she came back. Ordered quickly and without complaint. She must have made her point.

When she turned around, she found Storm standing, with his arms crossed over his chest, glaring at the people. As she passed him to turn in the order she spoke. "I can handle them, Mountain Man."

"It never hurts to have a little backup." He sat back down.

She gave him a slight nod. He was right. Even without his memory, he was protecting her, or did he do that for all the waitresses here?

Mike came back out with Storm's meal. "Heather, I'm sorry, but Bill just called in sick. His two-year-old son, actually. I'm going to have to fill in for him tonight so I can't take you."

"It's okay, Mike. I can still go on my bike."

"I'll take you."

"Excuse me?" asked Heather.

"What?" questioned Mike at the same time.

"Did I speak a foreign language?" Storm growled. He didn't look either of them in the eye.

Heather wanted to laugh. That was her mate. But she didn't want to force him into anything he didn't really want to do. She also didn't want to give in too easily. That could raise questions.

Mike seemed very shocked by his offer. Bert had told her he was a bit of a recluse so this must be totally out of character for him. "You sure?"

She thought about arguing with him, but she wanted to

spend time with him and see if she could figure out why he couldn't remember her. It would be smart for her to remain quiet and let Mike do all the talking for her.

"Yes." Storm sighed. "I need to go there myself so I can take her."

"That would be great, Mountain Man." Mike slapped him on the back. "I'd really appreciate it."

"Excuse me but I'm not some helpless female here." Heather wanted this but knew she had to act like she didn't appreciate them making this decision for her.

"No, but you are new to the area, and I would feel bad if something were to happen to you because you took a wrong turn and got lost." Mike touched her arm. "I would sure feel better if you'd let him take you."

"Fine." She sighed, only to make it seem like she didn't need a protector. This would give her the perfect opportunity to spend time alone with Storm without a bunch of people around them. "Give me a half an hour. I need to shower."

Storm nodded.

Princess came dancing up to the counter when she saw Storm sitting there. "How are you?" Her voice sounded sing-songy.

Heather hesitated. She leaned on the counter toward Storm, her white t-shirt gapping open to allow him to see her lacy bra and a bit of cleavage. This child didn't have designs on her mate, did she?

"I had hoped you'd show up."

Storm gave her a bored look. "Princess."

"Oh, come on, I thought you'd call me by my real name by now."

"Fine, Meagan." He took a sip of his coffee. "Don't you have tables to take care of?"

"Thought you were going upstairs to get ready?" Mike's voice sounded in her ear. She jumped when she heard it.

"I'm on my way now."

"You don't have to worry about the Princess. Mountain Man has been shooting her down every time she tries to grab his attention. I think she wants him because of his work. She wants to be a model and he would be her meal ticket."

"He's just going to take me to the mall, Mike."

"Right. Mountain Man attracts a lot of attention from the female gender. You're not immune. I can tell."

"Maybe I should go to the mall myself."

"I'll back off." He held up his hands and stepped back. "But don't think you've done a good job of convincing me."

Great, now she had to act like she wasn't after him and compete for her mate's attention.

———

Why did he volunteer? He didn't really need to go to the mall. He hated being surrounded by so many people. His 'condition' kept him isolated. He didn't want to lose control around a crowd so he normally ordered whatever he needed online and had them delivered to Mike's place. Mike knew that too. That was why he looked at him like he had lost his mind. Yet here he was volunteering to take this woman to the mall. Was he crazy?

He took a deep inhale. Her scent still lingered, and he knew the answer to his question.

———

She came back down in better spirits. At least she didn't have a strange pheromone causing trouble with the men she encountered. Cim had scanned her and found nothing out of the ordinary. The men were just reacting to her naturally. Before she met Storm, she had personal shields in place that kept anyone attracted to her at bay. Storm had lowered those defenses, making her feel beautiful and sexy, and that was what the men were picking up on. That was still a problem, but one she could handle.

She wore a pair of soft jeans and a form-fitting short-sleeved t-shirt made of a soft jersey that Bert had created for her. The light violet color of the shirt accented her eyes.

Her suit was versatile. When she broke the seals, they became different pieces of clothing. The boots she now wore were from the suit as well as the leather jacket she had draped over her arm. It was nice right now, but the temperature was supposed to drop once the sun went down.

Storm stood when he saw her. "Ready?"

"Yes." She felt so many people staring at her as she walked out with Storm. Opening her mind a little she felt their shock. Storm has never done anything like this before. What made this woman so special? Heather also felt hatred blossoming in one mind. It had to be Megan's.

Being the center of attention wasn't what she wanted, but her goal was to bring Storm home. She hoped spending time alone with him would free up his memory and if that was going to make people talk so be it.

"My truck is the mostly blue one." He gestured to a Dodge Ram four-wheel drive, four-door pickup truck. It had a lot of dents, and some parts were a different color from the original paint, but it ran like a dream. Her brother taught her a lot about combustible engines. As long as the engine was good you could fix anything else.

She found the fact that her mate had picked up her brother's habit with the fixer-upper funny and couldn't fight the smile she wore as she climbed into the cab. He thought the truck Kuarto owned ridiculous yet here he was with one of his own.

Storm pulled out of the parking space once she snapped her seatbelt in the slot.

They rode in silence, so Heather took the time to look at the nature that blurred by. The sun was setting. Vibrant colors of red, purple, and yellows filled the sky. She sighed at the beauty. Nervousness filled her. Not knowing what to talk about with him had her trying to figure out what else she could do. She decided on meditation to relax her. Something to help her focus on something other than her mate. So close yet untouchable.

———

God, she smelled good. When she came back into the restaurant in the tight-fitting jeans and t-shirt he just about drooled. Now with her in his vehicle, he picked up on her scent again. Storm tried to ignore the woman sitting next to him but couldn't. He had to get a grip.

Glancing at her while trying to keep his eyes on the road, he noticed she had closed her eyes and tilted her head up a little. She had a grace about her that drew him. Why? He had been around lots of beautiful women and had always been able to remain professional. Yet this woman had him wanting to feel her body beneath his. Make those sexually charged images he saw when he first met her real.

He needed to keep his desire under control, but he wasn't sure if he could with her. Why did he volunteer to spend time with her alone? It just made matters worse. The erection he would have to hide was embarrassing. He wasn't some high school kid who couldn't control his body, yet just looking at her made it throb.

He had to be out of his mind.

———

They arrived at the mall to find the place packed. Heather wasn't sure if this was a good idea. That was a lot of thoughts to block out. Another new talent she hadn't quite gotten under control. Once she started to read minds that were open to her she found it hard to keep them at bay in large crowds. Her steps slowed as they got closer to the main doors.

"You okay?"

"Yeah." Heather straightened her shoulders. "Not a fan of large crowds."

"Me either. We can go back and try another time if you like."

"We're here. I'll muddle through." She nodded her thanks as he held the door for her. Inside was a wonder. Large, airy, people everywhere, and lots of bright lights. Heather had never seen anything like it. She found it easy to keep the thoughts away since most were just focused on why they were there in the first place. It allowed her to relax and enjoy being with Storm.

Not knowing where to start, she looked at all the display windows. Storm walked with her, sighing every once in a while.

"You okay?" She looked at him.

"Yes." His words were clipped.

"You don't like crowds either."

"Not really." Several young men walked past them making lewd comments about her, but she chose to ignore them.

"Okay." She pulled out her phone and pulled her list up. "Let's make this painless then. I need to pick up a few things for the man cave Mike is letting me use. I can't handle the bare bulb over my head and need something better than a throw blanket with a sixteen-point deer on it."

"There's a Bed, Bath, and Beyond here. We could start there."

"Perfect."

Storm took her to the store, but as she walked, she continued to look. One store looked very promising. She wasn't sure what was Victoria's Secret, but the items in the window showed it had just the foundations she wanted. Would Storm go in with her? Could she get the bright glow of arousal in his eyes once again?

Only time would tell.

———

For someone who was only planning to stay for a few weeks, she sure bought items like she wanted to put down roots. Lamps, sheets, comforter, she even bought a new coffeepot, complaining that the one Mike had in the apartment gave the worst cup of coffee she ever had. He'd had coffee from that pot, and she was right, but the restaurant was just downstairs. She could always trot down the stairs for a better cup.

They passed another store, and he was suddenly alone. He turned to find her in a small mom-and-pop-like store, eyeing an area rug. It was an attractive pattern. Held a lot of colors he liked. It reminded him of the woods near his cabin. She came back out carrying the thing.

"A carpet?"

"The floor is extremely cold first thing in the morning, and I can hear every noise from the restaurant when I'm off. This will help fix both problems." She stopped once again. "I need to go in there."

He looked at the Victoria Secret store and hoped she

meant one of the stores on either side. She smiled as she took his hand.

"I promise to be quick." Half dragging him in with her, she walked to the back and pointed to a chair. "Have a seat while I look around."

Not what he wanted. He saw a young woman walk up to her and the two of them worked their way through the store, picking up things for her to try on. The items she decided to keep without trying them on ended up on his lap. He tried not to look but found it hard to resist. Most looked safe enough, but there were a few bits of lace or silk that had his imagination going wild. His thoughts were broken by the employee helping Heather.

"She needs your opinion."

"What?" About underwear? Oh hell no. "No."

"Please?" She popped her head over the top of the stall she was in. "We're having a debate over whether or not I can wear this down to the restaurant. I'm not sure."

She planned on exposing herself to everyone? She couldn't be talking lacy items now, could she? He sighed as he untangled himself from the packages. If she was, she was finally showing her colors, probably had something skimpy on to arouse him. He was already aroused, but she didn't know that, and he wasn't going to fall for her tricks. Looking over the top of the door, he found her body incased in flannel and sweatpants. Not what he expected. "Flannel?"

"I know. I don't want to frighten the patrons away." She turned back to the mirror. "But I would like something casual to wear when I need it."

"The pants are fine. Seen people walk into the restaurant wearing them, but you need something different for the top. That isn't flattering on you." He knew if all she was wearing was the shirt, he would have a different reaction.

She nodded, turning her attention back to the items still

hanging on the small hooks. There were a few more things she had to try on. He backed up when she pulled the top off, but his height allowed him to still see her. Without the hideous top on he realized she took good care of herself. Muscles in her stomach showed she worked out regularly. But he couldn't help but notice the lacy bra she had on. It hugged her breasts and exposed a lot of tissue. Tissue he wanted to touch. He had to look somewhere else before she caught him and couldn't miss the discarded pile of items on the floor.

He turned around and sat before he exploded. Watching her was so wrong, but he couldn't help it. Her body kept calling to him and seeing all that skin turned his arousal into a hard-on again. He had just gotten his body under control when he heard the door open.

Heather came out with several of the items he spotted on the floor in her arms. "Ready?"

He nodded, still seeing her standing there in the pants and her bra. Oh, he was in trouble.

The young woman took her to the register and started to ring up her items. There wasn't a lot to it but he felt like the sales clerk wanted to be sure he saw every bit of lace Heather bought. She lifted it up before folding it then wrapping it in tissue.

She gave him a bright smile when she had her package in hand. "Thanks for putting up with that. Didn't mean to put you on the spot." Heather reached for the carpet.

"I got it." He shifted it so she couldn't take it from him.

"I didn't want you to be my pack mule. I can carry it."

"Anywhere else?" He ignored her.

"I need to get a few pairs of black shorts and white t-shirts for work. What I'm wearing now doesn't fit. And since I decided against the flannel number, I still need something to lounge around in."

He remembered what had happened and agreed, although having her in tighter clothes might not be a good idea. "There is a clothing store right there. How about I take what you have bought and put it in my truck then catch up with you?"

"Sure." She headed into the store he pointed to.

———

Heather stepped into the store feeling a little guilty, but she got what she wanted. Storm's eyes were glowing. She wondered if he knew about that. She found several pairs of shorts that would work as well as tops. She also found a couple of pairs of yoga pants and long-sleeved tops to go with them. By the time he came back, she was done.

"Why don't you wait by the doors here while I go get the truck?"

"Okay." Standing outside the doors of the mall, she waited for him to return.

Her phone sent her a warning before she found herself surrounded by five young men. They looked her up and down then leered at her. Did she have a sign on her asking to be harassed? "Look, boys."

"Oh, honey. I'm a man. One that will rock your world."

"Don't need rocking." Another one who thought he was a man. They didn't hold a candle to her mate.

"A woman with spunk. I like that." He laughed. "You're something I want to tap."

"Really?" She gestured toward her body. Heather ignored the people passing by as she spoke to the stupid male. "You can't handle all of this. I'd break you."

"Like to see you try." He placed his hand on her arm. His plan was to bring her toward him, but he found himself on his knees with his hand twisted behind his back instead.

"I don't have to 'try' to break you." She leaned forward so she would be sure he heard her. "You are messing with the wrong woman. I floss my teeth with little punks like you. Now, here's your choice. You either go with the police who, by the flashing lights getting closer and closer, are on their way, or try something stupid so I can prove to you that I'm not as soft as I look."

"Is there a problem?" Storm pulled the truck up to where she had the boy on his knees. Sirens filled the air as the flashing blue and red lights got closer.

"I don't know." She twisted his hand a little more. "Is there?"

"No."

"And you will stop harassing women or I'll come after you. Do you understand?" When he didn't answer she pulled his hand to the breaking point. "Do you understand?"

"Yes," he screamed. He whimpered at the pain radiating from his wrist.

The police stopped in front of where she had the boy on his knees.

One pulled a pad out of a pocket and focused on her while the other cop dragged the boy to his feet.

"Are you harmed, miss?"

"Annoyed." She crossed her arms over her chest. "He thought I would be easy prey. I'm not."

"Do you want to press charges?"

"And what will happen to them if I do?"

He turned to look at the police car his partner had wrestled the boy into. "He has no record so will probably be let go."

"Let me talk to him." She opened the door and spoke to the young man quietly before closing the door of the car and walking back to the two officers. "We've talked and he's promised not to try to tap any other unwilling women. I'm not going to press charges."

The young man looked at her from inside the car. Relief on his face.

"You sure?" asked Storm, who had climbed out of his truck.

"Oh yes. He won't be causing any trouble anymore." She smiled at the officer then she looked at Storm. "I'm ready to leave."

Storm escorted her to his truck. She was livid. He could smell her anger. He found it fascinating. He decided to remain quiet and wait for her to speak. He helped her into the truck before walking around to his door and climbing in.

"Can I ask you a question?" Her voice was soft.

"Sure." As mad as she was, he wasn't sure if he wanted to hear what she had to say.

"Is there some sort of sign on me that tells these stupid males that I enjoy bringing them to their knees? That for a good time annoy me?"

"No." He laughed. "You're a beautiful woman, Heather, and they have no brains."

"I'm going to kick the next one who thinks he can rock my world and is dumb enough to try." She looked out the window. "I want a man, not a boy."

"Are you ready to go back or would you like to get something to eat?" He wanted to be that man. Every facet he saw of her he liked. The desire to make the fantasy he kept having a reality was getting stronger by the minute.

"There are a few things on my list that I didn't see in that mall."

"More shopping?"

"Sorry. There isn't a lot of space on that bike. I'm running out of shampoo and such, but I can do that on my own."

"I know just the place." He pulled into a small parking

lot. "They are a little more expensive than some of the chains, but they will give you personalized service, and the food at their counter is just about the best around here. Besides Mike's. He knows I come here but made me promise that I would always go back to his diner."

She laughed as she climbed out of the truck.

He held the door for her to enter the small store. A jingle of a bell warned the owners they had company. The moment they saw him they were all smiles.

"Mountain Man! Good to see you!" A gray-haired man came up and shook Storm's hand. He looked at Heather with appreciation. "And who do we have here?"

"This is Heather. She is filling in for Patti at Mike's place."

"We heard she had a very healthy boy."

"Yes. Mike has been bragging." Storm walked with the other man while he left Heather behind with the man's wife.

"She is pretty enough to be one of your models," he commented as he stepped behind his counter. "Something to drink?"

"We're going to eat once she picks up a few items. Go ahead and give me my usual while we wait."

He nodded and picked up a tall glass. After filling the glass to the top with ice he poured freshly brewed sweetened tea into the glass. The man didn't say anything, but Storm could feel him waiting.

"What?"

"You never brought any woman here before. Is she special?"

"Why would you think that?" This was all he needed. People thinking that he was attracted to her. He didn't need the headache.

"Don't know." He shrugged. "What does Mike think of her? He needs someone to help him forget."

"Not her." Then he realized what he blurted out. "Mike told me he wasn't ready to date yet."

"Give him time." He looked at Heather. "If I was thirty years younger and not happily married, I'd be trying to make her mine."

Storm turned to look at Heather. She had a small basket over her arm, and he could see items sticking up out of it. Looked like she was finding what she needed. He wished she'd hurry. He didn't like the questions being asked and if she was sitting with him, they might just stop.

———

She had no idea what she was looking at anymore. Too many choices. If it hadn't been for the lady helping her, she'd be lost. She now had most of the items she needed, and a few she didn't. "The last thing I need is laundry detergent."

The lady nodded. "Are you one of Mountain Man's models?"

"No." Heather laughed. "I was in the military."

"You should be. He needs a muse. Such a nice man carrying the weight of the world on his shoulders."

This version of her mate was a little darker than what she was used to, but he had no memory of who he was before two years ago. She understood that. She wished she could get him to give her his killer smile again. "You think he has secrets?"

"Oh, we all have secrets. I can see the shadow in his eyes. Love would pull that away." She sighed. "So, do you have everything?"

"I sure hope so. If not, I'll be back."

"Then come get something to drink." She brought her to the counter. Standing in such a way that Heather had to sit next to Storm, even though there were plenty of other stools available. Heather couldn't help but smile.

"What?"

"Huh? Nothing." She settled on the stool and picked up a menu.

"If you feel a little adventurous let me pick what we have." He touched the menu. "I promise you will like it."

"Sure. I've been picking out things for the last few hours it would be nice for someone to make a few decisions for me." She grinned. Storm was always making decisions for her, even when she should do it herself. He was still the same man deep down inside.

"Great." He gave her a smile that reached his eyes for the first time since she found him. "Two of your burritos, extra everything."

The woman leaned close to Heather. "See? The shadow is fading already. Because of you."

Heather hoped so. Being with her mate had her desire rising. She was very close to the breaking point, and he hadn't even touched her.

———

He pulled the truck into the parking lot of the restaurant. Opened twenty-four/seven there were always cars in the lot. Storm pulled around the back, close to the stairs of her apartment.

Heather slipped out of the seat before he could make it around to open her door. She seemed nervous all of a sudden.

"Thank you for taking me."

"You're welcome." He opened the back door of the cab and found her right in front of him. He couldn't help but notice the tightness of her jeans as she leaned into the truck.

It had remained warm so she only had the t-shirt on and it rode up her waist as she reached for some of her packages. All he could think of was what she exposed versus what was still hidden from view. And he badly wanted to see what was beneath her clothes.

When she turned around, she looked up at him with such trust. Then she smiled and moved around him. After climbing the stairs, she unlocked the door and walked in, only to come back out a few minutes later for more.

He had grabbed the rest of her bags and was heading toward the stairs when she met him halfway.

"You don't need to do that." She tried to take everything from him.

"Heather." He moved his arms so she couldn't make him drop anything, but she also couldn't take anything from him. "I'm going to lose all of this if you keep it up."

"I'm sure you have better things to do than carry my packages up to my apartment." She reached for them once more.

"I don't mind, and I already have them." He looked down at her, glad he had a handful, or he might have grabbed her and pulled her to him.

"Okay." She didn't sound convinced but gestured up the stairs.

He climbed them, wondering how the small place would feel with her presence. He had been up here to watch sports with Mike when he had problems sleeping in his house after the death of his wife. It had been his haven. It surprised him that Mike allowed anyone to use the room. He still had nights where he couldn't stay in the house.

The first thing he noticed was the smell when he entered the one-room apartment. Instead of the stale beer and chip smell it had a fresh scent that carried her essence.

She had dropped her packages on her bed so he placed

the rest of the items there. The only thing he had to do was bring up the carpet and the lamps she bought. Heather was already working on putting her things away.

The carpet wasn't very big, but he had a little trouble getting it out of the back of the seat.

"You wrestling a gator there?" asked Mike.

"No. Heather went a little crazy. There's two lamps in the cab too, if you want to grab them."

"Sure. I'm still running the grill, but I got a few minutes." He took the two lamps and carried them up. "She didn't care for the deer throw blanket, did she?"

Storm laughed. "No. Called the apartment your man cave."

"There is nothing wrong…whoa." Mike stopped when he spotted Heather. She was changing the sheets on the twin bed. One knee on the bed, she was bent so her jeans hugged all the right places. Storm felt his heart beat a little faster and knew Mike was probably reacting the same way. Her shirt rode up halfway up her back. That soft skin begged for his touch.

Mike looked at him and winked. "Got to get back to work now."

Storm found himself alone, standing there, wishing for something he shouldn't. He didn't understand why she affected him. He had always kept to himself. There had been lots of models who tried to throw themselves at him and he had always said no. All of a sudden, he wanted a woman to throw herself at him, but he knew she wouldn't. Maybe it was for the best.

He called it his 'condition' but only one other person knew he could shape-shift. It was a secret he had fought hard to keep. How he wasn't sure, since he felt he had no control over it. What would happen if he was with a woman? Would he start shifting in the middle of it? He couldn't take the chance of hurting anyone. One of the reasons why he had never been with any of his models, no matter how hard they tried. Or how badly he might have thought he needed to.

Yet here he was, wanting this woman with all his being. What was it about her that broke through all the walls he had built?

She got the fitted sheet wrapped around the corner of the bed and turned back to grab the top sheet. Heather looked up at him with her bright violet eyes. "You going to stand there and stare or help me get this thing made?"

That got him moving. The faster he helped her, the quicker he could get out of there. Taking the bottom of the sheet, he tucked it under the mattress while she straightened her end and filled the pillowcases with new pillows. Her new comforter was next.

"There. The man cave is starting to disappear." She took one of the lamps and placed it on the small table next to the bed. The other she put on a matching end table near the recliners Mike had in there. When she bent over to plug in the lamp, she was facing him. The view he received when he looked down her blouse made him swallow hard. She no longer had a bra on. Her soft full breasts called to him. His body screamed to touch them, kiss them, lick them until she screamed in pleasure.

Oh, he was in trouble.

THREE

She looked up at him, then straightened, like it suddenly dawned on her what he could see. "Makes it a little more cozy, don't you think?"

All he could do was nod.

Next, she picked up the Victoria's secret bag.

"I got to go." Watching her put away her underwear could be his undoing.

"If you're sure." She set all of the delicate pieces on the small bureau and walked him to the door.

He looked once more at the items on top of the dresser before he looked back at her. "You have things to do."

She wrapped her arms around him, resting her head against his chest. "Thank you for all your help."

He found the move a little awkward, but he returned the gesture. She fit against him perfectly. When she tilted her head back to look up at him instinct had him lowering his face to hers. Her lips were soft under his. Storm had planned on a simple kiss but when she opened her mouth for him his desire took control and his tongue swept into her mouth, searching the recesses, drawing her tongue to swirl with his. He tightened his hold on her, feeling he couldn't draw her close enough.

He could smell her need for him spike as he kissed her. It surrounded him as his own grew. His hand slipped up under her shirt, capturing one of her breasts in his hand. His desire to taste it overwhelmed any common sense he might have had. He revealed that breast as he lifted her up and pressed her against the wall so he could take the sweet tip into his mouth. He sucked the tender skin, causing it to pebble under his attention.

Part of him told him to stop before it was too late. Another part screamed for release. She tasted so right. Like she belonged in his arms and in his bed. Without realizing what he was doing he had removed her shirt and moved his mouth to her other breast.

The soft touch of her fingers on his chest made him aware that she had opened his shirt, exposing his skin to her hands. She brushed her fingers against the odd tattoo he had and his need became overpowering. All he could think of was being inside her.

He made short work of her jeans, pulling them off her legs and throwing them to the floor. Desire taking control, he couldn't shed his pants fast enough. His mouth moved back to hers as he centered himself to enter her.

Heather's legs wrapped around him, pulling him to her. He couldn't stop if he wanted to, but it relaxed him to know she wanted this as badly as he did. She looked at him, desire etched on her face, but there was something else. He saw trust. Her trust in him. All his fears filled him. What if he harmed her? Would he start shifting as he lost control? A strange warmth spread through him when she brushed the tips of her fingers against the tattoo again and he forgot everything but his need to be buried deep inside her.

She wanted to cry with joy when she felt him fill her. He had been at war with himself since they walked in. Heather wasn't sure if his libido would win over whatever battle he was having, but she hoped it would. This was what she wanted so badly. Her fear that he would walk out of her little apartment without touching her made her want to bar the door and throw herself at him, but she knew he had to make this decision, not her. Thank goodness he made the right one. A sigh escaped her as her muscles rippled along his length.

"Heather, I don't want to hurt you." He continued to pound into her even as he worried about what he could do to her. Concern etched on his face, she could see that war starting again.

"Oh God." If he stopped now, she just might scream. She so badly wanted to tell him she knew about his shape-shifting, wanting to ease his mind but knew this was the wrong time. It would raise too many questions. "You will never harm me."

"How can you be so sure?" His voice came out ragged as each stroke brought him closer and closer to his orgasm.

Instead of answering him, she brushed her fingers against his mark, knowing it would make him forget about anything but the two of them. He shook as the simple stroke rocked him to the core. "Because you have too much kindness in you."

A moan escaped her as he filled her again and again. Her muscles tightened against his staff, intensifying what they shared. The wildness of their intimacy showed how long it had been for them. For Storm, it had been two years, for her two weeks. Her orgasm blossomed in the pit of her stomach, spreading throughout her until she was one with the stars.

He never disappointed her. Just as she hit the height of her orgasm, she felt the first tendrils of their mind meld re-bond.

———

What had he done?

He looked at her, eyes closed, mouth slightly parted. The image of his fantasy had become reality, but at what price? "I'm sorry, Heather."

She opened those soul-searching eyes of hers and looked at him. "Sorry about what? You didn't enjoy what we just shared?"

"God, no. That was wonderful, but I shouldn't have taken advantage of you like that."

She laughed, causing her muscles to ripple against him, making him harden again. "I believe we both wanted that. I couldn't have told you no anymore than you could stop. Even now I'm experiencing little aftershocks that are so delicious."

He felt them too. Each time her body reacted to one of those aftershocks he felt himself pulse. His mind said get out now, but his body wanted to go for round two.

"Heather. I have you pinned against the wall for crying out loud. There was no finesse. No romance."

"Did you hear me complain?" She brought her hand up to his face then rested her hand on his shoulder. He thought she was going to brush her hand along his jaw before she must have decided against it. The gesture seemed right so why did she change her mind? Did she think it was too intimate after what they shared?

"I didn't really give you a chance." He eased out of her and allowed her feet to touch the floor again. "I didn't even use protection."

"There isn't another person in the universe I'd rather be

with right now, sharing what we just shared. If you feel that bad about this then make it up to me." Heather brushed a few strands of hair out of her face as she looked up at him with a smile. "There is a bed right there as well as a brand new carpet we could break in. And as far as my medical history I have birth control and no diseases."

"Me either." It didn't make him feel any better. He looked at the twin bed then the floor. Why was he even contemplating this? Then he looked at Heather, beautiful, naked, waiting for him to make a decision.

He pulled her comforter off her bed and walked back to where she stood. With gentle hands, he wrapped her in it, then lifted her to the recliner facing the television. "Give me a few minutes."

She gave him a heart-stopping smile.

That was why. She trusted him. Knew he wouldn't hurt her, and she had been right. He hadn't shifted, he had remained in control even as he spiraled out with his orgasm. And what they had just shared was something beyond sex. He knew that.

He took a flat sheet she had been sitting on the second recliner, picked it up, and spread it out over the top of the carpet. Next came another top sheet she had out. She had an awful lot of sheets out for the one bed. "You trying to figure out which one to use first?"

"What can I say. The ones Mike had were a bit scratchy and I couldn't decide which one went best with the fitted sheet I bought."

He grabbed the deer blanket.

"Oh, please, no." She stood and handed him the new comforter. "Use this one."

He stopped and stared when she revealed herself. "You are so beautiful. My camera would love you."

Once he had the comforter in place he walked to where

she stood. With gentle hands he caressed her, sliding his fingers along her velvet skin. He picked her up in his arms and carried her to their makeshift bed. He lowered her to the floor. He wanted it to be romantic and sexy but a couple of sheets on the floor didn't measure up. Storm scratched his head. "You know this went much better in my head."

Heather laughed as she wrapped her arms around his neck and pulled him to the floor with her. "You are over-thinking this. Just follow your instinct, Storm. It has never failed you."

"You call me Storm. Why?"

"It is your name, isn't it?" A soft sigh escaped her as he pressed his weight into her.

"Well, yeah, but just about everyone calls me Mountain Man. A few even call me Heath. I can't think of anyone who calls me Storm." There was Princess, who for some strange reason called him 'Stormy,' but he kept that to himself. The tone she used and the way she said it annoyed the crap out of him.

"It seems to fit you." She looked up at him, their faces only inches apart. "If you don't like it I can stop."

"No." Her lips called to him. He couldn't help but take a sip from them before he spoke. "It sounds right coming from you."

"Good." The smile on her face was infectious. He couldn't help but smile back. "Now. You wanted to make up our first time together to me?"

"Right." Her reaction to him relaxed him. Like they had been partners for years. He pressed his lips to hers before blazing a trail to her throat. For some reason he felt drawn to the left side of her neck and found when he brushed his mouth against one area, she reacted like he had hit an eroge-nous zone. He hovered there, drawing a sigh and a moan from her. It was music to his ears.

But he wanted to show her he could be gentle after the way he had first taken her. It was wild and wonderful, but he needed to prove a point. He slowly kissed his way down her throat, across her collarbone, and down the slope of her delicate skin to the tip of her breast. Capturing her nipple in his mouth, he suckled her, causing her flesh to pebble against his tongue. After getting that reaction, he gave the same attention to her other breast.

Her need called to him, making him want to forget everything but the desire to feel her body take him in again. Storm fought the urge until he felt he had it under control. That would have to wait. He continued down her stomach to her mound. Proving he could be a good lover was important. Why he wasn't sure. He seemed to know what he was doing. The moment his mouth latched on to her, she started moving beneath him, soft words escaped her, begging him to fill her. He didn't let her beg for too long before he climbed back up her body and entered her. She arched against him as he slid in deep. Her muscles clamped down on him.

"God, Heather. You feel so good." He started moving, setting a pace that he found pleasing. She met him thrust for thrust.

———

Tears formed in her eyes as he pressed his lips to her mark. Storm might not know who she was, but his body did. It knew exactly what to do to bring her to the heights he always brought her to. She felt her release race toward her as he filled her again and again. The heat of his mouth on her mark only heightened the intensity of the orgasm overtaking her. It filled her with joy as her muscles tightened against him and she soared along its powerful wave.

It took her a few minutes before she opened her eyes and looked up at his smiling face. She touched his cheek softly. "Wow."

"You don't hold anything back, do you?"

"Not with you." She smiled up at him. Her fingers skimmed along his jawline.

"Um, you know I'm still hard, right?"

"Oh, yes." Her smile brightened. "I might be a little boneless, but I can still handle another orgasm or two."

"You sure?" He pulled out and drove back into her heat.

She arched up against him as he stroked a very sensitive spot. "Very sure."

———

Storm closed the door to her apartment quietly, not wanting to wake Heather. She had curled up beside him afterward and they talked about nothing really, but he enjoyed the intimacy of the moment. As hard as she tried to stay awake, she ended up falling asleep in his arms, so he picked her up and put her in her tiny bed, comforter and all.

He looked at his watch as he hit the button on his keys to unlock the door to his truck. "Wow. Didn't think it was that late."

The slight movement of a curtain at Mike's place made him hang his head. The man was far too nosey for his own good. Storm knew he could just drive away, and Mike would never question him, but he also knew he'd probably try to get information from Heather in his subtle way and Storm wasn't sure if he wanted that.

He walked to the steps that led to the porch of Mike's home and didn't even get one foot on the first step before the front door opened. "Thought you'd be asleep by now."

"Thought you'd be home by now," Mike returned.

"You going to let me in?" He had climbed up the three steps to the wraparound porch.

"Of course." He moved aside so Storm could enter. "Want coffee?"

"Sure."

Mike made two mugs and offered one to him. "Bret called to confirm the shoot in three days, and he grumbled about not having a number for you."

"I have no need for a cell phone. He'd be the only one calling me besides solicitors and you. Not having one gives me an excuse to come see you."

"I'm wondering if you have another reason now." He looked at the window that would reveal Heather's room if he were to move the curtains.

"You know that is none of your business." Storm didn't want to talk about how being with her had moved him so profoundly.

"I know." He took a sip from his cup. "Heard Bret's bringing three models with him and he's giving Princess the nod. He wants to do the shoot using the backdrop of the mountain again."

"Must be doing another shoot for the jewelry people. If he's allowing Megan to model that means she'll be in my hair all day." He sighed. "Should have made a living taking pictures of wildlife."

"Hey, if you had taken advantage of all those women who threw themselves at you, you could have had your own wildlife." Mike laughed. "Sometimes I'm just too funny."

"I didn't shift." Storm wasn't sure why he said it out loud.

"What?"

Mike knew about his secret. The only person who knew the truth about him. "I didn't shift with Heather."

"Great, now you have no excuse for your grouchiness."

Mike grinned. "When one of those models arouses you, you can take advantage of it. I know they'll be happy."

"We'll see."

———

Storm drove back to his cabin, wondering about Heather. Besides not wanting anyone to find out about his condition, he had remained celibate because every woman who offered themselves to him didn't really care about him. He could tell by the scent they gave off. All they wanted was either the prestige of being his bed partner, hoping he would launch their career if he was intimate with them, or his money. They all assumed he made good money as a photographer.

She seemed different than the others. Heather had no desire to be a model, so that eliminated the first of the two things most women wanted him for. Didn't seem to need money. Not the way she spent it last night. She acted like she had no designs on him at all. Yet he smelled her need. For him. When she was accosted before, she was annoyed with the men. If all she wanted was sex, she could have taken any of the offers she'd had, but she shot every one of them down.

Was she playing a game with him, or for real? He hoped she was for real after what he did.

———

Heather woke the next morning with a smile on her face. Each time Storm had an orgasm their minds connected a little more. Some of the mindmeld things they took for granted were gone and she missed it. These little tendrils reconnecting were giving her a touch of the constant contact she had grown accustomed to. The tiny thread connecting them made her miss his mind all the more.

She took a quick shower and straightened her bed before she went outside and down her stairs. Heather didn't need to be at work until late in the afternoon so she thought she'd do some exploring. Maybe run. Not being able to exercise the way she was used to was driving her a little crazy. She did it two to three times a day on Vespia, normally with Storm.

There was a slight nip in the air so she put on a pair of yoga pants and one of the shirts she bought then her jacket and her sneakers. The ones Burt gave her were a hundred percent better than anything she could buy. She started walking to warm up and when she felt ready, she took off at a quick pace. The view was beautiful. She found one spot that called to her, and she started walking so she could cool down enough to sit and meditate. The air wasn't as clear as she was used to in her timeline, but it wasn't too bad. Sitting cross-legged, she closed her eyes and centered herself.

She slowed her heartbeat and focused on the tiny mind connection she had with Storm. Their minds had been so entwined. What happened? What was blocking her ability to meld with him? It didn't make sense to her.

Heather sat there for a long time just clearing her system of the fears and questions she had been carrying. She found him. Now all she had to do was make him remember. Opening her eyes, she found a large white wolf sitting opposite her. She tilted her head. It wasn't Storm but she sensed something that reminded her of her mate. As Heather studied the wolf, she realized it was also female and beautiful.

"So what do you want?" She kept her voice soft so she wouldn't scare her away.

The wolf just stared at her.

Great. Now what should she do? The way the wolf studied her showed the animal had no fear of her. Time to see what she wanted.

"Hello." She looked at the beautiful wolf sitting in front of her. She opened her mind to let the animal know she meant her no harm. "You looking for someone?"

The wolf tilted its head as it stared at her like it expected something more.

"What confuses you?" Heather then smiled. "You smell Storm on me, and you don't understand, do you?"

The wolf whined her answer.

"I'm sorry. You're looking for a mate, aren't you? He's sort of taken. Or was. The whole thing is a bit confusing to explain."

Although she wasn't the darker gray animal that Storm turned into, she was magnificent. Silky coat, bright blue eyes, Heather had never seen anything so gorgeous.

"You should have no problem finding a mate. Your coat is clean and shiny. I'm sure there is a mate out there for you somewhere. Be patient. It will happen."

The wolf sighed.

"I know it is hard. I waited a long time before mine showed up."

A soft growl filled the air. A blur of fur caught her attention before she found another wolf in front of her. This wolf she recognized. Storm.

———

He had been following Heather for a couple of miles. He had watched her apartment and waited to see what she would do. When she started running, he trotted close enough to keep her in sight.

The smart thing to do would be to just ignore her and head back to his cabin, but he hadn't done anything smart since he met her. When he saw the female who had been following him around for several months, wanting him as a mate, approach Heather, he feared she might harm her.

Yet Heather had been talking to the female like it was her best friend. She knew the other wolf had noticed his scent on her. How? And what was all that about a mate? What did this woman know?

He looked at the young female and growled low in his throat. She might want him as a mate, but he wasn't interested.

She whined again before taking off.

"I think she got the message." Heather looked at him. "Unless you are interested in her. If you are you should go after her."

Storm looked in the direction the other wolf had taken then sat down.

"I see. Not your type, huh?" She closed her eyes. "I need to meditate so if you have things to do I'll be fine. She meant me no harm."

Storm tilted his head at her. She had to be crazy. She spoke to him as if she understood her. He did, but she didn't know he was a shifter. Did she? He watched as she tilted her face up toward the sun, totally ignoring him. Her body relaxed as she meditated.

Her unique scent called to him. He took a deep breath, breathing her in, feeling his body relax as her essence settled deep inside him.

She opened one eye and looked at him before closing it again and going back to her meditation.

He snorted and he laid his head down.

"You sure are noisy for a wolf."

He lifted his head to look at her.

"I'm finding it hard to concentrate with you breathing deeply and snorting. It's distracting." She patted the rock she sat on. "Come on, settle down so I can clear my mind. If I don't work it properly each day I get a massive headache and have been known to pass out. It upsets people when I do that."

He moved to her side and lay down. She didn't fear him at all. She rested her hand on his head and petted him as she went back to her meditation. He found her touch comforting. Enjoying the simple contact, he rested his head on her thigh. Her pheromones enveloped him, making him hard with need.

Maybe this wasn't such a good idea. A distant noise made him raise his head. Someone was coming. Heather knew as well because she opened her eyes and stopped petting him. "I'll have to meditate later, looks like we're about to get some company."

Mike came into view right after she spoke. He slowed when he saw her sitting there with a wolf, even though he knew it was Storm. "Whoa, Heather. Why are you sitting with a wolf at your side?"

She smiled as she ruffled his fur. "He's watching over me."

"You sure it is safe?"

"He's quite docile, but I understand if you don't feel comfortable near him." She looked up at Mike. "Were you looking for me?"

"Yeah, I needed to talk to you." He moved to the other side and sat down. "Storm is doing a photo shoot in a few days, and I need help with the catering."

"He's doing it here? I would think he would go wherever they do shoots."

"They can do it anywhere, and the backdrop of the

mountains really makes his pictures pop." He shifted so he could look at her. His eyes cut to Storm before he continued. "I asked Susan, and she doesn't want to do it. And Princess is going to be one of the models so helping me is a little beneath her at the moment."

"I've never catered before."

"Figured that, but you never waitressed before and you picked that up quickly. All you really need to do is make sure they have food when they need it and drinks." He shrugged. "It's not that much different than taking care of tables."

"Why doesn't Susan want to do it? She has seniority."

"The last time she dealt with them wasn't pretty. She had a few choice words I won't repeat when I asked her if she wanted to do this."

"I guess I could if it would help you."

Storm looked up at her. A part of him wanted her to say yes. Of course, having her that close all day would probably distract him. She seemed to have that effect on him.

"It would, but I wasn't sure how comfortable you would feel being around Mountain Man."

"You mean after last night." She petted Storm's head.

Storm was surprised at her honesty. She wasn't embarrassed by what happened between them.

"Yes." Mike shifted in his seat. "Look, it's none of my business what you do or who you do it with, but if it is going to cause trouble I need to know."

"It won't cause any trouble." There was truth in her voice. She meant it.

"You have feelings for him."

"I'm here for as long as he wants me here."

Storm wondered what she meant by that.

Heather had everything set up for the staff and models of the shoot. She never realized how many people worked in the background. There were people who did hair, others who did make-up, and then the people who handled the clothing, the props, and the lights. She didn't know how Storm handled being around all these people. They seemed to get in his way more than help.

She stood off to the side and watched the chaos. Voices raised as things weren't going the way they wanted or when someone got in the way. People were setting up areas for the makeup artists and the clothing department. Sets were being erected as the lighting department was trying to make sure everything was lit properly. It amazed her.

She felt his presence just before Storm came to stand beside her.

"Crazy, isn't it?"

She nodded. "How do you put up with it?"

"I don't. Normally, I stay away until they call for me. One of the perks of being the photographer."

So why was he there now? She hoped it was because of her.

She sensed another person approach just before he slapped Storm on the shoulder.

"You ready, Mountain Man?"

Everybody called him that. Obviously, this man worked with Storm, and they probably had to discuss the job today. Heather figured she should go stand behind the tables she had set up and leave them alone, but as she turned, she found her hand encased in the stranger's hand. She looked up to find their ancient friend Bert smiling at her. What was he doing here?

"And who is this?" He didn't act like he knew her, and Heather didn't understand why.

"Heather." Storm frowned. He didn't seem happy about the way Bert was focusing on her. "Heather this is my boss, Bret, Bret this is a new waitress at the restaurant, Heather."

"You are beautiful. Did you know that?" He studied her, head to foot.

What kind of question was that? "I see you're a flatterer."

"Mountain Man, have you taken her picture? See if the camera loves her?" He looked at Storm. "I need to see. We're short a model and she'd be perfect."

"Oh, no thank you." Heather held her hands out in front of her. Why would Bert, or Bret which was what Storm called him, want her to model when he knew she was a time traveler? Unless they hadn't met yet. "I've never modeled before."

"Take her picture, Mountain Man." He totally ignored her comment. Then he walked to where the models were and began to prepare them for their turn in front of the camera.

"Sorry about that," Storm said. "He does have a good eye for beauty and has made a lot of money because of it."

She looked at Storm. There was no way she was going to get in front of a camera. She was sure that would cause time-line issues. "Right. Time to get to work."

She was a time traveler, not supposed to make waves. How could she get out of this? She knew how well she photographed. The image of her in the middle of an orgasm popped into her head. That showed her beauty in a way she had never expected. Her phone vibrated, which made her frown. Why would Cim be trying to get her attention? She dragged it out of her pocket and found an image on the screen. It was her, with a large cat, and the mountain as a backdrop. At the bottom was an ad blurb. "Great."

Since she couldn't talk to Cim she typed her question. 'Does this Bert know me?'

'No. He should know you are the prophecy, but he hasn't met you, Sam, or Skye yet.'

"Great." She said again, not wanting to show her frustration over the situation. Heather checked the coffee urn then made sure the water and sodas still had plenty of ice on them. Mike couldn't stay with her. He had to run the kitchen. He had promised to come and check on her from time to time, but if she needed something she would have to go and get him. As skinny as these women were she doubted it would be food.

Dropping her phone into her pocket she found several of the models staring at her. Now what?

———

Storm watched her as she checked her station. Bret was adamant about him taking a picture so he would. The idea of her posing for his camera had been on his mind, but he hadn't planned on doing it while surrounded by people. He wanted it to be very private.

He had forced himself to stay away from her the last few days, and it had been painful. He had found himself outside her little apartment each night, wanting to go up to her room and enjoy her body like he had before. It took all his willpower to turn away.

Bret saw him with his camera in his hand. It didn't take him long before he walked over and talked to Heather to give Storm something to work with.

Storm lifted his camera and started taking pictures.

———

"Hello, Bert." Heather didn't look up from what she was doing.

"It's Bret, honey."

"It's Bert. Short for Bertanthus." She looked up at him. "And don't call me honey."

He was taken aback by her comment. "You know me."

"Yes, I do." She continued wrapping silverware in napkins. "Just like you know me."

"You are the prophesy."

Heather nodded. "I must assume we haven't met yet in your timeline, but we have in mine."

"You are here for him." He turned to look at Storm for a moment. "Is he the catalyst?"

"He is my mate." She looked at Storm as well. "I don't think of him as anything other than that."

"Of course. But he has no memory of who he is. Has he remembered you?"

"No." It broke her heart to know he was so close, yet she couldn't tell him the truth. "But I'm hoping to fix that."

"Why haven't you told him who you were?"

"I can't." Anger filled her as she glared at him. "You told me not to. Your exact words were he had to figure it out on his own."

"Then you must pose for him. It could trigger the memory to free his mind." Bert smiled. "He is taking pictures right now to show me."

"Are you sure it is wise?" She tucked a piece of hair behind her ear. "I would think it would be smarter to stay out of the limelight so to speak since I'm not from here."

"You have seen the future, what does it show you? Is there a picture of you in an ad? If so you already have your answer."

Heather didn't answer.

"Look, none of the models here will pose with the white

tiger I have brought in for this shoot. That is all I need you to do. I promise to leave you alone after that." He looked back at Storm. "I don't even know if they'll like your picture, but I need to come back with one. If you won't do it I'll have to get someone else."

"I don't know." But she knew it would happen. She had already seen the picture.

"Think about it." He turned and left her with one last parting comment. "You could be the one he has to focus on unless you'd rather it be someone else."

Heather hated being pushed into a corner like this. She didn't like being the center of attention unless it was coming from her mate. Knowing she could monopolize his time and have his undivided attention had her thinking.

"He's been pushing you to pose, hasn't he?"

She looked up into Storm's golden eyes. She hadn't noticed he had come up beside her again. Their mindmeld hid the fact that he was so light-footed. Heather nodded.

"Look, he does this all the time. It doesn't mean he'll use it." Storm put the strap around his neck and allowed the camera to rest against his chest. "And he won't stop until he gets his way."

"Mike won't like it. I'm supposed to take care of this." She gestured to the food and drinks she was babysitting.

"I'll talk to him."

"You want me to do this?" She wasn't quite sure why, but he seemed to be pushing a little too.

"Believe me it is better to give in than to listen to him harp all day."

Heather wasn't too sure about that.

———

It took about an hour before Mike came to check up on her. She stood behind the table, watching as Storm whispered in the ears of the different models. Using gentle caresses or his bone-melting smile, he got them to act the way he wanted in front of the camera.

"Something else, huh?"

"It's like he's making love to them before he puts that camera between him and the women."

"Jealous?"

"Why is Princess staring at me like she wants to stab me?"

"Not going to answer my question, are you?"

She just looked at him. It didn't deserve an answer.

"She has designs on Storm and doesn't like it when someone draws his attention away from her. Even though he has shot her down so many times everyone around knows he doesn't want to have anything to do with her. She just doesn't get the hint." He crossed his arms over his chest. "Did something happen recently to make her jealousy flair up?"

"Not that I'm aware of." She thought about it. "Unless the fact that Bret wants me to model could be causing the problem."

"Has Mountain Man been talking to you at all?"

"He came over a few times, but it's not like he's showing me any undivided attention. Got coffee, introduced me to Bret." She shrugged. "That kind of thing."

"And what did you say to Bret when he asked you to model?"

"That I'd think about it. It's not something I feel driven to do. I'd be so much happier staying right where I am, but they are pushing this."

"They?" That piqued Mike's curiosity.

She sighed. "You'd think Storm would only want professionals, but he seems to want me to do it too. When I tried to use me being here because I'm working as an excuse to get out of it, he said he'd talk to you."

"Bingo." Mike laughed. "That was it. Mountain Man wants you to pose for him and you aren't jumping at the chance. She doesn't understand why you would say no. She never would, unless it got her Mountain Man's attention. That's what she thinks you're doing, trying to get him to beg you to pose. You're stealing her thunder." He turned to look at her. "So what are you going to do?"

"I don't know." Heather crossed her arms over her chest. "Will it piss off our little Princess?"

"Oh, yeah." He grinned. "Mountain Man has tried to get her to turn her attention away from him time and again, but she ignores anything that would get in the way of some fantasy she has about him and her. This could show her she doesn't have a chance."

"Then I guess that makes the decision for me."

Mike's grin widened.

———

Storm pulled the memory chip from his camera and slipped it into the small case before putting it in his pocket.

"She said yes." Bret was giddy. "I was afraid I wouldn't be able to get this ad done. They are giving us a shot but have very strict ideas about what they want in this picture. Ones you have to stick to."

Storm gave him a bored look, but inside he was just as excited as Bret was. The thought of her making love to the camera made him hard. "Like what?"

"The tiger, the dress, and the diamonds."

"Don't tell me they're basing their ideas off of an ad they saw forty years ago."

Bret shrugged. "We need to make them happy."

"Fine." Storm slipped a new chip into his camera then looked at him. "When will she be out?"

"I promised her she could go last."

"Last?" Megan's voice cut through the air. "I thought I was last."

"Sorry, darling, but we had to give that slot to Heather because of the tiger." Bret turned toward the girl and gave her his best smile.

"Why can't I do that ad?" She pouted as she held her head high. They were giving her this chance, and she acted like she was the highest-paid model here. "You asked for me, didn't you?"

"Of course I did, but this particular shoot is the one you turned down because of the 'wild animal.' I believe you balked at the idea of coming within ten feet of the tiger. I have to hire her, or I'd lose the ad company. Sorry Darlin', but we have to make money."

She huffed. "Well, why can't you do her first?"

"Because, my love." Bret put his arm around her and steered her away from Storm. "The tiger can be a bit temperamental with too many people around. He hasn't even been delivered yet and I need to thin the crowd out before we bring him onto the set once he gets here. Now if you're willing to be a snack for it then you may stick around, otherwise, it will be essential personnel only."

Storm was glad his sensitive hearing could pick up what they said.

"But I was hoping to spend time with Mountain Man."

"Not this time, sweetheart. He is so busy making sure he gets the best pictures he can get. Perhaps you can talk to him back at the diner once this is all done?" He didn't wait for her to answer. "You know I have another shoot in a week, it will be with another photographer, but it would mean more exposure for you."

And she completely forgot about him. She was one of the ones who wanted him because she wanted to further her career. Storm was glad Bret could distract her. He hated whiners and that was all she seemed to do. If Bret could get her out of the diner, he would probably visit Mike more often.

The next few hours dragged for him. His desire to see how Heather would be transformed got stronger and stronger. One of the makeup artists had taken her back about an hour ago to get her ready. He kept looking toward the back area to see if he could catch a glimpse of her.

He still did what he needed to do. Normally if he had already taken the picture, he knew was the best one he would let the camera continue to snap images to keep the models happy, but not this time. He wanted to clear the area as quickly as possible.

"You okay?" Bret watched the pouty Megan climb into her car to take her back to her place.

"I'm fine. Why?"

"Never seen you clear the area like this. Normally you give these women what they want and make them believe they have a chance with you. What changed?" He looked back to the area where Heather was getting ready.

"Nothing. You said yourself that the tiger didn't like a lot of people around."

"You heard that?"

Storm realized his mistake too late. When did Bret say that? Before or after they walked away? He shrugged. "Yeah."

"Have to remember to keep my voice down. I forget how well it carries." He slapped Storm on the back. "Hope you don't mind working a little later. She's never done this before so I don't know how well she'll follow direction."

Storm wasn't worried. There was something about her that told him whatever picture he took would be one of the best ones he'd ever taken.

———

Heather watched as the hairdresser teased her hair until it stood about six inches above her head. Good Lord, now she knew what people meant by big hair. Then they sprayed it so it wouldn't move. Makeup came next. When they were done, she didn't recognize herself. False eyelashes, shade upon shade of color on her eyes. Foundation so thick she thought it would crack when she smiled and a lipstick color that had her thinking 'here comes Heather's lips.'

The dress was the worst. She was larger than the dress so they put her in this spandex contraption to make her fit. The zipper wasn't their friend in the beginning, making the costume manager as well as her assistant wrestle with it, but it did finally close. Heather looked in the mirror and was amazed at the image that stared back at her.

Bret popped his head in and smiled broadly when he saw her. "Perfect."

"I can barely breathe." She pressed her hand against her chest. "And I'm revealing a little more than I like."

"That can be fixed." He pointed to the woman who helped her into the dress. "Pop of color, right here." He gestured to her breasts which were trying hard to spill out.

"Have it."

"Good. Bring it out and attach it once we get her situated." He offered her his arm. "You ready to meet your partner for the shoot?"

"Is the tiger really as bad as everyone has been saying?"

"Of course not. We couldn't use it if it was too wild, but you can't think of it as some sort of kitten either."

She couldn't help but smile. Her mate could shift into a wolf, and she could hear the thoughts of most of the people in the area. It shouldn't be hard for her to bond with the tiger.

He brought her out of the room, and she had Storm's undivided attention. The glow of desire brightened as he watched her approach. The tiger was brought in on a leash, bearing its teeth when it came close to Storm.

Heather touched the mind of the cat, feeling it recoil from her at first then welcoming her calming thoughts. Her handler placed the tiger on the small platform she was to lay on then Bret brought Heather over. The handler showed her how to greet the animal and some of the holds she might need to know to keep the cat still and quiet while the pictures were being taken.

When Storm stepped up to her the cat growled.

"Show your manners." She patted the cat on the side of its neck. It looked at her and roared before licking its lips and laying its head down. Storm looked at her with curiosity.

"What I want to do now is pose you for the picture." There was a small stool in his hand. "This might not be the most comfortable thing to sit on but it puts you at the height I need." He set it next to the platform and held her hands as she eased herself down. She looked up at him to see his eyes fixed on her breasts. The glow was a little brighter now. Once she was situated, he moved the dress around. The gentle swish of her skirt, a fluff of the hem didn't bother her, but when he worked on her bodice, giving it a few tugs while gently brushing the exposed skin until he was happy with the draping, made her heart beat hard.

"Now I want you to place your hand." He looked at her unadorned hand. "Where's the jewelry?"

"Right." Bret smiled. "Be right back."

"Wonder what he would have done if I hadn't noticed them missing." Storm turned back to Heather. He looked down at her and swallowed hard. Her breasts were pushed up, the creamy flesh calling to him. "How much did you plan on exposing?"

She looked down. "Not that much, but Bret promised a bit of color to help hide them."

"I want to see if we need the color. Place your hand on the tiger's head like this and I want you to lean forward." He started walking backward as he saw the image he pictured in his head. "That's it. Just like that."

He lifted his camera and took a half dozen shots. He looked at the images and realized she might need a little more fabric to hide the fact that she was practically spilling out of the dress. Although her breasts looked beautiful and would show off the diamond necklace perfectly, one wrong move and she would expose herself. A nipple in the image might make the jewelry people a little upset. The head of wardrobe came out with several materials including a royal purple bit of silk, a lace piece that was bright red and a white crinoline.

"Thought the purple would match her eyes but wasn't sure if it was enough color." She draped it across the front of Heather's gown.

Storm looked at it through his lens. "I'll need to change a few filters to make it brighter, but that should work. Leave the rest just in case."

"How do you want the cloth arranged?"

"Not sure yet." Storm looked at the young woman. "Leave them and I'll take care of it."

Heather turned toward him. "Now what?"

"I'm going to try to get this cloth to give you a little coverage without taking away the overall look. I might get a little intimate." He tucked the cloth into the edges of her gown. Not happy with the way it looked, he pulled it back out. "Why don't you stand up and turn around."

She looked at him before she did as he asked.

His hand shook at the thought of touching her again. He eased the zipper of the dress down her back enough so the top of the dress loosened. "Okay turn around."

When she did, he found himself mesmerized. Her soft skin had a soft pink glow. He remembered how it felt when he had touched her the other night. The silk he held started to slip from his hands as he stared at her. Storm needed to get a grip.

He lifted the silk and started to slide it into the front of her dress. His fingers glided against her silky smoothness. Each time he touched her he became more aroused. His nail inadvertently rubbed against a nipple, and he heard her sharp intake of breath. He looked up at her to apologize and found her staring at him with such passion.

The desire to kiss her overpowered him and he started to close the distance then he realized he couldn't, or he'd ruin her makeup. He licked his lips and stared down at her mouth. "You need to turn around again."

She presented her back to him again and he pulled the zipper back up. He adjusted her dress so it sat on her body properly then touched her shoulders so she would turn and face him once again. The cloth was tucked in deep, and he grabbed at little fragments to pull it up in spots. Once he thought he got his desired effect he backed up and took a few more pictures.

"Almost there." He came forward, had her sit back down so he could realign the skirt then gave the cloth a few more tugs. His lens didn't lie and that gave him the desired effect.

Bret walked up with a suitcase. Storm wondered how much he saw. It couldn't have taken him that long to get the case in his hands, yet he didn't come into the area until Storm was ready. He opened the case and showed them to Storm. "You want me to put them on her?"

"I'll do it." The thought of anyone else touching her made him want to growl. If he had to stand aside while Bret worked on getting the necklace to lay right on her he just might knock the man to the ground. He had felt the same way with the costume director, and she was female. It was better if he did it. Storm picked up the necklace with the large teardrop diamond and draped it over her throat. "Did they give you more than this chain? It needs to be longer."

Bret handed him another chain which Storm threaded through the eye of the setting. He nodded when he propped that against her neck.

"Pull your hair up."

Heather moved her hair so he could close the clasp. His fingers caressed her as he hovered over her nape. The clasp closed and he had to step back. He put the earrings on next. "These might pinch but they hang better as clip-ons."

"Is pain part of the process?" She tugged her ears a little once he closed the earrings on her lobes.

"Unfortunately, yes." He smiled, hoping to ease her discomfort. Storm readjusted them when she finished messing with the earrings.

"Great." She didn't look thrilled.

He draped the bracelet on her wrist and closed the clasp then slipped the ring on a finger. She flexed her right hand, making the lights bounce off the jewels. "Now I need you to place your right hand on the head of the tiger."

She laid her hand on the animal's head and waited. He maneuvered her hand so it would show the ring and the bracelet off, had her lean forward, and re-draped the necklace so it rested intimately between her breasts. He flicked the earrings so they fell softly against her throat.

"Don't move." He backed up and pressed his thumb against the button so the camera would take shot after shot. "Now tilt your chin down a little, that's it. Tilt your head to the right. Perfect. Now think about the best sex you have ever had."

Her eyes widened a little as a sultry smile spread across her face. Was she thinking about their night together because he sure was. The raging hard-on he had was getting painful. Bret came to stand beside him.

"How's it going?" he whispered. "Have you got it yet?"

"I've gotten several I believe are very close but I'm still waiting." Storm continued to watch her as the camera continued to snap away. "It's coming, I can feel it."

The tiger sighed.

"Hey! I know how you feel." Heather spoke softly to the giant cat. "Not my favorite thing to do either."

The cat moved her head and looked at Heather who had forgotten about the camera. She lifted her hands. "What? You don't agree?"

The cat stood and turned. Fear filled Storm at the thought of her being harmed and he felt the change start to take over. He fought as hard as he could to stop it. The tiger inched closer and closer. Heather sat there, unmoving. Then it leapt forward and dropped its arms on Heather's shoulders.

Laughter exploded from her as the tiger started to lick her face. Heather tilted her head back and wrapped her arms around the cat. She ended up exposing the jewelry just the way he wanted. The camera continued to snap away, and he knew he had what he was looking for.

"Got it." He turned and grinned at Bret.

"Then that's a wrap."

Storm stepped forward and the tiger turned and growled at him. Was it protecting Heather? The animal's handler stepped forward as well, took its leash, and led it back to its large cage. Once it was out of the way he came within inches of Heather. "I swear she was trying to protect you."

Heather laughed. "Came for the baubles?"

He nodded as he removed the different pieces of jewelry. He knew he didn't need to stand so close to her, but he couldn't stop himself. His desire for her was too strong. "What are you doing later?"

"Once I get out of this thing, I'll be helping Mike clean up. Why?" She looked up at him with innocent eyes.

"I need you."

"My door is always open for you, Storm."

"You ready?" Bret walked up to them and slapped Storm on the back. "I can't wait to see what you captured in that camera of yours."

Heather turned to head back to the dressing rooms.

"Heather, you should come too. You'll be amazed at his work."

"I need to change and help Mike."

"Go and change, but Mike always looked at the pictures too. I'm sure he won't mind, so come to the trailer when you're ready."

Storm watched her go, wanting to follow her so badly. Instead, though, he turned as well and headed to the trailer where he could download the pictures for Bret to see.

———

Heather felt her insides melt when he uttered those three words—*I need you*. She wanted to fling herself at him. It took all her control to turn away. A sigh escaped her when the dress was pealed from her body, and she could climb back into her uniform. Next was the chair in front of the mirror where one woman removed her makeup while another brushed out her hair. The makeup only took a few minutes, but her hair was taking longer.

"You need to stay away from him."

Heather looked in the mirror to find Megan glaring at her. She felt sorry for the young girl. Princess just didn't understand. It was time to make sure she did. "How old are you? Seventeen?"

Megan didn't answer, just crossed her arms over her chest.

"Right. I thought Bret asked you to go back to your place." This young woman wasn't going to get to her. Storm had wanted Heather since she arrived. She knew he had sat outside her apartment the last few nights, watching her. That proved to her he didn't want anyone else. Part of him did remember, but this young woman didn't know their history. Heather felt for her. The poor girl had no clue how far out of her league she was.

"Yeah, well, I came back." She pushed a bit of hair out of her face. "I saw how he flirted with you today. He does that with all the models. Don't think you're special to him."

"I've been watching all day. I know how he is with the models." Heather smiled. She was pretty sure he hadn't been aroused so badly by them that he wanted them though. She was the only one who put the glow in his eyes. "And I know how he was with me."

The hairdresser placed her hand on Heather's shoulder, letting her know she was done. "Wash it a few times and it will go back to normal."

Heather leaned in to see her hair was still pretty full. How much shampoo would it take to get it back under control? Picking up an elastic, she pulled her hair back and put it into a ponytail. She looked at Megan's reflection in the mirror. "If you'll excuse me, I need to get to work."

"I'm not done talking to you."

Heather sighed as she turned and faced Megan. Being confronted by a child wasn't at the top of her list. "What?"

"I want you to stay away from him."

"Why? Have you slept with him?" Heather braced herself for a yes. She knew her mate and his libido.

She hesitated before she answered. "Of course."

"Really?" There was something in the way she hesitated. The girl was lying. "What is his favorite position?"

"What?" She seemed shocked by the question. Maybe searching for a way to answer.

"You said you had sex with him, how did he take you?"

"I'm not going to discuss what Stormy and I shared." She brushed her hair like she was above Heather's question, but looking in her eyes, Heather knew she didn't know how to answer her. Nothing had happened between them.

"Stormy?" Heather fought the laughter bubbling up inside. "Fine. Then we're done."

"Are you going to stay away from him?"

"Tell me, Megan. How does Mountain Man feel about you walking around making decisions for him?"

"I'm not."

"But you are. Although who Mountain Man wants to be with is his decision you are telling me to stay away from him. How do you think he will feel when he learns?"

"He wants me, not you."

Heather stepped close, using the intimidation tools she had learned from her mate, one of the best intimidators she knew. "Look, I don't have time for this. You can pretend you know what is best for Mountain Man or for me, but it won't do any good. I'm a military officer and I can chew you up and spit you out. Yet I have let you stand here and try to tell me what to do even though we know I'm not going to listen to you."

Megan put a hand on her and in seconds Heather had her on her knees, twisting her fingers enough to draw a small cry from her.

She bent down so her mouth was inches from the girl's ear. "You can pretend all you want but it isn't really up to you, is it? Mountain Man will choose who he wants. A little girl or a woman."

FOUR

Storm saw Megan head toward Heather and followed her. All he needed was a catfight because someone said the wrong thing. The moment Megan opened her mouth he wanted to slap his forehead. She still didn't get the message.

Heather tried to be nice. He could tell by her sigh she didn't want to stand there and listen to Megan, yet she did. When she asked Megan what his favorite position was, he came close to barging in. Megan might be a pain in the ass, but she didn't need to be humiliated by Heather flaunting what happened between them. But she didn't. The question caught Megan off guard and Heather read right through it. She was right. It was his decision. He found he wanted Heather, but was that all there was to it? Was it just sex with her?

He wasn't sure if he wanted to answer that question. Storm only knew he wanted her.

———

Heather walked to the tables where she had been working. She started putting covers on the large trays of food, making sure they were sealed, then stacked them on carts. Seething over the audacity of Megan, she worked quickly.

"Hey, take a break." Mike's voice penetrated her anger. "You've got to see these pictures of you. They're gorgeous."

"But I'm almost done." She was a little too angry to be in a cramped little room with anyone, especially Storm.

"It will keep for a few minutes." He grabbed her hand and pulled her with him. They climbed the steps of the trailer into a darkened interior. It wasn't as small as she thought it would be, but it was still crowded. A large screen dominated the left wall, below it was a console covered with buttons and slides.

"Wait 'til you see them," he whispered, not wanting to disturb Storm as he worked.

Storm had dozens of pictures, taken of one model, up on the screen. At first glance, they looked almost identical. When she studied them a little closer, she did notice the little nuances between them. He stared at them for a moment before he picked one to fill the screen. "This one."

"Whatever you think," said Bret. He didn't seem concerned about Storm's choices.

Heather looked at him. He trusted Storm's opinion so much he was letting him make the decision. No matter what her mate was he was still the leader she knew.

He began to move buttons and adjust a few of the slides until he was happy with the image then he saved it. He did the same thing with several others until he came to her pictures.

Mike jabbed her in the ribs, grinning from ear to ear.

"Cut it out." She kept her voice low.

Bret turned when he heard her whisper. "Good, you're here. This is what I saw when I first met you."

Image after image popped up, showing the slow progression of the shoot. She watched as a smile filled her face. That had to be when Storm asked her to think of the best sex she had. Her eyes sparkled above the sexy smile she gave him. Holy cow. No wonder he got aroused. The look she gave him made her blush.

"The jewelry company wants a particular image, but I like that. Enhance and save it on the thumb drive I brought."

Storm marked it to work on later. Another picture popped up that was the image that the company wanted so Storm marked that as well. The images continued to fill the screen.

"Good Lord, how many did you take?"

"I don't count. Each model gets her own chip so I can shoot as many as it takes." Storm kept looking at the screen. "I look for the right one and know when I get it."

The images where the cat wrapped his arms around her came up next. He froze one where she had her head back, laughing as the cat licked her face. The one earring hung against her throat. She had turned just enough to show the necklace against her breasts. The ring and bracelet rested against the fur of the white tiger in perfect relief.

"That is yours."

"Wow." Heather moved closer. "My hair looks three feet tall."

All three men laughed.

"Not a big fan of the big hair?" Storm asked.

"It's just hard to get rid of once it shows up." Heather ran her hand over her hair, even after the hairstylist had straightened it and she pulled it back, her hair was still out of control. "I can't wait to take a shower and wash it about twenty times."

"Oh." Mike touched her arm. "Um, you're going to have to wait a few hours."

"Why?" Heather turned to look at Mike after his comment.

"Because of all the dishes from this shoot I have been running that ancient dishwasher of mine overtime and it sucks the water pressure right out of the building when I push it. You try to take a shower now and you'll feel like you're being spit on."

"Wonderful." Now she had to wait to tame her hair.

"You could use the shower in one of our trailers." Bret leaned back in his chair. "There's no water pressure problems and they're bigger than that tiny thing above the restaurant. I have had to use it one time and couldn't move inside. I think I'd rather do without than use it again."

"There is nothing wrong with the shower," Mike shot back.

"Not if you don't need elbow room." Bret rubbed his elbows.

Mike laughed.

"Heather, you can use either trailer," said Bret. "It's up to you."

"Mountain Man's is bigger. Take that one," said Mike. "I've used both of them and Mountain Man's is the nicer of the two."

"You just said that because I complained about your precious shower."

"You were being honest and so was I." Mike grinned as he bounced on his feet.

"You two can stop this any time," Storm grumbled. "It's hard to work when you start this kind of banter. Heather, to shut them up, use my trailer. That way if they decide to keep this up, I can kick them out and they can go into Bret's trailer to continue."

"Bret, you got those great cigars?" asked Mike.

"Of course."

"And the whiskey?"

Bret laughed. "You do have good taste."

"Then let me and Heather finish cleaning up and I'll join you as soon as we're done." Mike straightened and signaled for Heather to follow. "I have several large carts loaded with food that we didn't use today."

"You're kidding."

"No." Mike shook his head. "But that is the way it goes. The carts are in the walk-in fridge. That comes out for the crews when they start breaking down everything in the morning. They love to eat. Anything that has been out too long today gets dumped, but anything left over that is still good I make care packages and give it to anyone who wants it. I hate wasting food. Now Mountain Man will forget to eat so I normally put one plate in his trailer, and I give Bret one as well."

She nodded. Most of what she had wrapped earlier was the sandwiches she thought were good so she pulled the trays back out, working to set up plates for the two men as well as the costume, makeup, and hair department, anyone who worked behind the scenes. Mike piled other plates high with different sandwiches and then wrapped them with plastic wrap. He took as many as he could carry and headed toward the crew cleaning up. While he was doing that, Heather took the brown paper bags he had handed her and put four sandwiches in each bag. By the time he came back, she had all the leftovers bagged and back inside the trays in the rolling rack or trashed for pickup in a few days.

"Have you eaten anything?" he asked as he grabbed the rolling rack she had filled.

"Never got around to it."

He handed her one of the bags. "No excuses. Take it. I know you like your veggies and fruit so take a couple of apples and bananas, whatever you want."

She had learned not to argue with the man. Heather took the bag as well as several pieces of fruit. She turned to find Storm standing in front of her. Her heart started to flutter. His eyes had a definite glow to them, and the glow was for her.

"Here." He handed her a key. "I've had a little trouble with someone trying to get into my trailer without my permission in the past so I've been locking it."

"I can wait until the dishwasher is done. I don't want to take advantage of you." She wondered if Megan was the reason he kept his trailer locked.

"I'll be in the other trailer working for several hours." The look in his eyes sent a little thrill through her. "Please, I insist."

"If you're sure." That look had her heart beating faster and hoping he would join her despite what he said.

"Yeah. Get your stuff and enjoy the shower."

She nodded. Once Mike told her she was done she went to her room and gathered her things. Clean clothes, shampoo, soap, and lotion. She never had to worry about lotion at home, technology kept her skin soft and subtle, but here she had found without lotion her skin dried out too much.

Excitement filled her as she crossed back to his trailer. What would she find? Would there be some hint of their life together even if he didn't remember it?

The key slipped into the lock easily and opened for her. After locking it behind her, she looked around a little. There was very little to show this belonged to Storm. He must not use it very often. There were a few things though. A statue of a wolf that looked very close to the form she had seen him change into many times. She ran her fingers over it lovingly. Touches of violet popped in odd corners. Was it part of the basic decoration or did it represent her eye color? A snippet of memory? The bedroom didn't surprise her. A massive bed, probably specially ordered because of his size, filled the room. She continued through the room to the bathroom. She turned on the light and stopped.

"Wow." It looked just like the bathroom they had on Vespia. She had worked hard on the design, making it natural yet functional. Part of him had to remember. Now she had to find a way to unlock all those memories.

———

Storm was working on one of the photos when an image of Heather moving about his trailer popped up on the screen. "Well, crap." He had forgotten about the motion sensor cameras. "I'll be back."

"Why not turn off the camera from here?" Bret sat beside him, waiting for Mike to return.

"Wish I could, but I didn't get a chance to set that up." Bret gave him an odd look. "I put the camera in the last time I used the trailer, but the installers didn't get it done in time for me to set up a remote in here. It was something I had planned on doing the next time I had a few minutes and the trailer nearby, but it hasn't happened."

"Okay." Bert stood and stretched. "I'm going to see if Mike is ready and head back to my trailer. See you in the morning."

"I'll be right back." Storm stood.

"Uh-huh." He headed to the door. "You don't need me anyway."

Storm shook his head as he followed Bret out of the trailer, locked the door, and climbed down the three steps to the gravel which crunched under his feet as he walked to his trailer. He found his hand shook a little when he put the key in the lock. What would he find when he went in?

———

Hot water danced against her skin as she washed her hair for the fourth time. It was actually starting to feel normal again. Her senses picked up someone else nearby. She relaxed when she heard Storm talking to himself. He said he would be a while. Why was he in the trailer so soon? She went back to her hair, rinsing it once again. Heather wasn't going to rush her shower just because he came in.

Heather could feel him moving closer to the bathroom. Would he come in, or be too afraid and stay out? She knew he was questioning his desire for her. She picked up her liquid soap and started a good lather before she spread it down one leg, then the other. He was her mate and she wanted him back. There was no way she would make it easy for him to walk away from her if he did try to sneak a peek. Her heart beat faster when he entered the large bathroom, wondering how he was reacting to what he saw. It didn't take too long for her to know.

He groaned, drawing her gaze. Storm watched her as he shed his clothes quickly, joining her in the shower. His mouth claimed hers as he pinned her to the shower wall and drove into her. Her legs wrapped around him, pulling him in as deep as she could. He wasn't about to change his mind now. She was so glad he couldn't stop himself because she wanted this as much as he did.

"What is it about you that makes me throw caution to the wind?" He spoke softly against her throat. "To forget how I wanted to seduce you and show you I can be tender. Instead, I act like some animal."

"Wild or tender, I love the way you fill me, make my need spike just by your touch. A thrill races through my blood when you can't control yourself, knowing I drove you to this." She tightened against him as the pace he set hit a sensitive spot. He shuddered as her muscles rippled against him.

"You are addicting. The more I get, the more I want." Heather watched as he closed his eyes, lost in the sensations their intimacy brought out of them.

Each time he pumped into her she felt her release get closer. Spiraling tighter and tighter inside as her need took control and she met him thrust for thrust. Her heart pounded in her chest as her orgasm raced toward her, grabbing her and flinging her out with a scream. The walls vibrated with it. She turned boneless in his arms.

"You okay?" He brushed her hair out of her face, concern etched on his face.

"Oh, yeah." She smiled up at him. Her mate would have been proud he got a scream out of her, but the man who just got that scream looked worried. Did he think he hurt her? "I didn't upset you, did I?"

"No. Just wasn't sure if that was a scream of joy or of pain." He kept her pinned against the shower wall as little tremors still racked her body. A beautiful smile spread across his face as he watched her. "I have to say it was like music to my ears."

That made her happy. He loved it when she screamed before and now was no different. Once she felt she could stand again she made him aware of it. "You might want to put me down."

"Right." He withdrew from her and let her feet touch the ground. "Stay tonight. I have a little more work to do, but I want you to stay."

"If you have work to do, I can go back to my apartment." She wasn't sure if staying was the smart thing to do. Heather wanted to be with him but knew he had to be the one to initiate their intimacy. There was a fine line between being there for him and allowing him to take her for granted.

"But I have that big bed in there and we know that once isn't enough. Let me finish with my work then I'll wake you properly." His fingers slid along her jawline and down her throat to rest against her mark. He also didn't fight fair. His lips claimed hers, his tongue delved into her mouth, drawing a sigh and taking all the fight out of her. "Promise me."

"I'll stay."

"Good." He gave her a quick but heated kiss. "I'll be back as fast as I can."

———

Their connection was getting stronger. Each time they were intimate she could feel the mental bond reconnecting. If having sex with Storm was the way she had to get her mate back, she wasn't about to complain. After being used to having sex several times in one day, having to wait for it made her feel like she was starving when she did get it. It was one of the reasons why she screamed. Her body wanted it so bad she was ready to explode with a simple touch from him.

She toweled dry her hair then padded into the bedroom. Heather saw no reason to bother with clothing. Climbing between the crisp sheets, she curled up with a few pillows and turned on the large television facing her. She kept up with the news as well as some of the more recent history when she could find it. Things she should know to fit in.

Every once and a while someone would name a show or an event that she didn't know about. Most of the time she could blow it off by saying she was overseas, but not for the things that were around when she would have been a child. That she had to work on, and this was how she did it.

One person did give her an escape though. They asked her if she had a television when she was a child and she was honest. That saved her. But with shows and movies on television, DVD or accessible through the internet or streaming she tried to catch what she could so she wouldn't draw too much attention to herself.

She tuned into some reruns of a sitcom, curled up in the bed and watched.

———

Storm found it difficult to focus on the pictures. His mind kept going back to Heather. The way she was bent over as she soaped her legs. The look she gave him when she realized he was in the room. The way her body reacted when he drove into her. He had made her scream with pleasure. He couldn't help but be proud of that. She wasn't a vocal lover otherwise. She did enjoy the sex between them though. Her face showed her ecstasy every time.

He tried to work a little longer before giving up and heading back to his trailer. He didn't get far before he heard the whiney voice of Megan. Not what he wanted. He ran his fingers through his hair as he turned around.

"Why her and not me?" Megan's tear-stained face looked up at him.

"Megan, go back to your apartment." He took another step to the trailer. The girl was too young for him, and he had tried to tell her over and over. Maybe now she'd get the hint.

"I have tried everything to get you to notice me, yet you let a total stranger in and not me. Why?"

Storm turned to look at the young woman. "I'm too old for you. Princess, I could be your father."

"You're not that old, and I like my men older."

"You don't know my age. You never even asked." He wanted to say that the older men had most of the power and money too. Most of the young guys chasing after her probably couldn't rub two nickels together. She didn't want him. She wanted the prestige and power that came from his name. "If you wish to have Bret continue to use you as a model then you will go back into the restaurant or get in your car and head home. If you persist in this, I'll tell Bret I can't work with you."

Her face fell as she turned back toward the restaurant. She turned to look at him one more time before she walked inside.

He shook his head as he unlocked the door and stepped inside. Throwing the deadbolt, he sighed as he heard it snap into place. At least she wouldn't be bothering him anymore tonight. Music from the television floated to him. The thought of Heather in his bed filled him with excitement.

He found her curled up in the middle of the bed, asleep. Trying to keep quiet, he kicked off one shoe then another. He froze when she shifted in the bed, but she didn't open her eyes. Good, he promised to wake her properly and he was trying to keep that promise.

Next, he pulled his shirt off then slid his trousers down his legs. He sat on the bed and pulled his socks off. Now he gave his undivided attention to Heather. He closed his eyes and took a deep breath. Her personal scent filled his lungs. It smelled so good. He moved so he was behind her, lifting the sheet and blanket, he revealed her back to his gaze. It was so beautiful he couldn't keep his hands to himself. Pressing a kiss against her nape he slid his hand down her spine and then up over her hip.

Heather rolled onto her stomach, keeping her face away from him. She gave him all that lovely skin to touch.

"How long have you been awake?" He spoke next to her ear before he pressed another kiss to her back.

"I'm not awake. It's your imagination."

Storm laughed, his fingers gliding up and down her back. "Not if you're answering. What woke you?"

"I'm a light sleeper." She turned her head so she could look at him. "But I think it was the shoe that bounced off the wall before it hit the floor that caught my attention."

"Sorry about that." He continued to plant wet kisses down her spine. "Love the taste of your skin."

She smiled.

"Roll over."

"Why?" she rolled to her side, sliding her hand up his thigh.

"Because there is so much more I want to taste."

"I have a few things I'd like to taste too." She wrapped her hand around his erection.

"I'm about ready to explode and the way your body tightens around me is what I want to feel. If I let you do anything else that might not happen. Let me have my way with you and show you what you do to me. I promise it will be worth it."

———

Storm had never verbalized his reasons for not allowing her to explore his body that much when they were intimate. This made perfect sense. The glow in his eyes became so bright when they were intimate. Was he always that close to his release? How did he hold it back the way he did? This honesty was wonderful. She liked this side of him.

Heather relaxed back on the bed, wondering what he

had in store for her and how far he would get before his body took over and she found him deep inside her. He moved so he sat between her legs then started by brushing his fingers against her sensitive flesh. A gentle brush under the swell of her breast. A quick caress on her hips. Goosebumps followed his touch. A sigh escaped her when she felt the heat of his mouth follow the featherlike touch of his fingers.

"Like that do you?" His mouth closed over a pert nipple.

"Very much. You have a magic touch." She arched her back as he suckled her. He slipped his arms under her to help her keep the pose so he could focus on her breasts the way he wanted. His tongue swirled against the tip he worked on. Heather felt her insides clench.

His lips kissed their way down her stomach until he reached her mound. She sucked in her breath when she felt the brush of his tongue against her core. Heather wasn't going to last much longer herself if he kept this up. "Storm."

"I know my heart, you're close. I can smell it."

"Then please put me out of my misery. I need to feel you inside me now." He called her his heart. Joy shot through her.

He didn't need any more urging. Storm climbed back up her body and surged inside her. She moaned at the sweet invasion. Turning her head so her throat was exposed, she was blessed with his lips on her mark. Even though it was hidden from sight she could still feel the same arousing excitement from the heat of his kiss.

"This is a very sensitive spot for you, isn't it?" Storm set a wonderful pace that had her body humming quickly.

"Feel it to my toes." It took effort to speak when she could feel her orgasm trying to take over. She was so close that quickly.

Storm must have picked up on it because he changed his

stroke so her imminent orgasm backed off a little. He knew, somehow deep inside he knew. It brought tears to her eyes. She wanted her mate back one hundred percent, but it was nice to see that some things went deeper than memory.

"Please tell me those are tears of joy." He slowed his pace as he brushed a tear from the corner of her eye.

"I promise they are." One stroke stopped her from speaking for a moment. Heat blossomed deep inside. She arched against him again. "Oh my!"

"Hang on."

"I'm trying, my heart, but it feels too good. I can't fight it much longer." Her voice was barely a whisper.

"Will I get another scream?" he murmured against her throat.

"Are your walls soundproof?"

"As a matter of fact, they are."

"Then you just—" She arched up against him as her orgasm finally took hold. Speaking was beyond her. She didn't scream but moaned her pleasure as her body clenched against him. Her body soared through the stars. Storm shook a little in her arms as he followed her into his release as well. As they climaxed together, she felt their minds connect a little more.

———

Heather found Mike was right about the men who came to take down the sets the next day. They ate well and their tips made her happy. She had to keep filling up the trays, watching their leftovers slowly dwindle down. Several flirted with her and she smiled and laughed with them because she didn't want to be rude.

Storm though, showed his normal jealousy toward anyone who showed her a little too much attention. He glared at any man who spent more than a minute or two with her.

She waited until there was no one around when she confronted him. "Stop growling."

"What?" He looked at her. He seemed surprised that she noticed his behavior.

"I live off the tips. You keep giving them the evil eye and they won't tip me."

He growled at her next then stomped away.

"He doesn't look very happy for a man who should have a big grin on his face." Mike handed her another tray of food to put out. "You'd think the man would be a little mellower."

"Where did you come from?" She took the tray, wondering how long he had been nearby watching.

"What kind of question is that?" He pointed to the door that led to the kitchen. "I work here, remember?"

"I mean, I didn't know you were behind me."

"Ah, in other words, you want to know what I heard?"

"Yeah." She looked at him. "You know what is between Storm and me is private."

"I know. If I asked him anything he'd probably growl at me, too. He doesn't seem to like any man talking to you."

"Noticed that, huh?" She couldn't explain that he saw every man as a threat because of what they had been through. He just didn't know that so it surfaced as jealousy.

"Never known him to be jealous before."

Heather shrugged. What could she say? Storm was only trying to protect her? It would bring up far too many questions. Mike had already noticed the way they behaved around each other. She didn't need to feed his inquisitive mind.

Storm didn't wander too far from her side, but at least he didn't glare and growl at the men as they came up to get food. When she had a break, she brought him a sandwich or a drink. He needed to feel dominant, and she would cater to that to keep him happy.

She was happy when everything was done. Helping Mike, she placed the empty trays on one cart while he worked on consolidating the food into several bins. It didn't take them long before they had everything loaded and were rolling the carts up to the back door. Large trays sat, readied for them to place the empty bins and trays on the conveyor belt to send them through. The heat was overbearing from too much use. It seemed that the restaurant had twice as many patrons when one of these shoots was going on. The man she met the first day worked hard at running the dishes through, complaining about the water pressure and the heat.

"Can I speak to you for a minute?" Mike blocked her way.

"Sure." What did Mike want?

"In my office."

"Okay." She followed him into the tiny room he called his office.

Mike made a big show of sitting behind the desk and getting comfortable. Bear would do the same thing when he wanted to get her attention. Especially when she was in trouble. Mike was upset about something, and she was at the center of it.

"I know it is none of my business, but Mountain Man is a good friend of mine, and I don't want him to be hurt." Mike looked at her. He looked as uncomfortable as she felt.

"Mike." She smiled. It was nice to see that Storm had found a friend in this timeline. He didn't really have that at home because of his position.

"I know I sound like a mother, but he is very unique. It has taken a lot to get him where he is now, and I don't want to see him go backward."

"I would never do anything to harm him." She felt him like she did when her mind first started to expand. She knew he was looking for her and was getting frustrated because he couldn't find her. "Um, is that door unlocked?"

"I think so, why?"

"Because he's about ready to knock it down." Heather moved so when the door burst open, she wouldn't be hit by it.

"Where is she?" Storm filled the doorway as the door banged against the wall.

Mike just stared at him.

Heather waved from behind the door. "If you step back, I can come out of here. It is a bit tight."

"What are you doing back there? Hiding?" He glared at her.

"Avoiding a flying door. There isn't a lot of room in here." She placed her hands on her hips and glared right back. "Why are you here?"

"Looking for you."

"Well, you found me."

"I did." He fell silent then. Not sure what to say.

"Are we done, Mike?" She hoped he would let her go so she could take Storm with her and calm him down.

"For now, but we're not done with our conversation. Not by a long shot."

After what he just saw his comment didn't surprise her. She did have a lot of explaining to do. She brushed past Storm as she exited Mike's office.

"Why were you in his office? Alone?" He grabbed her arm to get her to turn toward him.

"Because I work for him and I assume he wanted to go over the catering event, but you never gave us a chance to start our conversation." He wasn't going to intimidate her.

She looked at his hand grasping her arm then looked up at him with a glare.

He didn't say anything. He just studied her.

"You don't trust me."

"I didn't say that."

"Then you don't trust Mike."

"Don't be absurd." He dropped his hand.

"Then we're back to me." She crossed her arms over her chest. "If you can't believe I don't want anyone but you, after what we've shared then we're done."

"Heather." He ran his hand through his hair.

Her heart pounded in her chest. She didn't want to walk away, but she knew him. Backing down wasn't an option. "What have I done to make you jealous?"

"I don't know." He looked around, realizing that anyone could hear them. "Can we go outside where we can speak privately?"

She gestured for him to head toward the back door.

He walked to it and opened it, waiting for her to exit first. She stepped out into the late afternoon sun.

"Talk." Heather turned to face him when she heard the door close.

"I lost my memory about two years ago. No one has stepped forward to claim me. I don't know who I am, or where I came from. I felt like I lost control. Then Bret found me and helped me find a life I could deal with. But I avoided intimacy. No one appealed to me."

"Until me and now you feel you're losing control again."

————

How did she understand what he was going through so easily? A flash filled his mind of her playing with two small tots, laughing at some antic one of the children had done.

He knew by their beautiful cherub faces they were their children. Could he have that with her?

"Storm. I am here for you and no one else." She placed her hand on his heart. "I might be flattered that other men find me attractive, but you are my heart, and it never wanders."

He placed his hands over hers then drew her close to him. His lips claimed hers, his tongue delved into her mouth. Tasting, exploring, enjoying the way she gave herself to him. The longer he drank from her lips the stronger his need for her grew.

Bret had left his trailer there for him to use for a few extra days. It had been done in the past so it wouldn't seem odd for it to be there, but Storm wanted it because of Heather. That tiny bed of hers would never hold him and he didn't think it was right to make love to her on the floor, even though he didn't seem to have any trouble using a wall here and there.

He started to maneuver her toward the trailer.

Heather broke the kiss. Mike had offered her the rest of the day off, but she wanted to finish her shift. "Storm, I have to go back to work. We have to wait until my shift is done."

"Mike will understand." His mouth moved to her mark, pulling the delicate skin in as his tongue swirled against it. Her knees buckled. He took advantage and scooped her up into his arms.

"The other women are depending on me." She didn't sound very convincing.

"I need you more than they do right now." He carried her to the stairs of the trailer before he put her down so he could open the door. "You are all I can think of. I want to feel your body accept me with the joy it does, feel your muscles tighten around me as you orgasm. Find the release I do when we're together. Don't make me wait."

The moment he got the door opened he picked her back up. His mouth went right to her neck again, stopping any sort of argument she might have used. Nothing mattered but feeling her moist hot sheath surrounding his length.

They reached the bedroom and he let her feet touch the ground once more. He peeled her shirt off, leaving the soft tissue of her throat long enough to pull it over her head. His fingers made quick work of her bra before he moved to her shorts. He eased them down her hips and his fingers slipped into her folds to caress her as he continued his assault on her throat.

She stood there for a few moments before her hands moved to his shirt, undoing each button with a deliberate slowness. Her fingers grazed across the weird tattoo under his right breast, and he felt it to his toes. He didn't want to wait any longer. Heather's hands slid down to the top of his jeans, and she pulled the zipper down. To him, she took forever to ease it down far enough to allow the jeans to drop down his hips. When her hand wrapped around his erection, he felt his body quake.

He forced the denim material down to where he could kick it off and be free. His desire to be with her had him touching and caressing until she lay beneath him. He surged into her, needing to feel her muscles tighten against him.

———

This was going to be difficult to explain. Mike expected her to finish her shift, not have sex with her mate. He wouldn't understand Storm's need to dominate her, prove he was in control, and she tried to delay this until she was done with her shift, but when his lips touched her mark, she could only think about how he made her feel. His desire sparked hers. By the time she felt him enter her, she was a roaring flame.

Being submissive was part of her job as Storm's mate, but when it came to sex she could be just as aggressive as he could be, and he loved it. She tilted her hips to give him deeper penetration. A groan escaped him.

"God, you feel so good." He picked up his pace, causing her muscles to contract around him. He shook at the sensation.

She smiled. Her hands roamed his chest, brushing against his mark without focusing too much attention on it. He hadn't talked about it, so she wasn't sure what he thought it was. Each time she touched it she heard him suck in his breath. He increased his pace again as his mouth found her mark.

The moment she felt the heat of his lips on her throat she couldn't focus. All she could do was feel. He pounded into her, making her body quake each time he filled her. His mouth on her neck spiked her arousal with each tongue swirl. Her muscles tightened as her release overtook her. It filled her blood and took her breath away. Each time was beautiful.

Once she could speak again, she could only say one word. "Wow."

———

While Heather showered so she could get back to work, Storm went to look for Mike. He needed to apologize for his behavior earlier.

Mike was walking to his house.

"Mike." Storm fell into steps with him.

"Mountain Man." The man didn't say anything else. He wasn't going to make it easy for him either.

"Look." He ran his fingers through his hair. "I don't know what came over me earlier."

"I think it was jealousy." Mike reached his porch and sat in a chair. "I have never seen you act like that before. There have been lots of women who have done their damndest to catch your eye and you totally ignored them. What makes Heather so different?"

"I wish I knew."

"If she's going to bring out the violent side of you maybe she's not good for you." Mike looked at him.

"It's not her." Storm wasn't sure how to explain what caused his reaction earlier. He started to pace on the porch. "It's the men who are attracted to her. There is a scent I pick up."

"So you think I'm attracted to her."

"Aren't you?" He had picked up that same scent from Mike, yet he knew he would never make a move on Heather if he thought Storm was interested. He felt the same way about any woman Mike might be interested in. He'd back off in an instant.

"Maybe a little, but I'm not ready and I've told you that. She's easy to talk to, people really like being around her. And she's beautiful. She's going to attract attention. If you can't handle that you're going to have trouble." Mike watched him. "You have to decide what you want."

"I know." Storm looked at his trailer where she probably stood naked as she spread soap over her body. Just thinking about it made him hard again. He couldn't get enough of her. "The problem is I'm not ready to make that decision."

"You're going to have to. She's only here for a few more weeks. What will you do if you wait too long and she moves on?"

———

Heather heard the door open as she was just turning the water off. She held a towel against her when Storm walked into the bathroom.

"Finished already?" He started unbuttoning his shirt.

"I've got to get back to work before Mike fires me." She watched as he exposed his chest. He was trying to distract her and was doing a very good job of it.

"Yeah, I spoke to Mike. He plans on giving you the rest of the day off. He needs you to work the dinner shift instead." He eased his arms out of the sleeves of his shirt.

"Oh." So the two men decided for her. Just what she wanted.

His hands went to the snap and then the zipper of his pants.

"Now we have a whole afternoon." He gave her one of his heart-stopping smiles. "You have anything in mind you'd like to do?"

She smiled back. Heather would never turn down time with her mate. "I'm thinking you already have something in mind."

His pants hit the floor and he stepped out of them. He stepped up to her and touched her face. "I do."

His lips claimed hers while he turned the water back on. Steam filled the air as he urged her backward until her back hit the warm, wet tile. He lifted her up, pinning her to the wall while their tongues danced with each other. When he broke the kiss, he blazed a trail down her throat to her mark. She sucked in her breath when he pulled the soft tissue into his mouth.

Her hands brushed along his muscles, at least the ones she could reach. He had his weight pressed into her to keep her in place as he focused on her neck. Her fingers glided over the muscles on his back, hitting the spots she knew aroused him. Heather smiled again when she felt him shake for a moment. That got the desired response.

"You aren't fighting fair." He lifted her up a little higher and captured a nipple in his mouth.

"Neither are you. This is the second time you have used sex to keep me from work." She arched against his mouth as desire blossomed in the pit of her stomach. Her heart started to beat faster.

"You want me to stop?" He murmured against one breast before moving to the other one.

"God, no." She raised one leg and wrapped it around his back. The movement brought his hands to her core. A small moan escaped her. Heather shuddered as he caressed her. Her desire spiked and her need climbed.

Storm let her slide down the wall a little when he turned his attention back to her throat. Her core touched the tip of his length. Using her other leg she wrapped it around him as well, trapping him against her heat.

Storm groaned and surged inside her, shaking when her body accepted him in. Her muscles contracted around him, her tight sheath hugging him as he set a pace that she knew would bring her orgasm fast. She tilted her hips, increasing the sensations. Her breath caught in her throat as she felt the tendrils of her release wrap around her.

It snaked its way up her spine, pulling her with it. Storm had to have sensed she was close because he shifted his hold on her and the tempo in which he drove into her. It didn't matter. She clung to him as he made her body sing.

"So close," she said, her voice soft.

"I know, my heart." He pounded into her, his release close too. She knew how he reacted to different things and when he started driving into her quicker or with more force, she knew he was almost there. Her body clenched around him as the fire from her release started to lick at her insides, racing through her blood and her mind. Her breath caught in her throat and her head dropped onto his shoulder as she felt herself go boneless once again.

———

Heather understood why Mike wanted her to work that evening. The dinner shift was slamming. The other waitresses slid by her in a hurry as they dashed about the restaurant. She knew what they were going through. Heather hustled as fast as she could to clear tables only to have them fill up again. It seemed to go on forever, but it did finally start to slow down.

"Go take a break."

"I'm fine, Mike."

"You have been moving faster than the rest of the girls and took on more tables when it got to be too much for them and promised the girls the tips from those tables even though you worked them. You have taken on more than you should. If you don't take this break, I'm offering then I'm going to fire you."

"What?" She wasn't sure she heard him right.

"And once I feel you have taken enough time to give yourself a rest, I'll rehire you to finish your shift."

"Aw, come on."

"Go, now." He pointed to the back.

"Mike."

"I'm a mean boss now go."

She laughed and headed to the back. Heather leaned against the wall in the supply area while she sipped a soda. It felt good to have a few moments to herself. It was nice to be away from Mike's watchful eye. He kept looking at her, making her nervous. What did he suspect? They hadn't finished their conversation earlier and she knew he had questions. She just hoped they were ones she could answer.

A frown creased her brow when she felt a wave go over her. It was weird, yet familiar and had her shields up quickly. Who had a mind strong enough to do a mindsweep? One that felt familiar? Fear filled her when she realized the last time she felt a sweep like that.

Ialog.

FIVE

She inched to the doorway of the dining room and saw him sitting at the counter. A few seconds later she saw Storm enter and spot the man. His face showed he wasn't happy to see him, but he sat beside the man anyway. They had to know each other. Heather got as close as she could to eavesdrop without being seen.

Why was *he* here? Now? Did he have something to do with Storm's lack of memory? It made sense that he did.

"Look Al, you come here every month and show me a picture of a woman I've never seen. Can't we skip this for once?" The tone in Storm's voice was laced with anger.

"Sorry, but the woman I am after is wanted by Homeland Security." He set the picture on the counter. "And she could show up any time. Knowing how dangerous she is, the sooner I find her the better everyone will be."

"You never told me why she is wanted." Storm picked it up and studied it then slapped it back down on the counter with a sigh.

Heather wished she could see it. One of the waitresses breezed past their seats and the picture fluttered to the ground, landing face up. Her heart skipped a beat. It was the picture Storm took of her yesterday. How did Ialog get a copy of it so fast? And what would Storm say? He took the photograph.

This couldn't be good. Ialog here? Looking for her. Would it ever stop?

———

Storm looked down at the image of Heather and frowned. It already had the jeweler's logo on it. How the hell did Al get this? The paper was thin and glossy like it had been cut out of a magazine. There was no way he should have this. Bret just left with the chip this morning. An uneasy feeling settled in his stomach. Was this the same picture he kept showing and Storm never recognized it until now?

One of the waitresses breezed by and knocked the picture off. Just as he was going to pick it up again Mike appeared and retrieved it from the floor. He looked at it and at Storm.

"Coffee?" He pulled up two cups from under the counter after setting the picture back down.

"Sure." Storm welcomed the interruption, but he didn't miss the look Mike gave him. He had to make his decision right now. He could ignore the fact that Al had a picture that had him questioning everything, turn Heather in, and be done with her. Go back to the calm, boring life he lived before she came. But did he want to? Especially to this guy? He never really liked the man. There was something that had his insides screaming not to trust him.

What should he do?

"Hi, Mountain Man." The voice grated on his nerves. Megan.

He looked up at the girl who was all smiles.

"I was hoping, maybe, we could get a drink together later."

"Megan."

"Sorry, Megan," Mike spoke up as he picked up a cloth to wipe the counter down. The picture floated to the floor again. "Your dad called, and he needs you home when you get off tonight. Don't forget your curfew."

She huffed as she turned to look at Mike. "My father is out of town."

Storm bent down to pick up the picture, folding it up and tucking it under his coffee cup.

"Shall I call him and let him know you don't believe me?" He draped the towel over his shoulder as he stepped back and leaned against the wall.

"No." She brushed her hair back, turned back to Storm, and slapped a smile on her face. "Perhaps another time, Mountain Man."

She stomped off to finish waiting on her tables.

"Did her father really call?" asked Storm.

"What do you think?" Mike smiled as he moved back in front of them and picked up the coffee pot. "Refill?"

─────

Heather feared Megan would see her and confront her, but Mike blocked her from view when he leaned against the wall. Not being able to see anything anymore, Heather wanted to use her senses to get a better idea of what was going on but didn't know what Ialog could pick up and she didn't want to give him any reason to suspect she was there. If Storm gave her away, she needed to escape, and every second would count.

A loud noise filled the air followed by clapping. Somebody must have dropped something. Storm had turned toward the sound and Mike had moved out of her sight to help, giving her the chance to see Ialog slip something into her mate's coffee.

After a few moments, Storm turned back around and took a sip. Heather felt their mental bond start to disintegrate. She fought it, keeping the older bonds open but the few that had just re-forged were gone. Mike stepped back where she could see him, spoke to Storm again, and turned to head to his office, spotting her standing in the hallway.

"What are you doing here?" He kept his voice low so no one else would hear them.

"Shh." She looked to where Ialog sat. "You need to get that cup from Storm."

"What is going on?"

"I'll explain later, but you have to get that cup. That man slipped something into it. I saw him and I think it is why Storm hasn't gotten his memory back."

Mike looked at Storm and the cup he had his hands wrapped around. "You have to come clean with me."

Heather nodded. Anything to get that stuff away from Storm.

Mike walked back out and stood in front of Storm. He picked up another cup and poured coffee into it.

"I haven't seen this woman." Storm slid the folded picture over. He jostled his cup, but Mike didn't move fast enough to take advantage and cause the cup to spill. Frustration filled her. The more he drank the more connections disintegrated.

"Keep it. I have other copies." Ialog stood. "Have a good day, Mountain Man. I'll see you in about a month."

Heather watched Mike switch out the cups with the finesse of a sleight-of-hand artist. He came back to her and handed her the cup. "I expect to see you on my porch in fifteen minutes."

She nodded. If Storm would let her. His libido had been working in overdrive since he had that trailer there.

———

Mike was sitting on the steps of his porch when Heather stepped out of the restaurant. She took a deep breath, wondering just how clean she had to get with Mike. He'd never believe the truth.

"Something to drink?" He looked up at her as she approached him.

"I'm fine." She brushed a strand of hair behind her ears. How was she going to do this? The truth would sound like science fiction to him. She turned and sat beside him.

"Okay." He remained silent as he looked at his diner, not Heather. "I guess I should start this, huh?"

"You are the one with the questions." She glanced at him before looking in the same direction, nerves getting the best of her. She wasn't sure how much she would have to tell, and she was a terrible liar.

"Who are you?" He shifted his weight on the top step so he could look at her.

"My name is really Heather. Heather Drexel." She glanced at him again before she went back to looking at the diner. Her uneasiness over this made it hard for her to make eye contact.

"Uh-huh." Mike didn't believe her. She could hear it in his voice. "And how do you know Mountain Man?"

"I met him here." She squeezed her hands together, hoping Mike would believe her.

"That is your first lie. You know him." Mike turned to look back toward his diner. A little muscle started twitching in his jaw.

She grinned. She had the ability to draw anger out in

people. Bear's jaw would do the same thing when she upset him or got in trouble with security.

"I've watched you around him, anticipating his wants and needs," said Mike. "Knowing when to defuse his anger and when to confront it. You couldn't have picked that up so quickly. It took me a while to get to know him that well."

She sighed. Something so simple and he noticed it. "I'm not sure how to answer that."

"Well, you better figure it out or I'll call Al and turn you in."

"He's not Homeland Security." Heather looked down at her hands. The memories of what she had been through because of this man flooded her mind. Would they ever be free from him?

"Figured that. But we'll talk about him later. Right now, I want to know who Mountain Man is to you." He touched her hand, making her look at him.

"He's my husband." She knew he wouldn't understand the use of mate, but using the human word just didn't sound right. Storm was so much more than the man she married. He was her life. A part of her felt empty when he disappeared, and she couldn't imagine what he went through the last two years.

Mike had been there for her mate when he needed someone. She wanted to be as honest as she could without revealing too much. There was a special bond between the two men. She had noticed that in the few times she had seen them together. If she didn't tell him the truth and he didn't trust her, he could try to force Storm to stay away from her. She could come between their friendship and didn't want to do that.

"What?" He grabbed her arm, shock laced his voice. "Why don't you tell him that?"

"The doctors told me my best bet was to interact with

him." She looked back at Mike. She didn't try to hide her frustration. "They hoped it would release his memories on their own. They felt that would be the best way to help him remember. The only way he would remember."

"But it hasn't." Mike was quiet for a moment. "What kind of quack doctor would tell you that?"

"Someone I trust." She grinned. Bert was no quack. "I know it doesn't make any sense. It didn't to me until a few minutes ago."

"You're talking about Al."

"Yeah, I didn't want to go along with this either. I didn't understand why I couldn't just bring him home then fix his memory, but I was told to make him remember before I brought him home. Then I saw Al and it started making sense." The moment Mike had handed her the cup earlier she had pulled out her comm device and had Cim analyze the contents of the drink. Then she sent it to Bert along with one short sentence. Ialog was here. If Bert could come up with an antidote, she could get her mate back. "Whatever that man slipped into Storm's coffee has been pushing his ability to remember his life before away. He must have been dosing him every time he came here."

"Is that his real name?"

"Yes." She nodded. "It's short for one most people can't say."

"Come on. Let's move to the chairs. I have a feeling there is a lot more to this than you're telling me, but at least you're trying." He helped her to her feet. "That picture. How did he get it? I don't think Mountain Man has turned over his photos to Bret yet."

That was the question, wasn't it? How much should she tell him? What would he believe? She sat in the rocker he gestured to. "It might seem a little farfetched to you."

"Try me." He started to rock in his chair. "I have seen a lot recently."

"Okay." She rested her hands against her knees. If he was as close to Storm as she suspected, did he know about Strom's shape-shifting ability? If so, he might believe her. "He's from the future."

"Right." Mike laughed. But as Heather looked at him his laughter died. "The future? How far in the future?"

She looked at her hands again. That was a question she didn't want to answer. "Far enough."

"Okay, so let's say he is from the future and your silence is telling me that you and Mountain Man are too. I'm not sure if it's something I can believe, but it does make sense. Sort of. Are you saying he used it because he didn't know the picture hadn't been published yet so thought it would be safe to show to Mountain Man?"

"That's my guess. He probably knew Storm took the picture." She started to rock. "Bret told me at the shoot how long it would take before that image showed up in a magazine if it was picked up, and I was surprised at the long lag time between the shoot and it being published. He also explained the picture itself would be available for mock-ups as soon as the jewelry company gave their okay."

"That was from a magazine. I've seen Mountain Man's work enough to know the before and after difference."

"I wouldn't have. I never would have known any of that if Bret hadn't told me and I doubt Ialog knew the intricate details of how the picture ended up in a magazine either. If he had waited a week to show up, then we'd be having a different conversation because it could have already been sold and Storm might have turned me over to the man, knowing the company would have probably copyrighted it and added their logo as they worked with it. There's no telling how many people will see that picture in the upcoming weeks." She paused for a moment. "I was surprised he didn't anyway."

"He had a choice and he made it."

"I'm not sure I understand." She looked at Mike after his comment.

"His reaction to you confuses the crap out of him and he wasn't sure what he should do about it. I told him he had to make a decision." Mike looked back at the diner. "You seem to bring out a little bit of aggressiveness in him."

"He frightened you earlier, didn't he?"

"I had never seen him like that." He paused for a moment. "He was so hyper-focused on you it did scare me. What would he have done if he hadn't been able to find you?"

"Storm is aggressive, but I've never seen him violent." Heather knew Storm had a knack for being overpowering and it sometimes frightened people. "He's just a little over-protective when it comes to me. Whether he remembers why or not."

"So you think the crazy man I saw earlier was trying to protect you?" He looked at her again. "Why would he have this overpowering desire to keep you safe?"

"Because of what we've been through. I know my husband and he was trying to protect me." Heather wondered what she should tell him. "As a couple, we've had a few issues with my safety, so trust comes hard for him. He just doesn't remember why he feels this deep urge to protect me. Why it pushes him the way it does. That was why you thought he was crazy. He could be thinking the same thing."

"So how do you help him get his memory back?"

"I thought my presence would do it. That was what I was led to believe, but now knowing he's been drugged I don't know." She sighed. "I'm hoping I can find an antidote for it."

"If you can't?"

"I'll have to wait for whatever Al gave him to wear off."

———

She finished with her shift and headed up to her room. Storm didn't say anything about wanting her to stop by and she wasn't going to force herself on him. He was still sitting at the counter the last time she saw him. Let him make the next move.

The first thing she did was peel off her uniform. Smelling like salad dressing and fried chicken wasn't one of her favorites. The shower felt good. So did slipping into something more comfortable. She put on yoga pants and a long-sleeved t-shirt and stretched. Having time to herself, she meditated. The first thing she did was check the connections between her mind and Storm's. As far as she could tell what she fought to keep was still there. Could she get the new ones back?

With her eyes closed, she followed one of the tenuous lines that had been broken. Working slowly, she was able to reconnect it. Heather rubbed her forehead. It would take some work, but she knew she could repair the damage done. Pushing her mind like this hurt, but she would do what she had to in order to regain what she lost. Her phone beeped. She opened her eyes to see what it said. A shift in the shadows outside her door caught her attention as she picked it up.

You have a guest.

Please don't let it be Ialog. She knew better though. Cim would have warned her long before he would have climbed the stairs. It had to be Storm. So he was making the first move.

She crossed to the door and opened it. He stood there looking a little lost. Her heart went out to him. "Should I close it and let you knock?"

He grinned then. That heart-stopping, bone-melting one she loved to see. "No, but you did catch me trying to get up my nerve to knock. Why didn't you come to the trailer?"

"Well, this is my apartment. You know, where my stuff is?" She stepped aside to let him in. "The trailer is yours."

"I know." He stepped in and looked around. He seemed nervous. This was a side she hadn't seen before. Storm always knew what he wanted and didn't ever question whether he would get it or not. "But I thought you would want to take advantage of the shower and big bed."

"I'm not assuming anything." She felt a little nervous too. She found she needed to do something with her hands, or she'd be all over him. She grabbed a pillow and held it close. "If you want me there you need to tell me."

He took the pillow out of her hands, wrapped an arm around her waist, pulled her close then touched her face in his gentle way. Desire glowed in his eyes. "I do want you there."

She smiled at him. His libido was in control, the glow showed that, but she hoped there was more at play here now. Pressing her hand against his heart, she used the gesture to break his hold. She slipped her feet into her sneakers and grabbed her keys. "Let's go."

He followed her down the stairs but the moment her feet hit the ground Storm had scooped her up in his arms and carried her toward his trailer. She felt his lips against her throat, showing he couldn't wait to get them inside.

"You know I can walk." This was so like her mate. When

his need overpowered him, she normally didn't get too far on her own.

"I know, but this gave me the perfect excuse to touch you. I want you badly and need to feel your skin against mine. If I let you walk, we might not have made it into the trailer before my need had me pushing you up against the side of it. You deserve better." He reached the door and opened it. Once it slammed behind him, he let her feet down, but didn't let go of her as he reached behind him to throw the lock. Then he started his assault.

His mouth covered hers, a quick swirl of his tongue against her lips and she opened for him, letting him deepen the kiss and draw her tongue to dance with his. They swirled around each other, spiking their desire, their need.

He maneuvered her toward his bedroom, through the doorway, and to his bed. Storm only broke the kiss long enough to get her on the bed before he joined her and captured her lips with his once again. Soft fingers brushed against her skin, igniting her want for him. His hands caressed her and slipped under her top. She felt him work the hem of her shirt up to expose her breasts to his touch. Storm broke the kiss then pulled the shirt off her before his lips worked their way down her neck to her mark. The soft tissue begged for the heat of his mouth, the swirl of his tongue.

He wanted more. Slowly he kissed his way down across her collarbone to the tender flesh of her breast. He sucked on the delicate tissue as he removed the rest of her clothes, planting kisses as he exposed her skin. His tongue then dipped into her belly button before blazing a hot wet trail back to her other breast. She felt every one of those kisses to her toes.

As he undressed her, she did the same for him. His shirt unbuttoned easily, and she eased it off his shoulders.

Brushing soft strokes against his skin, she worked her way down to his jeans, easing the snap open and sliding the zipper down until she could grasp his member easily.

They sighed when they were finally free of their garments. Their legs entwined as they explored each other. Storm touched all the right places, making her want him buried deep inside only the way he could fill her.

Storm drove into her, his desire pushing him to feel her body take him in.

She felt the world slip away until it was just the two of them. Each stroke took her breath away. One of the connections she lost was reattached. Joy shot through her. She wouldn't have to wait for the bonds to come back. By the time they reached their orgasms, she should have all the connections back and maybe even get a new one or two.

Heather wanted more, though. She wanted her mate back.

Storm must have sensed something because he touched her face. "You okay?"

She smiled. Instead of answering him, she urged him on his back. "I am now."

"Like it on top?" His hands cupped her breasts as she settled around him.

"Very much, but I seem to like every position we've done." She licked her lips in anticipation of what would happen between the two of them. The joy she knew they would feel as they shared their bodies with each other.

"Even up against the wall?" His voice came out husky as if he was anticipating the same thing.

"Especially up against the wall." Heather took her time, sliding up and down his length, slowly taking him in as deep as she could each time. "That is when you lose control just a little because of me and I love that."

"And I love your moans and screams." He placed his

hands on her hips.

Her head dropped back as she got caught up in the sensations. Each time she slid down his length she felt him stroke one of her more sensitive spots. Exquisite desire filled her blood. He filled her completely, causing her breath to hitch. She wasn't sure she could take much more. "So close."

Storm slid his fingers into her folds and that was all she needed to be pushed over the edge. She shattered in his arms and fell boneless against him.

"Rest, my heart, because there is more where that came from."

She could only hope.

––––––

The trailer was picked up the next day. Storm was sad to see it go, but he knew he couldn't ask Bret to let him keep it any longer without raising questions. Ones he wasn't sure he was ready to answer. How did he feel about Heather? He knew he wanted her but was there more to it? He had been asking that question a lot lately but still had no answer.

He had an opportunity to walk away when Al showed up with the picture of Heather, but the fact he had a picture that he shouldn't have had made Storm want to protect her instead. Mike told him to choose. By not turning her in had he chosen her?

He needed time to think. Looking up at the full moon, he wondered what she would think if she knew the truth about him. Would she run away screaming?

Storm had told her he'd probably be away for a few days so she wouldn't expect him. The change should be taking him over at any time. It always did at this time of the month. It surprised him it didn't just force him into a change. It seemed to time itself, waiting for him to be ready.

He thought about Heather. Her body responded to his slightest touch. Having the heightened senses allowed him to pick up the subtleties of her scent. Each time he knew when she became aroused by something he said or did. Just being around her had him in some state of arousal all the time. Even now he was starting to feel the beginnings of his need for her.

He took off running, lifting his snout and taking a strong sniff. Her scent carried on the wind. Instinct took him in her direction. She must be running because he was now heading down the trail leading away from the diner and into the park that surrounded it. The fact she took good care of her body made him proud. Why, he wasn't sure.

He spotted her on the trail that weaved through the park near his home. In his wolf form, Storm was about ten feet above her so she shouldn't be able to spot him. He trailed behind her as she followed the path. He could see colors coming off her. If he had hands, he would slap himself on the head. He had looked at her aura several times but never paid any attention when he should have. As a wolf he could see the truth about her through her aura. If she had anything to hide, he would see it in the bright colors that surrounded her.

Focusing, he watched as her aura flowed around her. It was a beautiful color, deep violet with touches of blue. Pure colors surrounded her. He sighed in relief. She was pure in spirit. No hidden agenda.

A sound off to the side caught his attention and he went to investigate.

Megan? What was she doing here? She should be working or at home. Her promise to her father and the police was pretty explicit. He got close and growled at her, scaring her and sending her running to her car. Once he was sure she had left he went back to following Heather.

Heather finished with her run and climbed the steps to her apartment. The full moon lit the doorway, so she didn't have trouble finding the keyhole. A full moon? Really? Did Storm think he was a werewolf or something? The growl she heard earlier warned her she was being followed by him in his wolf form and she was pretty sure he had followed her back to the diner.

The fact that Ialog had been here had her wondering if he showed up about the same time each month. Could the drug he gave Storm interfere with his shifting to where he couldn't control it? She needed to talk to Cim.

She opened her door and crossed to her handheld device.

"Cim, what is the analysis on the drink?"

"It is an inhibitor. Bert is working on an antidote and will try to get that to you as soon as it is ready."

"Could the drug also affect Storm's shifting ability? Maybe make it uncontrollable for a few days after taking it?"

"It is possible. I'll rerun the data to look for that side effect and give you an answer in a few minutes."

"Thanks, I'll take a shower while I wait." The hot water felt good bouncing against her skin. She tilted her head back, enjoying the sensation. Storm had shifted before when she first met the white wolf, but it was close enough to the full moon for him to think that was what affected him.

Warning signals filled her. Someone was at her door. Her heart started beating harder when she heard the door open. She was sure she had locked it. Taking a protective stance, she waited. Whoever it was had no clue what she was capable of.

SIX

Storm sat in a copse of trees and bushes outside Heather's little apartment. His ultra-sensitive hearing picked up her voice, but he wasn't sure what she said or who she was talking to. He only picked up her scent so she must be alone, probably on the phone.

He couldn't stay away from her. It didn't make sense to him. He had abstained for the last two years because of the scents the women gave off, but Heather drew him to her. Even now, in his wolf form, he wanted her. His desire for her didn't seem to bother her either. She gave her body to him willingly, no matter how many times he demanded it. Storm was amazed he hadn't put either of them in the hospital as often as he wanted it.

The sound of water came from her place, and he knew she was in the shower. The thought of her naked and wet had him moving to her door before he realized what he was doing. He knew where Mike hid the key to the apartment. Storm had it in the lock and the door opened before he could stop himself.

Now he stood in her apartment naked. When did he

change back? Hell, he didn't remember turning into a wolf, just suddenly realized it had happened when he started to follow Heather's scent.

He wanted to call out but found his voice not working. Storm didn't want to frighten her. Movement behind the shower curtain put him on alert as she charged out of the small stall ready to do battle. Heather struck him in the face with her foot, but before she could do anything else he wrapped his arms around her and squeezed.

"Oh! Hell no!" She struggled against him, forcing him to pin her to the wall. It jarred her a little but stopped her long enough so she would look at him. "Storm? How the hell did you get in here? Mike have a hidden key or something?"

He nodded. Her softness relaxed, making him think of why he climbed the stairs in the first place. He wanted her. He always wanted her. "…need…"

She ran gentle fingers along his jaw. "That explains so much."

Storm didn't want to take her against the wall. She deserved better, but when she wrapped her long, beautiful legs around his waist he could only think of sinking his length into her wet heat. Bracing her with his arms, he captured her lips and he buried himself deep inside her. She gasped into his mouth as he filled her. Her muscles contracted around him, giving him a deliciously tight sheath for him to slide in and out of. "Heather."

"Shh. Just make me scream."

———

She hadn't sensed Storm at the door and now she knew why. They always lost their connection when he became a wolf. The moment he tried to speak she knew what had happened. His lack of clothing was also explained when she realized he had just shifted. He still hadn't figured out how to shift back with his clothes on.

His desire for her drove him to her doorstep. That made her happy. Now she needed to get him to admit how he felt about her, but she wasn't sure if he was ready.

He pulsed inside her, bringing her back to reality. His mouth moved from her lips to her throat. When they came into contact with her hidden mark she moaned. Her muscles tightened around him causing him to moan in turn.

The pace he set had her quaking in his arms. Each time he filled her he slid in deep, brushing the spot that caused her strongest orgasms. She clutched at his back, wanting more. He picked up the pace, making her moan again. It was exquisite torture. She was so close to her release, but it was still just out of her reach.

Storm slipped his hands down and grabbed her derriere and tilted her hips, which intensified the need in her. Her head dropped onto his shoulder as she met him thrust for thrust. "So close." Her voice was just above a whisper.

Then it started, everything inside her clenched as her release blossomed from her core to race through her blood. She felt like she was freefalling as it enveloped her. Storm's body tensed as he reached his orgasm as well. Heather collapsed against him, unable to move.

"You become quite boneless afterward, don't you?" He brushed some hair away from her face.

"Can't help it. Each time is always so intense," her voice soft.

"And up against the wall again. I can't seem to control myself when it comes to you." He eased himself out so she could put her feet on the floor.

"And you will never hear me complain." She smiled up at him. "I love the fact that I can make you lose control for a little bit."

"But I'm not showing you any respect."

"You showed me the best respect a woman can ask for. You waited for me." How would he interpret that? The fact that he was celibate until she showed up proved how much he loved her.

His brow furrowed for a moment. "It would be a little rude to reach my release before you reached yours."

Her smile widened. He didn't get it yet. She was going to have to push a little harder. "You are funny."

He moved to the door.

She could sense his unease. He had followed his instincts because of his need and now regretted it. "You don't have to leave."

"I'm naked."

"Hey so am I."

He looked at the twin bed and frowned again. "That is too small."

"How about the recliner? We could use the comforter and curl up together there."

He hesitated, looking at the door then the chair before he looked at her again. "Alright."

So he didn't want to leave her. He crossed to the recliner and sat while she grabbed the comforter on her bed and joined him. He shifted to the right so she could get comfortable. God how she missed this. The simple body contact was something they always shared.

She sighed as she settled against him. He wrapped his arms around her and held her close.

———

This felt so right. Storm rested his chin on the crown of Heather's head. She was nestled against his side, her head resting on his chest. Those wonderfully long legs entwined with his. He found he couldn't keep his hands still and he ran them up and down her back. He loved the feel of her soft skin under his fingertips.

Her odd comment kept running in his head. What did she mean by he had shown her respect by waiting? The look on her face when he responded showed she wasn't thinking about who climaxed first so what did she mean? He found it confusing. Yet here she was, naked in his arms, dozing. Her trust in him amazed him.

He should pick her up, put her in her bed, and leave, but he didn't want to. Why? Storm pulled the comforter close around them. Something about her had him wanting her near him all the time, but what did he know about her? Her aura told him she had no hidden agenda, yet he still wanted to question his attraction to her. Since she showed up his world had been turned upside down.

He needed to make sense of it all and having her this close only had him thinking of one thing. Maybe he shouldn't have come here.

———

Three days later Heather had a day off. She didn't know what to do with herself. So used to having her days planned, having this much time to herself was something she wasn't used to. and she was feeling a little lost. She needed to fix the situation.

The first thing she wanted to do was to check up on the information Cim had on the chemical Ialog had been giving Storm. Knowing what the man used would let them know how long it might stay in his system if they couldn't find an antidote.

"Can we counteract what Ialog has done to Storm?"

"Bert hasn't found anything yet, but he did learn the

chemical does dissipate. That is why Ialog comes to see him regularly. He needs to have a dose about once a month to keep his memories locked away."

"So since I stopped that last dose he should start getting his memories any time."

"Bert hopes so, but Storm has been taking those doses for two years. It could take months for it to leave his system."

"And there is nothing we can do that will help accelerate Storm getting his memories back?" She could be trapped here with her mate for months? What about the twins? Heather missed them so much and worried when she would get to see them again. All because of Ialog. But she had a bigger question to face. How was she going to keep Ialog from finding out she was there?

"Sorry."

Heather hated hearing that. "Then I need to push him. I want my mate back."

"Be careful. You could push him away."

"I refuse to think he would walk away when his heart knows who I am."

———

Heather felt like she was showering all the time. She had already run out of soap and needed to get more. Luckily, Storm had introduced her to that little shop. It wasn't too far from the diner, and she knew the way. She had the morning off, so she put on her riding suit, gloves, and helmet and jumped on the back of her bike. The people from the place Storm had taken her to a week ago made her feel so comfortable she knew it would be a perfect place to go to pick up what she needed. The huge conglomerates would just confuse her.

The small store had a few cars outside it when she pulled

her bike to a stop. Knowing others appreciated their business made her smile. They were very sweet and deserved to have people show their loyalty.

When she walked in, she found Megan in the store. Her smile melted. What was she doing here? Heather saw the schedule, wasn't she supposed to be working? She hoped she hadn't changed her schedule and would be working with Heather later that day. The girl never did any work and Heather knew she'd be covering most of the restaurant.

She studied Megan. This young woman was going to be a complication if she thought she could win Storm away from her. Why was she fixated on her mate anyway?

Heather removed her helmet and gloves and started to look around.

"Ah, the pretty lady Mountain Man introduced to us." The woman who worked with Heather said a bit loudly. Her words made Megan turn around. "How are you today?"

"Very good." Heather greeted her with a smile. Great, now Megan knew she was there. She had hoped to stay in the background until the girl left. "I need to pick up a few things."

"I'll get you a basket." The woman took off and was back quickly with a little plastic basket for her to use. "What do you need?"

"Shampoo, soap, and a good lotion. I seem to be drying out a little more than I thought I would."

"Not surprising if you're not used to mountain air. Switching climates can wreak havoc with your system. How bad is it?"

"Not too bad." Heather brushed her hand down one arm. "I just can feel my skin isn't as soft as I'm used to."

They worked together until Heather was happy with her choices. When she went to the register Megan was standing there. Heather didn't want another confrontation but didn't think she'd be able to avoid it.

"I want you to leave him alone."

"This again?" Heather looked at the woman on the other side of the register, wishing the girl had picked a more private time to confront her. Having an audience just made the whole situation stickier.

"He is mine. You need to back off."

"Have you spoken to St-Mountain Man?" Heather looked at Megan. "Does he agree?"

Megan refused to answer.

"Your total is twenty-five thirty-three."

"Maybe he's the one you should be talking to." Heather paid for her items and smiled at the woman who helped her. She then turned her attention to Megan again. "I'm not the one who keeps showing up on his doorstep."

Megan gave Heather her best pout. That might have worked on the men, but she wasn't impressed. Heather turned to the woman behind the register. Maybe if she ignored Megan she would go away. Megan did back off as they finished up.

"I see you have met the waitress," commented the woman who had been taking care of her as she bagged Heather's items. "She follows him all the time."

"Yes." Heather smiled. *Unfortunately.* "She works at the restaurant with me. We also got to work together during the shoot Mountain Man had near the restaurant the other day."

"Yes, we heard about that. You modeled too?"

"I helped Mike with the catering." She didn't want to make matters worse by telling them she did model as well. With Megan within earshot, she knew one wrong word would get the girl back in her face.

"Too bad. You'd make a beautiful model." The woman

handed her a folded-up glossy page. "Someone left this here. Will you give it to Mountain Man?"

"Sure. May I look?"

The woman nodded.

Heather unfolded the paper to see the same picture Ialog had shown Storm. No wonder why she asked if she had modeled. She had seen this picture. This meant Ialog had been here as well. What did they tell Al? Heather hadn't thought he'd be looking for her this hard. She never thought to make sure they wouldn't recognize her in a picture. Not much she could do now.

"The man who left this was a very unpleasant man. We had to ask him to leave after he asked questions we couldn't answer."

"I'll make sure he gets it." Heather wanted to kiss the woman. Her words told Heather they didn't reveal her presence here. She tucked it inside her suit. Heather took her bagged items, thanked the woman, and headed to the door.

"Give that to me and I'll make sure Mountain Man gets it." Megan blocked her exit, gesturing for the picture.

"Sorry." Heather moved around her.

"I said give that to me." She tried to reach into Heather's suit to find her hand in a tight grip that drove her to her knees. She cried out in fright.

"I don't think you understand just who you are dealing with." Heather looked down at the girl at her feet. "I am a military officer and have been trained in every form of martial art there is. I'm a master of those arts. If you try to touch me once more, I will make sure you will never be able to use these hands again. If you interfere with me in any way from this point on, I will make sure you won't be able to do it to anyone else. Go home, Megan. You can't compete."

The hatred that radiated out of her eyes let Heather

know she wasn't going to give up. Should she alter the girl's mind? Make her forget her infatuation with Storm? She didn't like doing that to anyone. What harm could this slip of a girl cause?

Heather decided to let her go, for now. But if Megan became a problem, she would have to do something to take her out of the equation.

———

Heather flew across the asphalt on her way back to the diner. She loved the freedom the bike gave her. It almost made her forget about the run-in with Megan at the store earlier. Maybe she should have gone ahead and altered Megan's mind. It sure would get the girl out of the way. Knowing she had no chance at taking her mate from her had Heather feeling a little sorry for the young woman instead.

Coming up around a sharp turn she caught movement in front of her. Something large and brown bolted onto the road. Her helmet identified it as a young doe. The thing was barely a year old, but large enough to cause some major damage if she were to hit it.

"Crap." The only way she could avoid the fawn now standing in her path was to throw her bike. This could hurt. "Cim, turn my suit up to protect me."

She hit the brakes and prayed it would work. The bike skidded, sliding sideways down the road as she flipped and rolled to a stop several hundred feet before the bike. She lay there, taking inventory. Nothing seemed to be broken. Heather tried to sit up only to find it beyond her capabilities at the moment. Everything hurt. "I thought I asked you to turn the suit up, Cim."

"I did, but you weren't the only one on the road and there are too many witnesses for you to come out of this unscathed.

I made sure you were protected to a point, but you had to have some damage, and bruises require no doctor."

She lay there in agony, wondering if she was going to be able to ignore the pain enough to steer the bike to Mike's after this. Her thoughts were interrupted when a shadow fell over her.

"You okay?" A young man kneeled at her side.

She nodded then grimaced at the movement. Pushing herself, she opened the visor of her helmet. "Just a little banged up."

"Can you stand?" He touched her shoulder.

"You can't move her," said another driver. "She needs to go to a hospital."

"No hospital." She offered her hand to the man who spoke to her first. He pulled her to her feet, which took a little longer than she would have liked. Her body screamed in torture as she regained her feet. Even though it hurt like hell to move, she lifted her hands to her head and released the seals on her helmet then pulled it off. "See? I'm fine."

"Where were you headed before Bambi decided to jump in the way?"

"To the diner down the road." Heather looked down the road but wasn't sure which direction that was at the moment. Pain sliced through her head as she turned to where her bike had slid. "My bike!"

"Don't worry about the bike. It can be replaced." He studied her, a frown on her face. "You sure you're okay?"

"Yes." She forced herself to walk to the bike and crouched down. A moan escaped her and white-hot pain shot through her as her legs screamed at the mistreatment. "Poor baby."

"It looks pretty mangled, but if you hadn't dumped it you would have been badly hurt. When you run into a deer you always lose." He helped her to her feet again. "I can take you and the bike down to the diner if you'd like."

"I don't want to take you out of your way." The words sounded hollow in her ears. His help would be wonderful right now.

"No problem." He helped her into the cab of his truck. The bike took a little more work, but he did manage to get it in, and the tailgate closed. "You know Mike?"

"I'm filling in for Patti."

"The new girl. Heard about you." He put the truck in gear and turned it around. "I'm Patti's husband."

"How's Patti and the baby?"

"Wonderful. They're home now and Patti was craving one of Mike's pot roasts. Made me come up here to get it." He laughed as he shook his head. "Lucky for you I came along when I did, or you could still be lying on the asphalt with a bunch of people staring at your form while they waited for an ambulance to show up."

"Thank you."

"That was weird the way that doe just stood there like it had been pushed out into the road or something."

———

Mike was surprised to see Bo back so fast. "Did you forget something?"

"More like found something." He looked out the door behind him to where Heather was just climbing out of the truck. She was moving very slowly like each movement was painful. Mike started moving toward her. "What happened?"

"She took a nasty spill."

"Is she okay?" He opened the front door and headed

outside, the din of the dining room fading to the sounds of tires crunching on the gravel parking lot.

"I'm fine." Heather wrapped her arms around her waist.

"She did several flips then rolled about one hundred feet but refuses to go to the hospital." Bo came out with Mike. "She's stubborn like a brother-in-law I know."

Mike cut him a glare before he turned his attention back to Heather. "You don't look fine. Let's get you inside."

"I don't want any more attention than I already have had. Can we please go to my apartment? All I need to do is rest for a while."

Mike looked at her. Her eyes held a hard edge. She was in a lot of pain. Rest wasn't going to fix the problem quickly. Why wouldn't she go to the hospital? "The doctors would give you something for the pain."

"No hospital and the pain isn't that bad." She reached into the truck to grab her helmet and grimaced.

"Right." He took the helmet from her. "Let's go."

"What about the bike?" asked Bo.

"Put it by the house. I'll look at it later." He slipped an arm around her waist.

"Don't worry about the bike, Mike. I'll fix it later." She moaned and removed his arm. "I'm better on my own."

"You are one of the most stubborn women I have ever met. Can you climb the stairs on your own or do you need help?"

She glared at him and headed to the stairs. Mike wanted to laugh. It was as good as the ones Mountain Man gave him. "I'll be up in a minute. Need to do something first."

Mike headed to his house. He had some ibuprofen she could take, and he needed to contact someone. Turning on the CB he tuned it to the right frequency. "Mountain Man? It's Mike. There has been an accident."

It took a few seconds before he got an answer. He smiled.

Mike hadn't been sure if Mountain Man was even near his radio, but the deep baritone voice filled the air as he responded. "Who?"

"Heather."

"Be right there."

He might be meddling, but if anyone could talk her into going to the hospital it would be Mountain Man.

———

Heather sat in the recliner. It was as far as she could get. Every muscle screamed as she climbed the steps to her apartment and opened the door. She couldn't even lift her hand to relock the door. Just fell into the chair, glad she could be still for a few moments. Cim said he put her suit at seventy percent. What would have happened to her if she hadn't had a chance to get the protective shield up? She looked down at the suit. She couldn't even get out of it.

Mike had come in and offered her a few tablets for the pain, tried to get her to go to the hospital again then left, promising to check up on her in a little while.

She had been dozing when she heard a knock on the door. "Let yourself in, Mike. I'm not moving."

The squeak of the door told her someone had come in, but when she didn't hear it close, she opened her eyes to find Storm standing there. He didn't say anything, just shut the door, moved to her side, and touched her face.

"What are you doing here?" She shifted in the chair to sit up better. That didn't hurt half as bad as it did when she sat down. Those pills must be working.

"Mike called me. What happened?"

"Mike has a big mouth." She sighed. Although Heather didn't want Mike meddling, she was happy to see him. "Had a run-in with a deer."

"A deer?" His gaze raked her body. "You could have been killed."

"I'm fine, Storm, and have been through worse." She shifted again. This time she leaned on her right side and moaned. That side hurt more. "Just a little bruised."

"Then why are you still in your biker suit?"

She bit her lip then smiled. "Because it hurt too much to take it off."

"Come on. Let me help you." He gently pulled her to her feet. Storm studied the suit for a minute. "How does it come off?"

"Seals. The main one is just to the left of my right collarbone."

His finger went to the edge of her outfit and felt around until he found the indentation that opened the seal. The brush of his fingers against her skin sent desire racing through her blood. His touch always did that to her.

He eased the closure open until he hit her right ankle.

"There is something similar on the other ankle and on each wrist. It will allow the suit to come off easier." She felt the other locations snap open then the heat of his hand as he continued to open the suit. Once he had everything open the suit dropped off her. Now she stood there naked.

"If you weren't in so much pain, I would take advantage of this." His hand trailed across her abdomen. "You are so beautiful."

She touched his face with her right hand. Even this slight movement hurt. Her body was covered with bruises. There was a heavy concentration of them on her right hip and thigh, her shoulder and upper arm. Some had already started to change colors. Some red, some green but all heading to the ugly purple that showed a deep bruise.

He smiled. "You need to remain still. What do you want to wear?"

"The easiest thing I have to slip on is a maxi dress in the closet."

Storm got the dress and slipped it over her head. It was a halter top, so she didn't have to worry about putting her arms through any sleeves, but it still hurt to lift them above the skirt. Her mate tied it behind her neck.

"All done." Once she was covered, he brought her to the chair and eased her into it.

"You should go to the hospital."

"Which is why Mike called you in the first place. All they are going to do is tell me I'm really bruised, and they want to keep me for observation. And while I'm there they will run a bunch of tests. Tests that will raise questions. You of all people should understand why I don't want to have a bunch of doctors get a hold of my DNA." She waited for the question he should ask. *Come on Storm ask me.*

He didn't say anything right away. Storm wanted to, she could see it in his eyes, but the internal debate on what he should do ended with the words, "I won't force you to go."

She wanted to sigh. He still wasn't ready. "Good because I'd go kicking and screaming."

"Stubborn."

"Just like you."

"I figured the reason I had to come here instead of a hospital was because you refuse to go. And you're right, all the doctors are going to do is give you some pain medication and prescribe bed rest. I don't think you're going to move that much for a few days, and I brought these." He pulled a small bottle out of his pocket. "It's ibuprofen."

Heather took the bottle and read the label. "I already took some of those."

"I figured that. But if they came from Mike, they were store-bought so not a high dose. These are prescriptions. How many tablets did he give you anyway?"

"Two?"

"And how long ago? About an hour or so?"

"Yeah."

"The ones you took earlier were only two hundred milligrams each. These are eight. I know you're not supposed to take someone else's medication, but I don't think this dose will hurt you." He handed one tablet to her. "Take it when you're ready."

She nodded. Heather closed her eyes for a moment. Not moving felt good. She heard another knock on the door but didn't budge. Storm could get it.

"That didn't take you long," said Mike as he walked in.

Heather opened her eyes to see him haul in a big piece of plastic.

"I have a pump at the bottom of the stairs. You think you could go get it?" he asked Storm. While Storm ran down the stairs, Mike unfolded the thing in his hands. It turned out to be rectangular and thick. Storm came back into the room with a small pump. He handed it to Mike.

"I figured you two would be more comfortable on an air mattress than the chairs or the twin bed. It is only a queen but should do the job."

Heather noticed he had just assumed they'd sleep together. She wondered how Storm felt about that.

While Mike inflated the mattress, Storm moved the twin out of the way.

"Sheets?" Storm asked.

"They're in the closet."

Storm went to the closet, found them, and brought them out. The two men made the bed. Storm grabbed the comforter from the twin and threw it on top. "Thanks, Mike."

"No problem." He headed out the door. "I'll be up first

thing in the morning with breakfast for you two." With that, he closed the door behind him.

"And why did he say that?" asked Heather. Storm didn't act upset about the way Mike assumed he'd be staying.

"I believe that was a warning that he would be back, and he didn't want to walk in on anything." Storm crouched down by the chair she was sitting in. "You ready to move?"

She wanted to say no but knew he would hover until she did. The bed did look inviting now that she knew her mate would be with her. "You aren't upset he assumed you were staying? With me?"

"Mike is my best friend and knows I would never leave you alone while you're hurt." He helped her to the bed. Once she was settled, he made sure she was comfortable. Using pillows, he propped her head up and covered her with the comforter. Then he moved to the recliner. "Hell. I can't leave you alone when you're healthy."

Heather sighed, wanting him beside her, not in the stupid chair. She laid on her right side and found that painful so tried her left side. That didn't work either. After tossing and turning she sat up and looked at him. "Can I have the chair back?"

"Why?"

"I just can't find the right spot. Guess I'm used to sleeping on my side and I can't prop my leg the way I need to here." She gave him a soft smile. "I was comfortable in the chair."

"What do you need?" He stood and looked around. "More pillows?"

"No. Only you." She watched as he turned to gaze at her.

"That isn't a good idea." He shook his head no even as he took a step toward the inflated bed. His mind was saying one thing while his heart was saying another. "You're hurt and I don't want to make it any worse."

"If you're afraid you could crush me in your sleep you don't have to be. You have always been gentle with me when we're asleep."

"Heather. I'm not worried about when I'm sleeping. My desire for you is so strong I'm afraid if our bodies touched, I won't be able to control myself."

"Let me worry about that." She waited for him to make the decision. If they had been at home, she could have been healed in minutes. Bruises don't take that long with their advanced technology. This was one time she wished for her modern conveniences. Her right side was more bruised than the left. She didn't remember much of what happened from when she dumped the bike until the moment Bo stood over her, but she must have landed on her right side hard when she dumped the bike, then her flipping caused all the other bruises she could feel developing.

He stood there, watching her for what felt like an eternity before he moved to the mattress. "I still don't think this is a good idea. Where do you want me?"

She wanted to say, inside her but smiled as she pointed to the right side of the bed. "I need to lie on my left side."

She gave him all but one pillow which she rested on his shoulder before she curled up beside him. A sigh escaped her, and she settled beside him. A few hours rest was all she needed.

———

This was not a good idea, and he knew it, but he didn't relish the idea of sitting in the chair all night watching her sleep either. The desire he felt for her was a constant thing. Touching or not, tonight was going to be torture.

She snuggled against him and closed her eyes. It didn't

take her long before she fell into a light sleep. How did she find this comfortable? Then he remembered her military background. She probably was used to sleeping on rocky terrain, probably with worse wounds, when she was overseas.

The bruises he had seen when he helped her undress angered him. Her body was covered with them. Seeing her hurt twisted his gut. His heightened senses picked up the blood causing the discoloration in her skin. Storm could almost see the pain she felt when she moved. He wanted to make it better but didn't know how.

The dimmed lights allowed him to see her aura. Normally a beautiful blue/purple, tonight it also had a healing yellow glow. Her system was trying to repair the damage. Where the bruises were the worst, he could see the area as a dark smudge against the healthy yellow tone of the healing her body was working on. What he found amazing was watching those smudges lighten as the bruises healed and faded. How was she healing so fast? No wonder why she didn't want to go to the hospital. This would be hard to explain to doctors.

He could also see how uncomfortable she was in the dress she wore. It had bunched up in several places, aggravating a few of her more tender spots. A soft sigh escaped her.

"You okay?" He kept his voice soft in case she was sighing in her sleep.

"I'm not used to sleeping in anything and this dress is driving me crazy." She sat up. "And I bet you don't normally sleep in your jeans."

"No. I normally sleep nude."

"Then you are probably just as out of sorts as I am." Heather held up the sheet. "Look, I know you're worried about hurting me but we don't need to be miserable. You could lie under the sheet, and I'll be on top of it. That way we still have something between us even if we're naked."

He wanted to say no. It would only get them in trouble, but the thought of having her soft body against his had him agreeing. He pulled his jeans off then undid the buttons of his shirt and let it fall to the floor. Once he had climbed back into bed Heather, who had already removed her dress, draped the sheet over him before she curled up against him again. True to her word she was on top of it while he was under it.

"Much better." She pulled the comforter up around them before she closed her eyes once more.

Storm wasn't sure if it was better. Now the only thing separating them was a flimsy piece of linen. The heat of her body penetrated the sheet and his side. He wrapped his arm around her, hoping he could keep his hands to himself for a few hours.

———

Heather woke up gasping. Pain forgotten, she pulled her knees up and wrapped her arms around them.

"You okay?" Storm touched her back.

"Yeah, just a nightmare." She looked back at him. "Go on back to sleep. It's going to take me a while to shake this one."

"Do you want to talk about it?" He sat up with her.

"Not really." She had gotten another jumbled-up vision. At least she thought it was a vision. She saw Ialog confronting her, then Storm standing nearby, watching as Ialog took her away. Flashes of monitors and panels filled with all kinds of data. She saw images of the canister her egg had sat in. Then rows and rows of large tubes. Faces filled her vision. Thousands of them, but this time no one's life was threatened. "It will sound crazy."

"I've had my share of crazy dreams."

Heather wondered how many of them might have been memories trying to surface. She had stopped his dose from Ialog but hadn't seen any change in their broken mindmeld. She could tell him the one part he might understand. "I don't know. I saw this strange blonde man wearing a dark suit. He was dragging me away while you watched."

"Why would you dream something like that?" He studied her. "Did you ever do anything you shouldn't have?"

"Well, sure. Who hasn't." She plucked at the comforter. "I used to get into trouble when the government wanted me to do something I didn't believe was right. Got reprimanded for it too. But I've never broken the law."

He eased her back against his chest. The sheet had pooled at his waist, and she got to feel the heat of his skin against hers. She wanted to burrow into his warmth but had sort of promised to behave. "What did the man look like?"

"Fair skin, blond hair, about my height. Can't say he had any discerning marks, but I'd know him anywhere. Gave me the creeps." She relaxed against him. Enjoying the feel of his warm skin and the sound of his heartbeat.

"You need to forget about your nightmare." He drew small circles against her arm.

"I wish it was that easy." She looked up at him. That wonderful glow only she could cause was present. "I'll be fine in a little while."

Storm didn't say anything and seconds ticked by as they gazed at each other, then his mouth covered hers. The kiss was soft and sweet before passion ignited between them. His tongue begged for entrance which she gave easily. Desire filled her as their tongues danced together. His fingers innocently stroked her throat, right where her mark was, ratcheting up her need to an overpowering level. She turned in his arms, wanting more.

Storm broke the kiss. "I don't want to hurt you any more than you have already been hurt."

"Good Lord, Storm, I'm not some fragile flower. My pain level is a lot lower than my desire for you. I want you and I need you." She pulled the sheet that had pooled on his lap from between them. "Your erection shows me you feel it too. Now you going to continue to fight this or come to your senses?"

She could see the war he was having. He wanted her badly, but he didn't want to hurt her. Heather didn't feel like waiting for the silent debate. "Get up on your knees."

"Excuse me?" He did what she asked though.

"I know the perfect position for us, and you won't have to worry about aggravating my injuries." She got up on her knees too. "Now sit."

He followed her instructions, allowing her to wrap her arms around him and straddle him. It didn't take him long to figure out what she was doing and helped her center herself so she could slide down his hardened length. The delicious sensation had her sucking in her breath.

"Oh, man." Storm's voice came out strained. He was as affected as she was.

Heather wrapped her legs around him, being careful of her bruises. Her body already humming from the sensation of him filling her, she wasn't ready to move yet. Muscles clamped down on him, drawing a groan from him. She understood why her moans and screams aroused him so much. Knowing she could get him to do that filled her with a heady feeling.

She started to move, sliding up and down his shaft. Each time she descended his length her body quaked a little. It wasn't going to take much to send her over the edge, she wanted to fight it and extend the wonderful friction as long as she could but wasn't sure how easy that would be.

Storm strove to make her have multiple orgasms and she had gotten quite good at them. Tonight, she wanted to hear him scream.

He held her steady, helping her as she set a pace that had her breathing heavy quickly. Already she was putty in his hands. One of his hands slid down between her breasts, over her stomach, and down to her mound, searching her folds for the spot that always intensified everything. Instinct let him find it fast, caressing her, bringing her close to the edge.

"So close." Her voice was barely a whisper, then she felt his lips on her throat, working their way down to her mark. The moment they closed over the delicate tissue she felt the heat building inside her unfurl, consuming her in a white-hot flame. Her release raced through her blood, filling her with a euphoria that took her breath away.

Her body clenched around Storm, causing him to shake as his climax took control. They clung to each other as their worlds spiraled away, freefalling through their orgasms.

"Wow." Heather relaxed against him.

"That was amazing." Storm gently slid his fingers along her jawline, making her look up at him. His mouth descended to cover hers. His tongue swept into her mouth when she opened it for him, drawing it with his by soft sweeps against it. Passion flared between them once again. He finally broke the kiss. "You should be resting."

"I'm pretty boneless right now." She heard him chuckle.

"I meant to sleep." He pulled the pillows behind him and leaned back, taking her with him.

"Uh-huh." She snuggled against him, already feeling the fingers of sleep taking her. He pulled the comforter up to her shoulders, tenderly drawing little circles on her back, relaxing her more.

———

A knock on the door woke Heather. She stretched then lifted her head to find Storm smiling down at her. "Unless you wish to be caught like this, I recommend you get dressed before Mike knocks the door down."

Storm helped her pull the dress up then tied the top around her neck. Once she was sure it was on right and he had pulled on his pants she padded to the door and opened it. Mike stood on the other side with a bag and a thermos.

"I hope you're rested because we have a problem." He looked around, grabbed the remote sitting on the small nightstand, and aimed it at the TV. It hummed for a second before the picture popped on the set. He tuned in to one of the news shows. On the screen was a clip of her flipping through the air. "Look familiar?"

SEVEN

"Crap." If Ialog saw this he'd be back. He'd know it was her in an instant. Whoever recorded this got a clear shot of her suit. Anyone who knew what to look for would know it wasn't your average bike outfit. She had to leave now before he got the chance to find her. How did it make it to the national news anyway? "Where did this come from?"

"Must have been a slow news day. Someone could have sent it in or someone in their newsroom could have found it on YouTube and added it to the newsfeed. It doesn't matter right now because they have it. I looked it up. It's gone viral. Whoever recorded it didn't load their name. The angle it was shot at is a little funny too. Like the person who was recording this hid behind a rock. I thought it was someone who was a passenger in a car until I studied it a few times. You can see the cars on both sides of the road, which proves whoever took this was behind all of that. It's looking down too." Mike's voice sounded frustrated. "This damn video has had over a million hits since it went live. Its popularity is probably what brought it to the news people's attention."

"When does Patti get back?" Heather ignored the pain she felt and picked up her bike outfit. Time to go. Ialog had to have seen that. Staying here wasn't safe anymore.

"She saw this and put two and two together from what her husband told her. She's ready to come back now, thinking you were in the hospital."

"Then I quit, Mike, and thanks for the apartment, but I have to move on."

"What?" Both men spoke in unison.

"It's not safe for me to stay here anymore." They stared at her like she had lost her mind. "Remember that man flashing my picture and asking lots of questions? He's going to come back here the moment he sees this." She pointed to the screen. "I refuse to get you involved."

"You can stay up here and hide."

"And how many regulars know where I've been staying? How many of the waitresses? You think Princess will keep her mouth shut when this would be the perfect way to separate Storm and me? No Mike, I can't. I know him too well. He'll learn the truth. He has in the past. If I leave now, he won't do anything to you because you won't be lying when you tell him you don't know where I am. If you tell him the truth, he'll have no reason to harm you."

"What does he want with you?" Storm asked.

Heather sighed. She couldn't lie but he'd never believe the truth. Not yet. "He wants me for himself. Whatever he has told you about some crime I committed is a lie. He's using it to make people fear me. Hoping someone will turn me in. I plan on staying one step ahead of him."

"Where will you go?" asked Mike. "Your bike is trashed."

"I can fix that." She couldn't tell them about the bike. All she needed to do was get out of sight long enough to switch

166

around those crystals, but she had to get going. Heather stood there with her suit in her hands.

Time to get dressed, but not with these two staring at her. "Gentlemen either turn around or leave because I have to change."

"What about your stuff?" Mike presented his back to her. Storm continued to watch her, silent.

"I'll take what I need, and you can give the rest to charity." She didn't have time to deal with this. Pain sliced through her as she pulled her dress off and slipped on the pants then the jacket, closing the seals quickly. Once her uniform was sealed, she took a moment to force the pain away before she grabbed what important items she needed then headed down the stairs to her bike.

The image in front of her made her want to cry. Bert had done such a nice job creating it and it looked like she tore it up. Now she knew why Mike kept trying to talk her into staying. The poor bike appeared a mess.

The front tire looked warped. The frame was dented in several places. Heather shook her head. The system did a good job making it look damaged, but it could have done her a favor and made it look moveable. She wasn't going to be able to ride the thing until she could switch the crystals and she'd have to push it pretty far before she would be in a safe spot to make it work. First though she needed to make it look like she had fixed the tire.

She scratched her head. How was she supposed to do that with them watching?

"Take my truck." It was the first time Storm spoke since he saw the video.

"I can't. You need it and I can't leave the bike." She moved about the bike, packing her things into the saddle-bags before she crouched down beside the tire. "Any evidence I leave behind could put you in danger. I'll be fine."

"You can't go anywhere. That bike is too damaged." Mike was working hard to keep her there. "No one will reveal your presence if I ask them to keep it to themselves. We'll take care of Princess."

He didn't know what Ialog was capable of, but she did. The panel was on the opposite side of where they stood, and they were at such an angle they shouldn't see the repair right away. She turned one crystal, then got up and pulled on the tire. It looked like she straightened up enough for her to move it now. "The bike will be fine, Mike. I'll walk it to the nearest gas station and have it running in no time."

"How? You going to walk it into the next town? There isn't a gas station for miles. Walking your bike will take you too long and you could get caught. We can keep a secret when we need it."

"Maybe with certain things, but this man has ways. If I stay here, he will know." Gloves on, helmet hanging from the handlebar, Heather started pushing the bike to the road. Her body complained, but she ignored it. Now wasn't the time to allow a little bit of pain to interfere. "A word of advice, Storm. Don't trust the man. He's after you, too. I saw him slip something into your coffee when he was here last, and I bet it is what is keeping you from getting your memory back."

"If you're determined to go at least wait until I come back." Mike ran into his house.

She sighed but waited for Mike to return. Glancing at Cim, she learned it was safe for the moment.

"You can't leave." Storm frowned.

"I have to." She looked at Storm. There was so much she wanted to say to him. If their link was stronger, she'd ask him to come with her, bring him home where he belonged, but he wasn't ready. Now she had to leave him before she had been able to help him get his memory back. "You are my heart, never forget that."

Mike came back out of his house, carrying an overstuffed backpack. "Here. Emergency rations."

"Mike." She shook her head as she tried to give it back.

"You're walking that bike. There is no way you'll make it to the next town before nightfall. This will help you through the night."

With logic like that she knew she couldn't refuse.

———

Storm watched as she turned the bike onto the road. She couldn't possibly think they were just going to stand by while she left, did she?

"You're not going to let her go like that, are you?" asked Mike. He echoed his thoughts.

No, but he couldn't tell Mike that. The man she kept calling Ialog had to be Al and he had always felt uneasy around him. As she said the man creeped him out. He also agreed the less Mike knew the better off he was. "What do you want me to do, throw her over my shoulder and keep her locked up at my place?"

That was what he planned on doing if she refused his help. She wouldn't get far pushing the bike and the longer she was visible the bigger chance she had of being found. If she was right that could be very dangerous. For now though, he was going to stay put and see if Al did show up. If she was right, he should be there within a couple of hours. And if she was right, he would start trusting her.

It took about an hour before the homeland security agent he knew as Al came in. Heather was right. He couldn't keep the annoyance out of his voice when he spoke to the man. "Didn't I just talk to you?"

"Now, Heath, is that any way to treat someone looking out for you?" He chuckled as he sat down beside him, but when he looked at Storm there was no laughter in his eyes.

"Everyone calls me Mountain Man. I'd rather be called that." His voice was flat. Storm wished the man would get to the point. He wasn't here for a social visit.

"Of course, Mountain Man." He nodded to Mike, who set a cup in front of him and poured him coffee.

"What brings you back so fast?" Mike asked.

Storm glared at him. Way to be subtle.

"I thought I'd pop by after seeing some footage of an accident not too far from here. It looks like the woman I'm looking for is in the area and I was hoping you knew a little about the accident."

"Really?" Mike wiped down the counter. "What accident?"

Al pulled out his phone and showed them the video. It showed Heather dumping the bike then flipping and rolling for several feet. It continued where the one they saw on the TV stopped. It also showed her removing her helmet before climbing into the truck of Patti's husband. The image of her face was not real clear and her hair looked darker, but they all knew it was her.

"This is the same woman you keep showing me? How come she never looks the same? The one in that other picture had blonde hair where this one looks like she has brownish hair." Storm shook his head. There was no way he was going to turn her over now. "Sorry. I haven't seen her."

Al smiled and nodded his head but didn't move from his chair. "I heard Mike has a new waitress."

"Had." Mike smiled as the door opened. He nodded at the person who entered. "Had someone fill in while Patti was having her baby, but my girl is back. The other one left several days ago."

"Did she have a name?"

"Hey, you thinking she was the one you're looking for? She was nothing more than a drifter who happened to be in the right place at the right time." Mike wiped the counter down.

"Do you know what happened to the other waitress?" Al studied Mike. "What was her name?"

"You talking about the girl who filled in for me?" Patti stepped up to the counter and grinned. "Heard her boyfriend showed up and they took off together. Gossip flies in a small place like this. I'm just glad she stuck around long enough to cover for me. Her name was Betsy or Betty. Something like that."

Al frowned. They didn't give him any information he could use. Hopefully, he would believe Heather hadn't been there and would move on. "Thank you."

"You brought pictures, didn't you?" Mike asked Patti, dismissing Al. "You can't touch a plate until we see pictures."

She laughed as she pulled pictures of Mike's new nephew out of her pocket.

Al didn't care to look at the images of the new baby. He stood. "If you do see her, call me." He set his card on the counter.

"Will do." Storm looked at the card, loving the way Mike changed the subject so easily. Heather had told him not to trust the man and she had been right about everything so far. Could he put something on the surface? Or was he just being paranoid?

Al looked around before he headed to the door. "I'll be around for a day or two to see if she shows up."

Great. Just what they needed. Storm breathed a sigh of

relief when Al drove his car in the opposite direction from where Heather went. Now he had to go get her before she got into trouble.

———

Storm had been up and down the road four times and found nothing. No evidence of her anywhere. Where the hell did she go? She couldn't have walked that far pushing her bike. Not as badly damaged as the bike was or as hurt as she was. That thing had to have slowed her down. If she was heading to the nearest gas station, he should have run across her.

He thought about it and as frightened as she was of Al, she could have taken one of the paths that led into the woods, pushing the bike until she could hide it and herself. Bikes were illegal in the federal park area, but if she was worried about being found she still might follow it. It would get her off the main road and still allow her to put distance between her and the diner.

He inhaled deeply, hoping to pick up her scent but found nothing. How did she disappear so completely? It didn't matter. He was going to find her. He drove his truck back to his cabin and parked it. The backpack he used to store his clothes in when he shifted leaned against the cabin. Could he switch when he wanted to? Storm removed his clothes and packed them into his backpack. Time to find out.

———

"There is an uninhabited cave nearby you could utilize. It is near a fresh water supply and will allow you to stay close to your mate."

"Show me, Cim." Heather saw the information load into her helmet and followed the directions. The cave wasn't very big, but it would do. There was a pile of pine needles in one corner and evidence of a fire. "Looks like someone has used this recently. Are you sure it is abandoned?"

"Yes. Evidence shows it hasn't been touched in about two years."

Data continued to fill her helmet. "Is that Storm's DNA?"

"Yes. He used this cave for about a month or so when he first came to the area. I'm picking up his wolf DNA more than the human."

"I'm not sure this is the best place to hide then." Heather looked around. It would have made a good hideout. "If Storm has been here, he might know to look for me here and I don't want to risk Ialog finding us together. He has left Storm alone so far, but if he knew I was here I don't think he'd be so nice."

"As long as you wear this outfit Storm can't track you."

"And what about Ialog? If he saw the feed, he would know I'm wearing an advanced outfit. It wouldn't take him long to know how to track it."

"He has been searching for you since we arrived. He knew you should show up. It could be because of that picture he had from the magazine. You haven't worn the uniform so far and that is why he hasn't found you."

"So you're saying if I seal this outfit so Storm can't track me Ialog will be able to?"

"Yes."

"Is there another place I can hide in nearby?"

"I'm sorry, but another cave like this is several days away."

"So I have a choice of having my mate track me or Ialog, the man I despise. Tough choice." She knew who she wanted to find her. Heather pulled her helmet off. "Wonder how long it will take Storm to find me."

———

Storm walked away from his cabin, wondering where he should start. She could be anywhere. He hadn't been able to pick up her scent, which made him wonder if she was able to get that bike working after all. She acted like it wouldn't be that difficult, but he saw the damage and didn't think it would be that easy.

He needed to shift but didn't know how to force it. It always just happened. He found when he ran, he emptied his mind and the shift would just happen, so he started running. Dashing across the asphalt he heard the clicking of his claws and relaxed. So now he knew he could at least control the shift a little.

Storm ran to the restaurant, looking for her tracks in the soft dirt. The bike tires were unique and easy to see. What he found strange was it had no scent. All vehicles had some sort of scent. The mixture of gas, oil, fluids, and rubber from the tires allowed him to tell makes and models apart.

He followed her trail for about half an hour before he found a place where she had stopped and moved around the bike several times. It was also where her footprints ended. Once she was able to ride the bike, he had no trail to follow, but something told him she was still nearby. So where did she go?

There were several paths in the area she could have taken. It wouldn't hurt him to check them out before he headed back to his cabin. She might have left the area, but he hoped she had just gone into hiding. The first three showed nothing and his heart began to sink. If she went this way, she didn't have the bike. The fourth did show evidence of a bike. Storm followed the trail for five minutes before he saw a clear tire track. His mood soared when he recognized the tread. She did go this way.

What was she looking for? The only thing this way was a cave. If he had hands instead of paws, he would smack himself. It made perfect sense. The perfect place to hide quickly. But how did she know about it?

Running, he took the path he had used many times. He skidded to a stop when he could see the mouth of the cave. Heather stood with her back to him, her hands on her hips like she was trying to figure out what she should do first. He wondered what he should do now. The form he was in would frighten her.

EIGHT

Heather had used Cim to sterilize the moss Storm had used for bedding. Then she went out and gathered more to give her a little more padding. Once she was happy with the height, she made herself comfortable.

"You should put your suit back on. It will protect you from the cold as the sun sets."

"I'll be fine in these jeans. They were made by Bert so I'm sure they will do the same thing. I'll put the top half of the suit on if the temperature drops too much for me." She grabbed the backpack and pulled it to her. "Might as well see what Mike packed for me."

"I can tell you without you having to look."

"That's okay, Cim. It will give me something to do." Heather pulled the water bottles stuffed into the mesh pockets on the side of the bag out before she unzipped the main compartment. Inside she found energy bars, matches, stuff anyone would need if caught in the wilderness. She even pulled out an inflatable pillow. "Thank you, Mike."

"For a piece of plastic?"

"This piece of plastic will allow my head to rest easily." She laughed. "I have spent my time on assignments where I had to sleep on the ground and never complained but having a few of these amenities is wonderful."

"There is also a silver packet at the bottom that will keep you warm while you sleep. Although your suit will do the same thing."

"You sound like you're whining. The only way to make the suit work is to seal it and you said Ialog could track that. I'm not willing to take that chance. This will be fine."

"That suit doesn't need the helmet to seal your body heat in and I thought my voice modulation was as it always is."

Heather laughed. "Stop pushing the suit. I know you're concerned about my welfare, but I have made my decision."

"Understood."

Heather pulled out the blanket and laid it on the makeshift bed. "I'm assuming a fire would be out of the question?"

"We are far enough away for a fire to remain undetected. Do you wish it for heat or light?"

"Both."

"This cave has a natural chimney that will allow you to have the fire inside."

Heather had noticed the remnants of an old fire off to one corner. "Let's go find some firewood."

"There is a felled tree not too far from here. You should be able to gather enough small pieces for the night."

"Great. Lead the way."

———

Storm sat on his haunches and watched her walk out of the cave and head into the woods. He tilted his head. What was she up to? He trotted parallel to her, trying to keep his distance and still see what she was doing. She bent over several times before he figured it out.

She was gathering firewood.

He would have thought her bruises would make that difficult. If he hadn't seen them himself, he'd be questioning if she had really been hurt by the way she was moving. Then he heard the sharp intake of breath when she reached for a piece that wasn't easy for her to grab.

So she was still hurting.

He heard another voice as she worked. One he didn't recognize. Was she talking to someone on her cell phone? If she had friends nearby, why didn't she go to their place? Storm shook his head. Perhaps it was a new phone app he hadn't heard of. He decided to watch a little more.

After she had gathered all the firewood she could carry, Heather headed back to the cave. Once she had gathered several piles she came back out and looked around then she gathered more of the moss he had used for the bed. He bet she planned on using that to get the fire going.

He didn't think she was a survivalist. He forgot she was in the military and was probably trained to survive worse. The fact she wasn't frightened or scared made him realize she might not think his sudden presence a good thing. He thought she'd see him as her rescuer, removing her from the hardship of living out here. Now he wasn't so sure. Heather knew what she was doing and being in a cave didn't seem to bother her at all.

Time to reevaluate his plan to rescue her.

———

"Your mate has been following us for over thirty minutes now," Cim commented.

"I know." She smiled, happy about how fast he found

her. "Our mindlink is reconnecting. I can now sense his moods and when he's near. He's not very happy with me either. Guess he was expecting a weak, helpless female instead of someone who could protect herself."

"Is that why he hasn't approached us?" asked Cim. "I would think he would remember that you were trained by the military and was ready for this scenario."

"True, but he also wants to swoop in and rescue me. That's the macho male that he is used to being. I kind of messed all that up."

"By being efficient? I don't always understand the way the humanoid mind works," Cim responded. "He shifted to his human form twenty minutes ago and has been pacing and talking to himself but has made no move toward you."

"His desire to protect me is so ingrained. Even with no memory of who I am he can't help himself. He wanted to sweep in and save the day, not expecting me to be able to protect myself. I threw him for a loop so right now he's trying to figure out a different way to approach me. I can feel his frustration."

"Are you going to speak to him?"

"No." Heather looked out where Storm was probably hiding. "He needs to figure this out on his own."

———

The sun had set, and he still hadn't approached her. It was going to get cold soon too. Should she make the first move? Tired of waiting, she walked to the edge of the cave. "I know you're out there. You might as well come on in."

Heather sat on her makeshift bed and waited. It didn't take long before she heard the crunch of his shoes on the leaves near the opening.

"How did you know?" Storm stood at the mouth of the cave looking uncomfortable.

She shrugged, wanting to tell him she could always sense his presence. "Sixth sense. Seem to know when someone is watching me."

"How did you find this place?" He looked around, taking in the little things she had done to make it comfortable for her. The fire burning in the corner kept the cave warm. The bed had new padding and there was a small, inflated pillow next to a silver blanket. That had to have come from Mike.

"GPS." Heather could see he wasn't happy with how quickly she had made herself at home.

He laughed. "If your GPS can show you where caves are I'd love to get the app for that."

"I mean I was able to find the cave pretty easily with the use of my maps, plus a few other applications." She tilted her head at him. "How did you find the cave?"

He didn't answer right away. "I stumbled across this one when I first came to this area. I lived here for a short time."

"Ah, you're the one who left the bed and the small pile of wood that started my fire. Thanks. A little comfort goes a long way when roughing it."

"You don't have to rough it. You could come back to my place." He took a step toward her. "I have all the amenities, including satellite."

"Thanks, but no." She smiled. "I'll be fine here, and you can visit any time you want."

He frowned. "It isn't safe here. There are all kinds of animals that could try to invade."

"Storm, I was in the military. I have seen things you wouldn't believe. There's nothing in this forest that will frighten me." She stood. "Plus there was no evidence of anything living in here in a while so the wildlife has avoided it."

He looked at the bed, then her, and she knew what he was thinking. The makeshift bed wasn't big enough for two, but they didn't need to use the bed. The cave walls looked smooth and sturdy enough.

"I'd feel better if you'd come back with me." Storm continued to push.

"Why?" Time to push back a little. They had been going along like they had all the time in the world, but they didn't. Not anymore.

"Because it's not safe here." He gestured around the small cave.

"Yet you lived here for a while." She stood and confronted him. "Why was it safe for you and not for me?"

He blinked, not quite sure how to answer her. She could see him trying to figure out what to say next.

"Look, you have a choice, either come with me peacefully or I'll make you."

"And how do you plan on making me?" That was how he planned on getting her to go with him? Being a Neanderthal? Was he out of his mind?

He frowned at her answer. She knew that wasn't what he wanted to hear. Then he came right at her. Heather figured he was assuming her injuries would make her slow, but she wasn't feeling the pain she was earlier. Storm could overpower her easily just by his size and had tried to use that on her in the past, so she knew how to counteract that. One side step and she slipped past him.

"You plan on overpowering me?" She turned to face him, anger radiating off her. "Really? You think brute strength is going to let you get your way? What will happen when you get me back to your place and I'm still angry? How are you going to handle that?"

He growled his frustration. "How the hell did you move so fast when you're hurt? I saw the bruises."

"Guess I'm a fast healer." Cim constantly monitored her wounds, alerting her to how fast they were disappearing. Good thing she didn't go to the doctors because her rate of healing was unheard of. It was never noticed before because of their modern technology. "But I'm not going to let you sidetrack me with the fact that I stopped your attack. I'm going to fight you if you try to take me by force."

"What do you want?" Storm ran his fingers through his hair. "Me to stay here with you?"

"Would that be so bad?" She jammed her hands on her hips. "You want to be with me. You wouldn't be here if you didn't."

"This is no place for a lady."

She had to laugh. "Storm, I'm not some fragile thing, although you always want to see me that way."

"I don't want you to get hurt," he growled.

She watched him for a few seconds, expanding her mind to see what she could pick up from him.

"That man came by the restaurant, didn't he?" He was a little too worried about her. Something had happened and that was the only thing she could think of.

"He was there within a half hour."

"That means he's near and watching." Heather nodded. "Does he know where you live?"

"No one does. I have kept my cabin's location to myself. You'll be safe."

"He is very resourceful." She tucked a stray piece of hair behind her ear. "Did you check for a tracking device on your truck?"

"I did and found nothing." He grinned. "Your parting words made me paranoid so I searched everything before I came here."

"I would still feel better staying here. What if he put it on months ago and removed it before you thought to look? He could be waiting for me to show up at your cabin. I don't want to give him the upper hand if I can avoid it." She looked around. "I know it's not much, but the cave is big enough for the two of us. A few things from your cabin and we could be quite comfortable."

"You can be quite stubborn, can't you?" He growled again.

"I learned from the best." She smiled, knowing he knew she was right.

He sighed, then nodded. "Don't go anywhere."

"Like I've got somewhere else to go."

He took off, leaving her alone.

"I recommend you move your vehicle so Storm doesn't realize it is in here." Cim's voice came from her pocket once he was out of earshot.

"Good idea. Not sure how he'd react to stumbling over an invisible bike." She grabbed her cycle and pushed it outside. "But I need to push him, force his memory to come back. We need to get him home before Ialog catches us together."

Storm came back to the cave weighed down with several large duffels. He expected Heather to greet him at the mouth of the cave. Trepidation crept in when she didn't. Setting everything down, he inched toward the entrance, fearing what he might find.

Wrapped in silver, with her plastic pillow cushioning her head, she was lying on her makeshift bed sound asleep. He sighed in relief.

The last twenty-four hours must have taken their toll on

her. He knew if he had gone through what she had he'd be beat too. Storm let her sleep as he unpacked the items he brought with him. Being as quiet as he could, he set up everything but the airbed he had borrowed from Mike. Blowing it up to half its height just outside the cave with a foot pump, he carried it in to finish inflating it. Once he had it ready, he gently lifted Heather, placed her on the mattress, made sure he didn't disturb her, then worked on pulling out the makeshift bed to make more room for the airbed.

He made enough noise to wake her several times, but she was out. Storm was able to push the bed close to the wall without waking her. He had everything set up before he joined her. He had put flannel sheets on the bed. Not very sexy but it would help keep them warm. So would the two thermal blankets he had added.

Not sure what to do, he lay there, wondering if he should pull her into his arms like he wanted to. She must have sensed his presence because she turned and draped her body along the side of his. Wow. So simple, but it had a strong impact on him. He didn't want her to ever move.

He loved her scent. He had been drawn to it from the beginning. Now he understood why. She smelt familiar. Why, he didn't know. Did she know him, but kept it to herself? If so, why?

A contented sigh escaped her as she settled against him. So trusting. Could it all be an act? Before he could dwell on it any longer, Heather's eyes opened.

"Sorry." She looked around, noticing all the changes before she looked back at him. "Guess I needed to rest."

"It's okay. You have been through a lot." He felt his words were a little inane. Her beautiful violet eyes mesmerized him.

"The least I could do is fix dinner." She went to sit up, but he kept his arms around her and held her close.

"No need. I brought dinner. Actually, Mike forced it on me when I went and borrowed the bed." Storm reached behind him. "All I did was ask if I could borrow this thing and he came back with a care package."

Heather took it from him and opened the bag. She laughed as she pulled out several thermoses. "He wanted to make sure I had enough coffee, didn't he?"

"Keep looking." Her laugh sounded like music to his ears. Mike knew where he was going without him having to say a word. Everything in that bag was Heather's favorite. The man had to be baking all morning to have all the items ready, freshly made donuts, sandwiches, and cookies. He also packed her favorite fruits and a few of the vegetables she liked as well. "I didn't say a word, but he knew."

"If he was here right now, I'd hug him."

"I'm here."

She smiled. A beautiful knowing smile that made his blood heat up. "You're right, but I think a hug won't do since you brought it all back for me." Heather got up on her hands and knees so she could lean toward him. Her lips touched his, soft, pliant and so sweet.

Storm wrapped his arms around her, pulling her against him as he deepened the kiss. Their tongues danced as he slipped his hand up inside the back of her shirt, to find she wore no bra. He eased the shirt up her torso, only breaking the kiss long enough to pull her shirt over her head.

It seemed like she was thinking the same thing he was because she had unbuttoned his shirt and was pushing it off his shoulders when he reclaimed her lips. He loved the feel of her skin against his, but it wasn't enough, he wanted nothing blocking their bodies from touching.

His fingers worked at the snap of her jeans. It came apart easily and he slipped his hands inside to find her heat. She moaned into his mouth as he started to stroke her delicate skin. He felt her hands work on his jeans, undoing the button and sliding his zipper down. Her hand wrapped around his erection, and the intimate contact made him shudder. Desire in control, he pushed her jeans down her hips, wanting to feel her body accept him in. He broke the kiss to pull her pants off and remove his as well. Storm kissed his way back up her body, sliding in deep when his mouth reached hers once again.

She shook in his arms as her muscles stretched and molded themselves around his erection. He could explode right now, but he wanted to extend the wonderful feelings grabbing him for as long as possible.

"Storm." Her voice was soft as those deliciously long legs wrapped around his hips.

"Shh, I know." He pulled out and drove back in, causing Heather to take a deep breath as she arched against him. He took that moment to pull her up with him, so they were in a sitting position. He knew the last time she had such an intense orgasm he wanted to see if he could give her that experience again.

Heather tilted her head back as she slid down his length. So beautiful. A flash filled his mind showing an image close to this, eyes closed, mouth slightly open caught in the beginnings of her release. Heather looking her most beautiful.

Was it something he wished to catch on camera or was that a memory?

When she started moving, he forgot about the image in his mind and concentrated on what he was feeling now. She knew just what to do to make his orgasm try to take over. Her muscles tightened against his length, creating a delicious vise around him. His fingers slipped between them, brushing and drawing small circles until he reached the delicate tissue that intensified her orgasms. Her breath hitched the moment he touched her. Anticipation made her quiver.

His caresses were gentle, each brush had her moving faster, building friction between them. Her breath came out in short little pants as she grew closer to her climax.

"You are so beautiful."

"You make me that way." She sounded breathless. Heather slid up and down his length a few more times before her body clenched around him. "Oh!"

He could feel her release like it was his. From deep inside it bubbled up, filling her blood and her mind with euphoria. The joy zinging through her sent him over the edge with her.

———

As she reached her orgasm, she felt another section of their mind bond connect and she could feel his orgasms once again. The intimacy they shared was heightened by the connection and she was happy to have it back, but how was he handling it? When it happened before he knew what her mind was capable of, but not this time. She touched his cheek, searching his eyes for anger or fear. What she saw was surprise.

Not what she expected.

"That was phenomenal." He brushed a few hairs out of her face.

"It always is with you." She smiled at him. The first time their minds connected during their orgasms they weren't sure what happened. Perhaps it is the same for him this time. Should she say something, or let him work his way through it? Because it would happen again.

"You don't seem surprised." He frowned.

Was he upset because she wasn't acting as amazed as he was? She couldn't say anything until he did. Bert was insistent about her keeping their past quiet until Storm remembered. He had to be the one to ask her. "About what?"

"What we share. It goes way beyond anything casual."

"I'd like to think so." It made her feel good to know he recognized how special their intimacy was.

"What aren't you telling me?" He tightened his hold on her. "I've been getting these flashes. Bits and pieces of things I don't remember, and you always seem to be in them. You knew me before, didn't you?"

"Yes." She had never lied to him before and wouldn't start now.

"Why didn't you tell me?"

"What would you have done if I had come charging in demanding that you remember?" It was what she wanted to do.

"Probably laughed at you." His fingers brushed against her jawline before sliding down her throat. "I have this erotic image of you in a picture like you're caught in the middle of an orgasm."

Heather blushed at his words. That picture was something she still had trouble looking at. She just couldn't see herself that way.

"And red underwear. You flashing me in a tent and then at a party."

"Your favorite. No matter what I wore after that one they never compared."

"You're my wife, aren't you?"

She nodded. Not a lie since they had been married by Earth's government and being his mate was basically the same thing.

"That's why you have the ring marks on your finger." He looked at his left hand. "But I don't."

"You never wore one, but you never held back about

how you felt about me." She shrugged. "I didn't see a need to push it."

"And Al?"

"Doesn't want us together. I think he has been giving you something to keep your memories buried. I stopped the last dose and hope now they will come back to you." It looked like they were, but Storm could have been getting these flashes all along. It might not mean he was in the process of regaining his memories.

"Why would he want to come between something so powerful?"

"He has other plans for me. Plans I don't want. I only want you."

"What is he, your father?"

How should she answer that? He wasn't. Not really, but he was the one who created her and that was as close to the truth as she could get at the moment. "I was a ward of the state. Raised by the government. He wasn't a father to me at all, but now that I'm an adult he thinks he can take control of my life."

"So you started running from him."

She nodded again. If only she could tell him the whole story.

"Why aren't you telling me everything now?" Frustration etched his face.

"The doctors I spoke to told me not to. They felt you needed to get your memories back on your own." She hated keeping anything from him. "Too much too soon could cause more harm than help."

"Did I do anything wrong? Murder someone?" The look of fear on his face made her want to break the rules and tell him everything.

"Of course not." She shook her head. "You need to remember when you're ready, that's all."

"In the meantime, you're going to hide in a cave to keep that man at bay."

She shrugged. "My fear is what he'll do to you if he were to learn that we're back together."

"I can take care of myself."

"I know you can." She touched his face. "But he works for some powerful people. Think about how he could make your life miserable if he wanted to. I don't want to take that chance."

"Let me worry about that." He lifted her so they could curl around each other. "The sun should be setting soon, and it is spectacular to see. Willing to face the cold a little to watch?"

"Sure." She moved off the bed to get dressed but found herself lifted into Storm's arms.

"Grab the blankets."

"Not going to let me get dressed, are you?" she asked as he dipped down low enough for her to snag the blankets.

"I like the way you're dressed." He captured her lips for a quick but heated kiss that made her knees weak then brought her to the mouth of the cave. Storm wrapped the blankets around them before pulling her into his arms so her back rested against his chest. The sky went from brilliant blue to crimson, pink, and orange.

"It is beautiful." She rested her head against him, enjoying the quiet moment.

"Not as beautiful as you." He tilted her face up so he could taste her lips again. He kept it tender, even though she could feel his need to deepen it flow through him. He was trying to show her respect instead of taking advantage of her state of undress. "Can I ask you a question?"

"Of course."

"The wall thing. Have I always done that?"

"Yes." Heather wanted to laugh. "In fact, it's one of your

favorite positions. I call it the up against the wall because I need to dominate you now position."

"Dominate? Please tell me I'm not that bad."

"You have always shown me great respect, but very protective. A true alpha male." She touched his face tenderly. "And I love you for it. When your need gets over-powering is when we don't quite make it to the bed. That intensity focuses you, and I have been at the winning end of that focus many a time."

"Not sure if that makes me feel better or not."

"It should. To know I affect you that way is something I can't describe. It humbles me, makes me feel loved." She shifted in his arms so she could place her hand over his heart.

"The first time you did this made me wonder why. Is that something we do?" He placed his hand over hers.

"Yes." She smiled up at him. "A gesture of love between us."

"I want my memory back."

"I'll do everything I can to help you get it back."

———

The last three days had been blissful. Storm went back to his cabin every day but joined her at night where they spent their time making love and testing his memory. A part of her wished it could go on forever. It was nice having him all to herself.

Cim warned her that snow, and a lot of it, was coming so she sent her phone with Storm when he went to the cabin to pick up a few more items for them. Heather used the excuse that her phone needed charging so he would take it with him, but the truth was she needed Cim to check his cabin.

The moment Storm learned of the snow he would want

her to go with him to the cabin and she had to admit it did sound better than spending a blizzard in a cave. Before she took that chance though she wanted to be sure Ialog hadn't put any sensors in Storm's place so he would be alerted when she did show up there. She wasn't sure what she would do if the system did find something, but knowing Storm, he would probably force her to go with him anyway and she had a hard time telling him no.

While he was gone, she went out to gather firewood. She also came across some wild berries and picked them as well. A quick snack to keep up her energy.

It would be hours before Storm came back so she decided to do some exploring. The area was beautiful. Heather weaved between trees as she followed a faint trail that led further up the mountain. The distance from the cave didn't bother her as she admired the flora and the fauna. What stopped her was the white wolf she had met before.

"Well, hello again." It was the same wolf; she was sure of it. There was something about the animal's eyes. A bright blue that showed so much intelligence.

The wolf tilted her head at Heather, studying her like she was making sure she measured up. Then the wolf moved toward her and bumped Heather's hand with her head.

"So you want your ears scratched, huh?" Heather dug her fingers into the thick fur.

The wolf looked up at her like she expected something else.

"What? I can't read everyone's mind. Not yet. And animals are the hardest. You guys don't think the way we do."

The wolf backed up and snorted.

"It's not my fault. I have been trying, but my mind hasn't figured out how to work the communication yet."

The animal sat there for a moment before it shifted in

front of Heather. Where the white wolf had stood now stood a woman with white hair and brilliant blue eyes. Her soft smile showed no hostility. "I had wondered how far your abilities had expanded."

Heather stumbled back. "You're a shapeshifter? Does Storm know?"

"No, your mate believes he is the only one. Heather, he needs to get his memory back. We need him. You need him to create the future you're supposed to be a part of."

"I know." The woman knew an awful lot about her and Storm. Just like Bert did. "My God, you're another ancient."

"Then you have met others of my kind?" Her voice sounded hopeful.

"Two. Ialog and Bert."

"Bert? You have met him? Good." She nodded approvingly. "He will help you."

"Who are you?" She didn't know what she should say in front of this woman. The fact that she ignored Ialog's name had her questioning her loyalty. Was she an ally or another one who wanted to keep her and Storm apart?

"I will explain everything, but not now. We have very little time. Ialog trapped me here. I have remained hidden from him in my animal form, but in this form, he can track me. I shifted because I needed to warn you."

"I have had dealings with Ialog before. I know he is involved with my mate's memory loss."

"Then you know what he wants from you."

"To build a race of his liking."

"That is how it started, yes. He can't capture you, Heather. Everything we did to protect you will be for nothing if he gets you."

"He has tried before and failed and what do you mean by we?" Did she know of other ancients? Or was she trying to feed Heather information to keep her from learning the truth?

"I wish I could explain more but don't have time. You're going to have to trust me." She pulled a necklace out of her pocket. "Take this."

Heather took the beautiful silver pendant in her palm.

"Ialog locked me in this timeline so I couldn't warn everyone. This device will let me go back to where I am needed. It will help keep us safe." She gestured for Heather to put it on.

"Safe? I don't understand." The moment Heather slipped it over her neck the woman pressed her palm against the aquamarine stone and disappeared.

Heather staggered under the pressure. She could feel the woman's life force trying to conform itself to the small space it suddenly found itself in. How she wished she had Cim with her. Not knowing who the ancient was had her questioning if it was safe to keep the necklace with her, but if she left it behind and the woman turned out to be an ally, she would feel the guilt for not trusting her.

Since the woman had jumped into the necklace and not her body, she would give her the benefit of the doubt for now and would have Cim scan the necklace the first chance he got. She hoped she was making the right decision.

Heather headed back to the cave. It was getting close to the time Storm would return and she wanted to have a little surprise waiting for him.

Her bike held what she wanted. Opening the pouches on the side she pulled out the flimsy lace material and went into the cave. The air was cool so she changed quickly then grabbed one of the blankets off the bed and wrapped it around her. The lacey underwear wouldn't keep her warm, but the blanket would help.

Time to add a few logs to the fire. Being careful of the

blanket around her, she tossed them into the flames that were starting to die. Three looked like enough. When she looked up Storm was standing at the mouth of the cave. "Didn't hear you come up."

"Have a light step." He looked around, his gaze lingering on her backpack where she had laid her jeans and shirt. She saw the spark of excitement fill his eyes as he tried to figure out what she was up to. "What is with the blanket?"

"Got a little cool." She straightened and turned toward him.

"You could have crawled into the bed."

"I might have fallen asleep and ruined the effect." Heather smiled.

"What effect?" He stepped in then. His curiosity peaked.

"You need to get undressed first."

He watched her for a moment, probably debating on whether or not he should just rip the blanket off her. Heather walked toward him, her bare feet and part of a leg slipped out of the folds. It was enough for him to do as she asked, and he removed his clothes.

"Now climb on the bed." She grinned when he followed her instructions. His desire for her overrode any argument he might have given her. Holding the blanket in front of her she lifted it and tossed it so it spread as it landed on the bed, making it easy for them to pull up later.

Heather watched his eyes as the blanket dropped, no longer blocking his view. His sharp intake of breath let her know he liked what he saw. The lacy lavender bra and panties had his undivided attention. He moved toward her as she climbed on the bed to join him.

"You are so beautiful." The heat of his fingers penetrated her skin when he brushed them across her stomach. "If I could get you to model, you'd be the most sought-after one out there."

"That one time will do, thank you."

"I know. You want to keep a low profile. A part of me likes that because that way I can keep you all to myself." His hands continued to roam, skimming across the lace of her underwear and well as bare skin. "But your body is so well honed and that is what companies want right now. Muscle is in."

"There is only one man I want ogling my body." She pressed her hands against his chest. "And that is you."

"You will not have to worry about that." He wrapped his arms around her and lowered her to the bed. "But first we need to remove some clothing from you. As much as I like this I don't want to destroy it in my desire for you."

That sounded so much like Storm before he lost his memory. Gone were the Earth idioms. He slipped the panties off her before releasing the clasp on her bra. A sigh escaped him when she was naked.

"Much better." He pulled the covers over them. "You trying to tease me makes it hard for foreplay."

"I have been anticipating this all day too. I don't always need foreplay." She brushed her fingers against his mark and watched as the glow in his eyes grew brighter.

"I hope so because I can't wait any longer." He surged into her, sighing as she accepted him into her body.

She arched against him when he filled her. He hit a very sensitive spot that escalated her need for him. "Do that again and I'm going to explode."

"What? This?" he slid out and back in again, hitting the same spot.

She moaned as she wrapped her legs around him. Tilting her hips, her body sent the silent communication that she wanted more, which he gladly gave her. Each time he drove into her she felt her excitement grow. Her muscles tightened against him, drawing a groan from him. He set a pace, trying to hit that same spot each time. Every time he did, she sucked in her breath. If he kept it up she was going to scream.

His lips found her mark and she moaned again. Each time he buried himself deep inside she got closer to her release. A few more strokes would send her over the edge.

"So close." Her words were nothing more than a whisper. Storm hit that one spot once more and her world fell away as everything shattered, and her soul sailed through her orgasm. The scream she knew would come echoed in the cave as all her muscles tightened inside her. She arched against him once again when he picked up the pace as he grew close to his release. She could feel his climax balancing on the edge. All it took was for her to shift her hips again and his world splintered around them.

"Wow." She looked up into his shocked face. Their bond was getting stronger. He knew the first time wasn't a fluke.

"You felt that, didn't you?"

"We have been sharing a lot for a long time." She touched his face with her fingers. "The bond we share is reconnecting every time we're intimate. Soon we'll be able to share thoughts."

"How?"

"I have the ability to do things with my mind. Just like you have an ability."

"What are you talking about?" His whole demeanor changed when she hinted at his shifting. He wasn't quite ready to talk about it.

"The fact that you could go again." She smiled up at him, her muscles tightening against his already hardening member.

"Oh, that." He grinned. "I can't get the image of you in

the lacey underwear waiting for me out of my head. I loved it and found it very arousing."

"I hope so, that was the point." She shifted her hips. Her eyes closed when he pulled out to drive back in again.

"You feel so good."

"You do too, Storm." She brushed his hair out of his eyes.

He watched her. "Our marriage. Is it a good one?"

"The best." She placed her hand on his heart. "You're a little overprotective at times, but you are kind, considerate, and very loving."

"Do we fight?"

"Of course. What couple doesn't? But we never stay mad for long and never go to bed angry with each other. We have far better things to do than hold a grudge."

"Like this?" He pulled out and thrust back in again.

"God, yes."

"Come back to my cabin with me." He withdrew and filled her again.

"Oh, now you're not fighting fair." She locked her legs around his waist and tightened her muscles again, creating a vise-like sheath that surrounded him. "But two can play that game. Here no one would ever find us. We could do this all day, undisturbed."

"I am highly tempted, but there is snow coming and we'd be safer in my cabin." He set a pace then. One that had them forgetting about their conversation.

Heather felt her need fill her, causing her breath to hitch when he hit just the right spot. Her mate, her heart. No matter what, the magic between them was still there. The memory would come.

NINE

"Come home with me." He touched her face, still pressing her into the air mattress.

"You're being a bit persistent." Heather hadn't had a chance to check her phone yet. Storm had handed it to her earlier, but they had been a little too busy for her to look. She reached behind her and snagged the device so she could check it. Storm took advantage of her movements by pressing a kiss between her breasts as she arched back.

"I just know that wherever we are when the snow starts, we'll be trapped there." He gave her some room so she could sit up and look at her phone. "They're expecting three to four feet and that will come into the cave. At my place, we can look at it from the inside where it is warm and cozy. I also have that great big bed we could take advantage of."

She laughed. "Not one-sided at all." She glanced at the screen of her phone and saw an all-clear from Cim. "If I say no?"

"I'll throw you over my shoulder and carry you there?" He said it as a joke, but she knew he would if she forced him. Storm stood and offered her his hand.

"You have done that before." She took his hand and stood then looked around the cave. "What do we do with all this stuff?"

"It should be easy to carry with the two of us." He pulled the plug on the bed to allow it to deflate. "You going to bring your bike?"

Heather hadn't thought about it. She heard the chime of her phone and looked at the screen. "Sure. We could probably prop some of the heavier items on it and move it to your place."

"We could ride it if your saddlebags aren't too full."

"I only grabbed what I knew I couldn't leave behind. All of that will fit in the backpack you brought from Mike. All it really had in it was food and water and most of that is gone."

"Good. If I can get the bed small enough, we can get it in one side that will leave the other for the sheets and whatever we can fit in it as well as the backpack."

Heather nodded, dressed in her bike suit, and went outside to get her bike. She brought it in a few minutes later. Storm had dressed as well. It didn't take her long before she had transferred the few items she had in the bike to the backpack. She slipped the blanket, and the pillow Mike gave her into one of the saddlebags before she folded up the sheets and blankets Storm brought and put them in the same bag as well. The half-empty backpack leaned against the wall, waiting for whatever else they decided needed to go.

Storm had deflated the bed and rolled it up as tight as he could. He stuffed it into one of the bags but couldn't close the lid. Heather stepped up to the bike and pressed a button, the lid slid into place and closed. He added a few more items that could fit into the other saddle bag. The rest barely fit into the backpack and Heather wasn't sure if she could get the zipper closed, but with a little force she closed it up and slung it over one shoulder. Storm doused the fire then spread the coals so it could go out quickly.

Heather handed him the backpack and climbed on. Her helmet hung from the handlebars, and she debated on whether or not she should put it on. It would give her total protection, but what about Storm? "Here. You should wear this."

"Why?" Storm swung a leg over the bike and settled in behind her. His voice, right next to her ear, sent little frissons of desire down her spine.

"I know you and I want to make it in one piece." Heather wondered if this was a smart idea. Walking would take longer but at least they'd arrive safely. If Storm tried to take advantage of the fact she had her hands full while she steered the bike they might not.

"What do you mean by that?" He wrapped one arm around her waist and pressed his front against her back. Storm let the helmet hang from his free hand.

"This much touching affects you." She started the engine, wondering if she should take the helmet back. If she put it on, she could seal her suit and keep him at bay, but did she want to do that?

"Let's go," he said, ignoring her words. He hooked the helmet on the back of the bike. "My place isn't that far."

Heather let out a breath, hoping Storm would behave himself, then took off. The moment the bike started to move Storm tightened his hold on her. With the other hand, he directed her to the path that went up toward his cabin. It challenged a lot of bikes, but hers had no trouble with the steep terrain. Her hair blew back and right into Storm's face. She felt the heat of his fingers moving her hair to one side so it was out of his face. Just the simple touch made her breath hitch, and he must have heard it. His fingers brushed her throat, moving any stray hairs, before she felt the heat of his mouth on her mark. The bike swerved as she got lost in her desire for a moment. She had to get a grip. "Hey, don't distract the driver here."

"Having a problem focusing?" He lathed the spot where her mark lay hidden.

"Just a little." She felt the brush of his tongue against her throat down to her core.

"Hmmm." He sucked on the soft tissue, and she knew he was going to try hard to break her focus. Keeping the one arm around her waist he spoke into her ear. "Follow this path for about a mile, then you'll come to a fork. Go right and it will take you right up to the cabin."

His other hand started wandering, moving from her hair to skim along the front of her suit until he found the edge of her jacket. As long as the helmet wasn't connected to the suit, it was programmed to remain in two pieces so she would fit in this timeline. Now she wasn't so sure that was the right move. Heather sucked in her breath again when his hand slipped beneath her waistband and inched downward. The heat of his hand sliding down her abdomen spiked her need.

"Storm." If he kept this up, she was going to have problems getting them to their destination. She was already having issues keeping the bike straight and he was just starting to explore.

His mouth went back to her mark. His teeth scraped against the sensitive skin before he sucked it into his mouth once again. Heather closed her eyes at the wonderful sensation.

Even though it couldn't be seen, and he had no idea what it was, he knew it was a spot that got her hot. His fingers continued to inch lower until they found her mound. He caressed her moist heat several times then slid in. The bike swerved before she realized she wasn't focusing on the bike again.

Oh God, she was in trouble. His caresses sent desire racing through her. Her blood filled with need. He took his time with her, his fingers set a slow pace, delving inside her then pulling out to slide around her core and dive back in again. His other hand worked its way up inside her jacket. Finding one of her breasts, he rubbed the tips of his fingers against the nipple then caught it between two fingers only to repeat the action again and again. The double assault made her forget about the bike once more until she felt it swerve again. She wanted to beg him to stop and beg him to continue.

"Please tell me it's close." Her voice was soft, her body pliant. Part of her wanted to stop and let him continue with his assault. Another part wanted to get to the cabin so she could show him just what his touch did to her.

He took a deep breath and grinned against her throat. "Oh, yes, it's close now."

She knew he meant her orgasm, not the cottage. His keen sense of smell told him she was close. Her breath caught when he fluttered his fingers inside her, hitting that spot that caused her most powerful climaxes. Everything inside clenched. Just as she hit her release and feared she'd lose control of the bike she saw the cabin. Taking her hands off the gas, she coasted into the area where he parked his truck. Heather couldn't move. Waves and waves of euphoria filled her. Her muscles tightened against his fingers as her climax had her seeing stars.

"Feeling boneless?" His voice was filled with need.

She could only nod.

He picked her up and carried her into his place, kicking the door shut before carrying her up to the loft area where he slept. Laying her on the bed, he eased her suit off her before he removed his clothing and climbed into bed with her.

"I have never seen a woman as beautiful as you when you're climaxing." He touched her face tenderly. "I want to see that face all the time."

"And you've worked hard at that." She smiled up at him.

"Talking about hard." He lowered his lips to her mark, drawing the delicate skin into his mouth for a moment, then pushed back up to gaze at her. "You had your release, which excited me so much you're going to have to do that again. You up to it?"

"Oh, I think so." Her fingers brushed against his mark, causing him to growl.

"How is that so sensitive when you touch it?" He sank his weight into her. "Others have touched it, and nothing happened."

"I have the magic touch." She slid a leg over one of his, urging him to fill her as quickly as possible.

"You sure do. Before you arrived, I never wanted to get involved with any of the women who were interested in me, but I can't seem to get enough of you."

"Not one?" She still found it hard to believe that he didn't have sex the entire time he was there. Two years? With his libido? How did he do it?

"Guess I was waiting for you." He surged into her, drawing a moan from them both. "God, you feel so good."

"So do you." Her eyes closed as he filled her. No matter how many times they were intimate she always wanted it. She grinned. He had created a monster.

"What are you smiling about?" He touched her face as he slid out then drove back in again.

"You once said you created a sexual monster in me, and I

have to agree." She shifted under him to give him a better angle. "I never grow tired of our intimacy."

"As often as we've made love, I'm surprised neither of us has ended up in a hospital."

"We have very strong libidos, Storm. We have been teased about it repeatedly. When I first met you, I learned you did put a few women in the emergency room. They couldn't keep up with you, where I can." She felt one particular stroke that made her shake.

"I'm happy to hear that because I seem to want you all the time." He found the right angle that caused her to shake and set a pace that brought a smile to her face as her body hummed in joy. "And you seem to be satisfied with our time together."

Her smile widened. "Very much. You always know what I need and push to make sure I am always satisfied."

"Let's see if I can continue my streak."

"I love it when you strive for perfection. I'm always on the winning side of that." A shudder raced through her when he stroked her sensitive spot. Her muscles reacted to it, drawing a moan from Storm.

Their focus moved from their conversation to what they were feeling. Storm's mouth captured her lips, drawing her tongue to dance with his. He continued to thrust into her. Each stroke brought her closer and closer to her orgasm.

Heather felt it deep inside.

Storm broke the kiss then worked his way down her throat to her mark. When his lips closed around it she sucked in her breath and arched against him. She was so close. It built slowly, deep inside her. Starting in the center of her core, she felt the flame of her release course through her veins. It filled her with a wonderful heat that wrapped her in a warmth that melted her body to ashes.

Just as she started to come back from her release she felt

Storm's, pulling her with him as he danced among the stars. It was wonderful.

Storm touched her face. "Wow."

"I know. Every time is glorious and makes me boneless."

———

Heather woke to the smell of coffee. Climbing out of bed, she expected Storm to greet her but was met with silence instead. She found one of his flannel shirts draped on the bed. Her bike suit was nowhere to be seen. It looked like he wanted her to wear his shirt. She smiled as she pulled it on while she descended the stairs from his loft. Pulling the material to her nose she took a deep breath and smiled. It smelled like him. A coffee cup had been placed next to the brewer with a note.

> Had to go to Mike's. Cream in frig. Sugar in the bowl. Be back soon.
> Storm

She had time to herself. The first thing she did after making her coffee was look for Cim. Storm had set it on the coffee table. Bringing her full cup with her, she crossed to the couch and sat down. Heather picked up her phone. "Morning, Cim."

"Good morning, Heather. Storm left about an hour ago. He didn't take his vehicle but decided to shift and run there. I estimate he'll be back in two hours."

"I thought he couldn't control his shifts."

"We both know he can, but he doesn't realize it. The chemical Ialog gave him did mess with his ability, but only for a day or two. Bert confirmed that. He seems to shift easily when he isn't thinking about it, and he has figured that out. That is why he runs."

"Running?" She thought about it. "It does empty your mind. He must get lost in the run and the shift takes over. Wonder how he handles the fact that he shifts back to human when he wants."

"That would be a question for your mate."

"You're right." Heather looked around. "You said he'd be gone about two hours?"

"Yes."

"That should give me enough time to get you to scan something."

"What?"

"Me." She set her cup down. "I have an ancient inside me."

"I'm not sure I understand."

"While you were with Storm scanning this cabin for anything Ialog could have planted, I did a little exploring near the cave. The white wolf I had met before came to me and turned out to be a shapeshifter. She talked about the future and how important Storm and I are to that future, then handed me a necklace. Once I had it on, she climbed inside it and the necklace sank into my skin like those medical scanners Kuarto gave Storm and me when I was pregnant. She said it would help her come to our timeline. The woman asked me to trust her, and I kept the necklace, but I don't know anything about her, and I was hoping you had something in your files."

"Just remove the necklace so I can scan it without interference from you."

"I don't know how."

"The scanners your brother created were modeled after ancient designs. How did you remove his?"

"Kuarto had a device he used."

"I see. He probably didn't know the regular way to remove them. Feel along where the chain is under your skin, you should be able to feel a slight rise. That is the point of extraction."

Heather did as instructed. "Okay, I have it. Now what?"

"Pinch it and it should raise to the surface so you can remove it."

She smiled as she pulled the chain off and placed it on the face of Cim's design. "Can you tell who this is?"

"The necklace belonged to Dianurosili. She was the one assigned to your family, keeping to the background, awaiting your birth. Bert already knew you would be sent from Vespia at an early age, and she was to be your guardian."

"How did she get trapped here?" Heather ran her fingers over the intricate designs on the necklace the ancient went into. It warmed with her touch.

"Unknown. Bert will be happy to know she is still alive though."

"Why?"

"He bonded with her."

"You mean she is his mate?"

"Yes. Understand as time went by females in the ancient race were very rare. To every six males, there was a female born. The women normally took more than one bondmate to help keep the race alive. It is where the sexual attitude of the Vespians came from. Bert is her primary bondmate."

"Why didn't you tell me about her when we first spoke to Bert, and he mentioned each of the families had an ancient follow them?"

"Someone blocked that part of my files. I cannot tell you who was assigned to watch Storm's family, but if that ancient were to join us their file would become unblocked. I can only access part of her file right now, but once she speaks with Bert, I should be able to access all of it."

"So someone built this into you?"

"I don't know. Bert noticed he couldn't access certain files when he tried to find out why my system kept blocking him. Until the person who programmed me to hide this information comes and unlocks my files, I have no answer."

"Can we bring this ancient forward?"

"If you wear the necklace, yes."

Heather sighed. She had only met two other ancients before this. She had a fifty-fifty shot that this woman was good. "What can you tell me about her?"

"If you are asking if she is more like Bert than Ialog, yes. She was the one who stood behind Bert when no one believed in his visions. She created me and programmed me to wait for you. She is trustworthy."

"Then she should be the one who will free your blocked files." She touched the face of the jeweled locket before she slipped the necklace back on and waited for it to sink into her skin again. Heather trusted Cim.

"Yes, if she is the one who made these changes in my programming. Being my creator doesn't mean she blocked the data. It could have been someone else."

"How many ancients are there?"

"I don't have an answer for that."

"Is that information blocked as well?"

"I assume so since I can't access it."

So she had to wait to see if the woman in her necklace held the answers to her questions. No need to pester Cim when he couldn't give her the info she needed. "Now what am I to do while I wait for Storm to get back?"

"He has several books that might interest you and satellite if you wish to watch television."

"I'll go for the television." She found the remote in a

small organizer draped over the arm of the couch. When she turned it on the TV was already on a news channel. "Let's see if there has been anything exciting going on."

Pulling her legs up under her, she made herself comfortable on the couch. Coffee in hand she took a sip from it as the weatherman confirmed the heavy snowfall that was coming.

"I would have been fine in the cave."

"If you were alone, yes. I could have put up a forcefield to keep the snow out, but if Storm had stayed with you, there would have been snow drifts inside it. This storm has very strong winds and will blow the snow right into the mouth of the cave. I wouldn't have been able to stop the snow without revealing myself."

"Whose side are you on anyway?"

"I am designed to keep you protected."

"I have that with Storm, and he does a very good job." The air was cool with just the shirt on. Heather grabbed a throw lying across the back of the couch and covered her legs. Resting her head on the arm she relaxed and watched the news.

———

Storm let Mike know he'd be at his cabin and probably wouldn't be back until the roads were cleared after the snowstorm. The news people were predicting a big one. They didn't talk about Heather, but Mike had a few more things ready for her so he had to assume she was at Storm's cabin. He didn't say a word as he picked up the few items Mike had for Heather, whatever he could fit in his backpack, and then ran back to his place. The snow that threatened started to fall. Big fluffy flakes stuck to his fur. He didn't care. Heather was waiting for him.

By the time he could see the door to his cabin, the snow was already sticking to the ground. He wondered how Heather would react to this shape. There were times when he wanted to shift and could, would he be able to maintain this form long enough to see how she could handle this part of him? Lifting his snout, he grabbed the pack with his teeth and pulled it off his back. The Velcro fastening he put on it for this reason came in handy now. He propped it with his mouth as best as he could against the wall and went through the large dog door he had installed.

Heather was curled up on the couch, a cup of coffee in her hand. She sat up when she spotted him. A smile on her face showed no fear. "Hello."

That wasn't the reaction he expected. What should he do now? He tilted his head at her and sat back on his haunches.

She patted the couch cushion next to her. Didn't she know he was a wild animal? Or did she know the truth about him? She was his wife. Was his shifting something he had been able to do for a long time? There was only one way to find out, but he wasn't sure if he could shift in front of her. Or if he wanted to. What if he was wrong and she ran off screaming? He didn't want to take that chance.

He climbed up on the couch beside her and was greeted with her fingers in his fur.

"Good boy." She settled down and continued to watch the news.

He rested his nose in his paws, wondering what he should do next. Heather had her legs tucked up under her but he could still rest his head on a thigh without looking like too much of a threat. So he inched toward her, watching for any sign that she didn't want him that close, but she totally ignored him. The only thing she did was rest her hand on his head when he placed it on her leg. She kept her hand there as she sipped her coffee. Then she patted him as she slid her legs to the floor.

Storm didn't miss the opportunity to sniff her core.

"Hey, now. We'll have none of that." She pushed his nose away. Heather got up and walked to his coffeepot. The shirt he left for her swam on her, yet he found it very sexy, but she could wear a burlap sack and he would still find her sexy. The front and back of the shirt hit her close to the knees. The sides rose nice and high as she stretched. Taking the pot, she filled her cup up and added what she wanted to sweeten the drink.

He had followed her to the counter and when she turned around, she bumped right into him. It would be so easy to stuff his snout under the shirt. It took a lot of control not to follow through with his thoughts.

"Back up, big boy." She moved around him and went to where she had been curled up before. Her phone dinged and after she picked it up and read whatever text she had received, she wrapped the throw around her and went to the door. She opened it and smiled. Snow was falling heavily, turning everything white.

"I have missed this." She stood there, watching. A sigh escaped her. "You know you should go look for Storm before he can't get back here. This stuff is sticking, and the roads are going to be treacherous. He needs to get back soon."

Storm looked at his truck sitting in front of them. Why would she think the wolf in front of her would know where he was? Unless she knew his secret.

"Oh, and when you find him, ask him to put my bike in the bed of his truck. The snow will hide it beautifully."

He looked up at her. She knew. She had hinted at it before, and he had cut her off. He huffed and ran out the door.

"Good boy." She stood there, watching the snow fall for a minute more before she closed the door.

He shifted and pulled his clothes on. After putting her bike in the bed of his truck and throwing a tarp over it, he grabbed the backpack and stomped into the house. "How long have you known?"

"Within a month after you shifted for the first time." She took another sip of her coffee. Her lovely violet eyes watching him.

"Why didn't you tell me?"

"I tried, but you shut me down so I figured you weren't ready to talk about it."

"What am I?"

"A shapeshifter. You can shift into any shape, but you shift into a wolf most. It's a comfortable form for you."

"Why?"

"You have to get your memory back before I can answer that."

"If I had my memory back, I wouldn't have to ask, would I?" He growled.

"No." She stood. "I don't understand why you haven't gotten your memory back either. I thought it would have returned by now."

"And this?" He opened his shirt to expose his mark. "I thought it was a tattoo until you touched it. I react every time. Other people have touched it and nothing happened. Why you?"

"That is your mark." She touched the side of her neck. "I have one just like it. Mine is just hidden from view."

"That is why your neck is so sensitive. You called it a mark. What do you mean by that?" He was close enough now to reach out and touch her throat.

"It proves we belong together." A flush filled her cheeks as he stroked the area where her mark was.

His touch on it excited her. He could smell it, but what she said made him frown. It sounded like she was holding back. "Having a mark that causes a reaction when touched by your wife but no one else doesn't sound very human."

"Neither does shapeshifting." She watched him, stepping back so he couldn't continue to caress her throat.

What was she getting at? They weren't human? He had never felt like he belonged here, was that why? Asking her would just frustrate him. Storm knew what she would say. It was her fallback answer every time. He dropped the backpack on the couch.

She stood there in his shirt, waiting for a comeback.

"You are very frustrating at times."

"I know." Those big violet eyes held laughter.

"And you think it's funny." He stepped toward her.

"I do." She stepped back.

"Why?" He stepped toward her again.

"Because I always frustrate you. In more ways than one." She smiled as she stepped back once more.

He wanted to wipe that smile from her face, and he knew one way that worked every time. He stopped moving when he realized that was a memory. Then just as quickly it was gone. He growled his frustration.

"Problem?" She clasped her hands behind her back, pulling the shirt against her. The top button had come undone. He counted, only five more to go and he would be able to see all the creamy flesh hidden from view.

"I remembered something then it floated away." He realized as he prayed for another button to come undone that was what he wanted too. It didn't matter if she kept things from him. Heather shared her body with him, giving all of herself every time. It showed him that she cared and that she was only trying to protect him. Deep down he knew he would have done the same thing.

"What did you remember?"

"How to remove the knowing little smile on your face." He stepped toward her again.

"And how would you do that?" She stepped back, this time she edged herself around the couch.

"By kissing you until you're breathless." He realized he was stalking her, but she didn't seem to mind.

"It has worked in the past."

He tried to draw her into his arms and managed to knock another two buttons loose, but that was all he accomplished. Now he had to watch as her breasts played peek-a-boo with him as she moved. Every time he stepped toward her, she smiled and stepped back. Pretty soon she would be backed up against the wall. What would she do then? She said it was his favorite position.

"Then I'm going to kiss my way down your body until I get a moan."

"That has happened before too." She moved to the right just a little bit. The little minx was heading toward the stairs. "But first you have to catch me."

"I do, don't I?" He noticed the minute changes in her stance. The moment she took off so did he. His long legs closed the distance between them quickly. She surprised him when she snuck around him. Storm turned around and looked at her. "You're quick."

"Have to be in my line of work." She put her hands on her hips, opening the shirt enough for him to see the gentle slope of her breasts. "You're normally faster."

"Probably, but you know what I should do. Perhaps, my mind isn't quite working the way you expect it."

"True." Mischief danced in her eyes as she looked pointedly at his jeans. "You normally don't remain dressed this long when you have a certain goal in mind either."

"I flaunt myself?"

"No, but you don't consider nudity that big a thing. You feel very natural in the buff."

"And you?" He could tell she chose her words carefully.

"A bit shy, but not with you."

"Then why don't you take that shirt off?"

"Not 'til you do. I only have one piece of clothing where you have at least two." She gave him a sultry smile. "In the past, you have always taken advantage of me undressing. It seems to be in your DNA so I'm not taking any chances."

"Okay." He pulled his shirt off. "Now we're even."

"You going commando under those jeans?"

"I find underwear uncomfortable." He made a grimace at the memory of how they felt on him. He wore them when he had to but went without as often as possible. "So I was right. We are even."

She just smiled. "Not quite but it will work for now."

"Does that mean you're going to take off your shirt?"

"Jeans first." She stepped up one of the steps to his loft.

"Why?"

"Because I know you." She went up one more.

He stood there with his hands on his hips, then he shrugged and removed his pants. As he straightened, he saw the shirt he lent her float through the air, the sleeves fluttering. Heather was nowhere to be seen. He bounded up the stairs and found her lying on the bed.

"What took you so long?" She lay on her side, her head resting on her arms. She looked like she had been waiting for him for a while. How he wished he had his camera. The image before him was breathtaking.

"Don't move." He couldn't help himself. The bag his camera was in was at the foot of the bed where he dropped it the last time he used it. He came back with it in his hands.

"I don't want my picture taken."

"This is for me, I promise. It's just that you are very

photogenic, and I can't pass this up." He had the camera up and shooting before she could say anything else. She sighed and laid her head back down for a few of his shots, but when he continued to take pictures, she sat up with the sheet wrapped around her.

"You done yet?"

Her words hit him. What was he doing? She was there in his bed, waiting for him and he wanted to take her picture.

"I'm sorry." He set the camera on his nightstand and climbed onto the bed with her. "Sometimes the camera takes over. How do you want me to make it up to you?"

"I get to choose?" Excitement danced in her eyes.

He nodded, taking her into his arms. Her excitement sparked his. What did she have in mind?

Heather touched his face, gently sliding her fingers along his jaw. "I believe you mentioned a hot tub?"

"I did." He smiled. He had built it on the second-floor deck then closed it in with glass. They'd be able to watch the snow fall as they made love. "Right through those doors."

She climbed off the opposite side of the bed. Heather dashed toward the doors. Her laughter floated behind her.

Storm jumped off the bed and ran after her. He skidded to a stop in front of the tub just in time to see her step into the hot water. Once it hit her hips, she turned to look at him. "You just going to stand there?"

"You going to stand still long enough for me to touch you?"

"Promise." She smiled that beautiful smile of hers.

He sat on the edge of the tub, swung his legs around, and dropped into the warm liquid. Heather stood there waiting. An image floated into his head of Heather with much shorter hair sitting in a hot tub just like this. Her face flushed, her eyes half closed like she was close to a climax. "Did you have short hair at one time?"

"Yes. I kept it short because of my job, but when I stopped working that job you asked me to grow it out." She touched her hair, smoothing it down.

"I do like it longer." He stepped up to her and touched her hair as well.

"Why did you ask me about my hair?"

"I saw you, in a hot tub like this, with short hair."

A slight blush filled her cheeks. "Oh. That was when we first met."

"You're embarrassed by it?"

"No." She touched his heart. "I just remember what happened while we were utilizing it. We were interrupted that first time, and you weren't happy."

"Did I make up for that?"

"Oh yes." She looked up at him with those violet eyes that let him see into her soul.

Storm wrapped his arms around her and pulled her close. Her softness felt so right against him. He lowered his head and claimed her mouth with his. Each time he touched her, he felt a connection with her deep inside. He just wished he could remember their life together.

Her mouth opened for him, allowing him to deepen the kiss. His hands roamed her body, delighting in the way his touches caused little goosebumps on her skin. Urging her backward, he worked them to the seat in the tub and eased her down. He moved his mouth to her cheek then down her throat to the spot he knew aroused her.

The beat of her heart increased as her excitement grew. "Please Storm, now."

"You need to be patient, my heart." He slid his fingers into her folds and was gifted with her intake of breath. Slipping two fingers into her heat he then pulled them out and circled those fingers around her core. He did that several times before he felt her hands on his chest.

She gave him a gentle push. He looked at her as she stood and continued to move him until he was seated. Before he could react, she climbed on him and slid down his shaft, her legs spread wide because of the back of the tub. The intimate contact brought a sigh from her. "That's what I wanted."

"Have you always been this dominating?" He wrapped his arms around her. Her heat surrounded him, making him wish for a nearby wall or bed so he could pound into her.

"No, but I have a very good teacher." She brushed her hair out of her face. "You have never complained when I took control before."

"Oh, I'm not complaining, just surprised." He rubbed his hands up and down her back. "You like this position, don't you?"

"Yes, why?"

"I have noticed you normally use this one when you take control. The night in your apartment after that accident you had me sit up."

She blushed.

"I embarrassed you again." He touched her face with gentle fingers.

"No. It's not like I don't like what you're saying, but I can't help the blushes. You have found them endearing in the past." She shook her head as she tightened her muscles against him. "Now I think we're talking too much when we can be doing something so much more rewarding."

"You have a one-track mind."

"So do you when it comes to sex." She set a nice slow pace. "I might need a little help with my knees so wide."

"I know just what to do." His hand slid down her stomach to her mound. The moment he touched her core she shuddered and sucked in her breath.

"Storm."

"Not what you had in mind? Sorry. I guess I have a one-track mind, too."

Heather laughed. Her muscles rippled against him. "You always have."

"You didn't let me enjoy you the way I wanted to. I have a feeling it's that way a lot. So I'm improvising to get my way." He kept his one arm around her to use a brace as his mouth lowered to her mark and was greeted with a moan. "That's what I hoped to hear."

———

Heather felt like melting. Storm knew her body so well that even without his memory he knew just where to touch her to get the responses he wanted. "Storm."

"Your reaction to my touch is so real, so genuine that I want to see it every time we make love."

Hearing him use the phrase 'making love' sounded so strange to her. But he had thought he was human. She'd love to know how he accomplished that since he spoke of doctors and hinted that he stayed in a hospital when he was first found. They should have picked up his unique DNA the moment they ran his blood work. His fingers worked their magic, drawing her closer and closer to her orgasm and making her forget her train of thought. Her muscles contracted around him, making him shake with need.

He slid off the bench onto his knees, bringing her with him. "Can you brace yourself on the sides?" he asked, his voice husky.

"Yes." He maneuvered her to the opposite side of the tub so she could get her grip. When she was ready, he set the pace. Long deep strokes that left her panting. He still kept an arm around her waist to give her support and his other hand still stroked her core. Each time he filled her he brushed the spot that created the stronger orgasms. Oh God, if he kept it up she was going to give him the scream he always strived for.

She felt her release building in her. Each time he filled her she inched a little closer. Excitement filled her. Muscles contracted. Her heart beat faster. Then it started, at her core, spreading out throughout her system, filling her with euphoria. Heather floated along her climax, caught in the aftershocks of her orgasm. Her body shook once again when Storm hit his release seconds after hers.

Storm lifted her into his arms and brought her to the edge of the tub.

"Wow." She reached up and touched his face. Joy filled her.

"Boneless again?"

She nodded.

"Stay put." He climbed out of the tub.

She watched as he gathered towels for them to dry with.

"Ready to move?"

"I think so." He offered her a hand and pulled her out of the tub. He wrapped a huge towel around her then took one himself to dry off with.

Heather turned to look out the glass walls he had surrounding the tub but the steam from the water blocked her view. Oh well, it was supposed to snow for a while, hopefully, she would get to spend a little time watching.

"You okay?" Storm had come up behind her.

"Yes." She turned and smiled. "Was just hoping to see the snowfall."

He gave her a heart-melting smile of his own. "Give me a few minutes."

Now what was he up to? She felt another section of their mind connect. She wasn't sure what they gained back. Each time it took a little bit of time before she realized what they had regained. He came back in with a huge robe, which he slipped over her shoulders. He had a blanket wrapped around him and two cups of coffee in his hands.

"You first."

"Where are we going?"

"The porch." He pointed to the door he wanted her to take. "There's no heat out there, however, I did get the storm windows up a couple weeks ago. It might be a little cold but at least we'll be dry."

She opened the door and held it for him. The snow fell softly outside. Heather took one of the cups then turned to watch the snow. Storm came up behind her and wrapped his arms around her, inclosing her in the blanket with him. A sigh escaped her, and she leaned back against his chest. Snow was the one thing she missed on Vespia.

"What is Vespia?" asked Storm, his voice soft.

Did she say that out loud?

"You must have since I heard you."

You can hear me?

"Heather."

She turned to face him. This way he would have to know she wasn't moving her lips. *I'm serious. I told you before we used to be able to share our thoughts. Each time we've been intimate some of those connections have regrown. You're answering comments I was only thinking.*

"This is crazy." He dropped his arms and stepped back.

No, it's not. Tell me, have you been feeling my orgasms or not?

But I'm not supposed to be able to hear your thoughts. It only happens in science fiction. She felt walls going up to block her out. Storm feared something he had always enjoyed.

You have for years and enjoyed the added intimacy. We don't share all the time, only when we want to.

So you can stop this at any time?

"Yes." She smiled at him, hoping to relax him. His fear

was palpable. Pushing this wasn't smart right now. "I will keep my thoughts to myself, but if you contact me mentally, I will answer." Heather turned back to the snow. "I love this."

"Is Vespia where we're from?"

So he wasn't so frightened by what happened that he wanted to walk away. That was a good sign. "Yes. We've lived there for several years."

"Is it an island I never heard of?"

How was she going to answer that one? She never lied to him before, but he had a problem with their mindmeld and wasn't comfortable with the thought of shapeshifting. How would he handle learning he was from another planet?

"Never mind. I can feel your hesitation and since you backed off the mind thing, I'll back off this. I'm not sure I'm ready to hear your answer anyway." He wrapped his arms around her again.

"I love you, Storm." She leaned back against him. "You're my heart and we'll work our way through this."

TEN

The next morning Storm watched as Heather took a sip of her coffee. This mind thing had him wondering how safe it was and if he could share his innermost thoughts with Heather the way she said they had in the past. It made him wonder if bringing her here was the right decision.

She looked at him as he watched her. A frown creased her forehead. He wondered what she was thinking.

Heather had kept her promise and stayed out of his head, but the damage was done. He worried that she had planted all those memories in his mind, so he'd believe she was his wife. With her abilities, it would have been easy. What did he know about her? She stepped in when Mike needed it. Bert seemed to trust her too. When that video came out, she didn't act like some scared lost woman or try to use her newly acquired friends but went into hiding. She wanted to put distance between herself and them. Storm was so confused. He was the one who went looking for her, but could she have put that thought in his head?

"Look, if you don't want me to read your mind you have

to stop telegraphing your thoughts." She stood. "And thanks for the vote of confidence. If you don't trust me then it's time for me to go. Where's my suit?"

"What?" Her words shocked him. Once again, she wasn't acting the way he thought she might. She wasn't begging him to give her a second chance. Heather was pissed.

"I don't think I'm speaking a foreign language. Where's my suit? I'm leaving."

He wasn't ready for her to leave. There were far too many unanswered questions.

Before he could say anything else he heard another voice. "Heather, Ialog has triangulated on my signal. He knows where you are."

"Crap! I thought we were safe. Cim, where is my uniform?" She ignored Storm as she went to her phone. "How much time do I have?"

"Bottom of his closet. Two feet back and on the right." The voice hesitated for a moment. "He'll be here in less than five minutes."

She was talking to her phone like it was a person.

"Thank you."

"You're welcome."

And it was answering her. Phones didn't do that.

She dashed to the closet and pulled her outfit out. Unfolding the suit, she climbed into it and sealed it. She looked at him with sadness. "I have to go."

Before he could respond his front door opened. Storm watched as the color drained from her face. Yet she kept her back straight, refusing to show her fear.

"Ialog."

"I knew you two couldn't stay away from each other. All I had to do was wait. Storm might not remember you, Heather, but that didn't stop you, did it?" He looked at

Storm and smiled. "You couldn't stay away from him and that was what I hoped for."

How the hell did Al know where he lived?

"He's my mate, Ialog. Whether you like it or not we belong together."

"Oh Heather, I had such high hopes for you. You are better than him." He gestured toward Storm. "If you didn't allow your hormones to control you, you'd see the truth of it too."

He was confirming everything Heather said. Storm went to move but found he couldn't. His voice wasn't working either. What the hell was going on?

"You are talking about my mate." She crossed her arms over her chest. "Insult him again and you will regret it."

"Really?" He laughed as he held out his hand and showed her a small cylinder. "Considering I can control him with this little device I'd recommend you behave, or I could cause harm to him you wouldn't like."

Storm strained against whatever was holding him, but he couldn't break it. He looked at Heather, wishing he had listened better.

"Storm, you have to remember." She pleaded with him as she focused her gaze on him. "We have run out of time."

"He'll do you no good now." Ialog walked up to Storm and slapped him. As much as Storm wanted to retaliate, he couldn't. "See? He can't move and won't be able to until several minutes after we leave. If you come with me nicely, I will leave him alone. Fight me and he'll pay."

Heather looked at Al, sadness filling her eyes again. "Why do you keep trying this, Ialog?"

"So, I have tried several times before?"

Heather glared at him. "I'm not falling for it. You know you have. When are you from? You knew to drug Storm to keep him from me."

"So where is your mark?" He pointed to Storm's bare chest, ignoring her questions. "It is obvious he has his."

"What mark?" She gave him a confused look.

Storm wasn't sure what she was trying to do. Was she trying to pretend she didn't know him? After what she had already said? He didn't believe her and knew Al wouldn't either.

"I see we're going to play that game." Al studied her for a moment. "I see the mark is still there just hidden. Let me fix that." Storm watched in amazement as a tattoo just like his shimmered into view on the side of her neck. "I also see you have had your twins."

Twins? What he saw was a memory, not a fantasy?

"You will not harm Storm." Heather stepped to where she shielded him from Ialog with her body.

She was defending him when it should have been the other way around. He felt a little part of his memory click into place. He had gone up against this man before. Now he knew he should have trusted her. If he had they might have gotten away before Al arrived. Storm wanted to kick himself.

"Then you'll come along peacefully. Good." He stepped to the side so she would be walking in front of him. "But I do need to add something to your outfit first."

"What?"

"This." He slapped a piece of metal to the back of her neck as she passed him. "It will keep you from running once I have you away from your mate."

He called them mates. Storm felt the truth of the words. This man kept trying to separate them but had never been successful. Right? That part of his memory was still evading him.

Storm, I'm sorry I am breaking my promise, but you have to listen to me. You have to remember. You need to save me from this madman, and you can only do that with your memories. I need to push your mind and it might cause you pain, but you can't show any reaction to it if it does.

This man knows you, us. We've had run-ins with him before, haven't we?

He has been after me for a while. He has plans for me I don't want. I only want to be with you. Every time he has tried to separate us you have defeated him, and he hates you for it. He felt her love for him fill him as they shared thoughts. *You need to do it again, my heart.*

He felt a strange sensation enter his mind. It started like a whisper filling his brain, then expanded. Pressure took over. It felt like a bomb exploded in his head. Whatever Al used to lock him in place helped him keep his feet. His head pounded. Heather gave him one last look that held such compassion then she turned and headed to the door, Al right behind her. He couldn't do anything but watch as Al followed Heather out the door and into the snow.

"Goodbye, Storm. I hope I never see you again." He laughed as he shut the door behind him.

Storm wanted to follow but his body wouldn't listen. Pain kept him from fighting whatever was holding him in place. His brain felt like it was on fire. If he could move he would have grabbed his head. It took a few minutes, but he found he could finally move his arms. A few minutes later he was able to move a leg and crumpled to the floor. So much information overpowered him. Images flooded his mind. Pictures and scenes of his life with Heather, their children, his life as a child and young adult, his family and friends all raced through his mind. He screamed at the pain as he pressed his fists against his temples. Slowly the pressure dissipated. He found he didn't need to keep his hands against his head. As he started to regain control of his body, he forced himself to sit up.

"Heather." His mate and his life. He looked up at the door. She freed his mind and kept him safe. Now she was with Ialog. Would they ever be free of the man? Why did he keep coming after Heather? Storm knew he had to rescue her. He needed a plan. Cim. She had been talking to Cim? How was that possible? The computer was from their future. "Cim?"

"Yes, Storm."

"How are you here? We're in the early twenty-first century of Earth."

"Bert modified me so I could accompany Heather on her quest to find you."

"Can you contact Bert?"

"Of course."

"I mean the one here in this timeline? Tell him I remember, and I need his help." He stood. "I also need to talk to Mike, but with the snow still falling I doubt if the roads have been cleared."

"You could shift or use Heather's bike."

"The bike? It would get me there faster than running." He dressed, slipped the phone into his pocket, and headed outside. Dropping the tailgate, he pulled the bike out from under the snow-covered tarp. "Bert designed this too?"

"Yes. It looks conventional but is a temporal travel device. You and Heather are to return on this. There is also a suit for you in the saddlebags. The travel back will be harder than the travel here. The suits are designed to withstand it."

"Heather only had one helmet."

"Bert built the other helmet into the bike."

Storm looked around. There, near the handlebars was the perfect hiding place. Disguised as part of the gas tank, no one would notice the slight hand indentation to pull it free if they didn't know where to look. "Why did he want Heather to wait until I regained my memory?"

"He never went into detail, just said you had to regain your memory before she could return with you."

Storm ran his fingers through his hair. Could it have something to do with Al? Bert was here, maybe he had already lived this and feared if she hadn't waited, she might have changed the timeline. "Have you gotten an answer back from the Bert who lives here?"

"Not yet, but I do know his location."

"What about Heather's?"

"Ialog hasn't left this timeline yet so I can track him the way he tracked me."

"Doesn't she have her chip?" He had a special locator chip inserted into her after the last time Ialog had taken her. This one couldn't be detected by ancient technology. At least not the technology Ialog used. Storm smiled. He had his mate lojacked.

"None of your technology works here. The time travel cuts off the power source. The handheld that holds me, the bike, and the suits were designed for travel. They have a lock on your timeline but draw power from this one."

"Set the GPS." He grinned. He had been here a little too long. He used to give Heather a hard time about her Earth phrases, but he wouldn't be able to do that anymore. Cim brought up the three-dimensional map for Storm to follow. Storm climbed on the back of the bike and took off. "Keep a lock on Heather's whereabouts. We need to get her back. Cim, if Ialog leaves this timeline before I can retrieve her will you be able to track them?"

"I will be able to tell you the timeline they travel to, but not where."

"It's a start." He headed down the mountain as fast as the bike and safety allowed.

———

Heather hoped the push worked, but there was no way to be sure unless Storm's mind reached out to hers. It was too early for her to try to reach for his. The power that flowed from her when she tried to free his mind startled her. She touched her chest where the medallion lay hidden. A burst of energy came from it when she used her abilities to force the block on Storm's memories to fall apart. Ialog hadn't detected it, or if he did, he didn't think anything about it. She was surprised he didn't feel the mental wave she focused on Storm. As powerful as it was, he should have.

They had transported to a small building in a heavily wooded area. She opened her mind enough to see if there was anyone nearby. Nothing. They were miles from any town. Oh, this was what she wanted, being stuck in another secluded area with this madman.

"So where are we?" She looked around. It felt familiar, but she didn't know why, she didn't recognize anything. The bracket on her neck didn't seem to dampen her mind. Maybe he didn't know what she was capable of yet. That would work in her favor. She needed to test the limits of the device in case what she just did was a fluke, and it didn't detect it.

"Some place safe."

That didn't tell her a whole lot. She had learned not to say too much to this man. Since he didn't know when she came from, he shouldn't know the outcome of their last meeting. He had to be from somewhere around the time when he kidnapped her while she was pregnant. He knew about the twins. Yet had to scan her to prove they were already born. So he must have suspected she was wearing something to hide her pregnancy.

A small rock sat on the floor of the cabin. Something that probably got caught in a shoe. Focusing on it, she watched it float up about eye level before she allowed it to touch back down on the ground. The device in her neck controlled her physically, but not her mind. What happened earlier wasn't a fluke. Now, could she reach Storm? Would he even answer? Had she given the push enough time to work? Did it work? Heather rubbed her forehead. So many questions she wanted answers to.

I am here, my heart, and I remember.

She smiled and her heart soared. He was back. *My heart.*

Where are you?

I don't know. It's a small cabin in the woods. Other than that, I haven't seen or heard anything that lets me know where I am. Hang on, Ialog suspects something. She glared at him. "What?"

"What are you up to?"

"Please, you have this stupid thing on my neck." She pointed to her nape. "You have control over me. I can't run away. What could I possibly be up to?"

"That is the question, isn't it?" He watched her.

All she could do was smile.

———

Storm didn't like Heather's silence. He wished she'd let him know everything was okay. He pulled up in front of Bert's home and knocked on the door.

"Mountain Man? What are you doing here?" Bert looked surprised to see him.

"An ancient named Ialog has kidnapped my mate." He didn't have time to explain everything so hoped Bert would fill in the blanks himself.

"You remember." Bert stepped aside to let Storm in, but he didn't seem surprised.

He nodded as he entered Bert's home. This was the first time he had been to the man's place. He could tell he had more advanced technology than what was available with a glance. "I see you brought a little bit of home with you."

Bert grinned. He gestured for Storm to sit. "I have to have my creature comforts, but it harms no one. So Ialog is here?"

"He's the man who came to see me about once a month looking for Heather."

"The one you complained about." He looked at Storm as he put the pieces of the puzzle together. "The one who was looking for the woman in the pictures he kept showing you. It was Heather?"

"Yes. He annoyed the hell out of me." Storm ran his fingers through his hair. "I'm not sure how he figured out Heather was here. I never told him she had showed up after I met her, and she always stayed out of sight. I know Mike never said anything. He cares for her too much."

"Is there anyone else who might have told him?"

Storm frowned. He tried to think about who didn't want Heather around. "The only person I can think of is Princess. She kept hitting on me, even after I told her to leave me alone, and wasn't happy when I showed Heather the attention she craved."

"You think that little girl is capable of this?" Bert was shocked. "I know you kept trying to get her to leave you alone to a point where I had to run interference from time to time, but I never saw her as a vengeful person. In fact, I was able to easily distract her when I made her my main focus. I thought she only saw you as a way to get into modeling."

"I know it sounds crazy, but she did have motive and I saw her following Heather one time. I scared her off, but what might have happened if I hadn't?" Storm shrugged. "I can't think of anyone else."

"There is only one way to find out. You need to go talk to her."

———

Storm didn't want to waste his time talking to Princess, yet here he stood, outside her door, wishing he was on his way to free his mate instead. He banged on it and waited.

She opened it, smiling when she saw him. "You came!"

He found her comment odd. Was she expecting him? Why? "I am not here for you. I only came to ask you a question."

"What?" she asked, her voice hopeful.

"Did you tell Al about Heather?"

"Heather? You came here to ask me about her? What is it about that woman?" She gripped the door, frowning. "I told her to stay away from you, but she wouldn't listen. Every time I saw her you were close by. Why? She wasn't that pretty, or smart, or rich, yet you couldn't seem to stay away from her. When Al showed me that picture of her, I saw a way to get you back and he seemed almost giddy when I told him that she had shown up and you had been lusting after her."

"How long has he known?" He wanted to strangle her. This woman's jealousy was the reason his mate was now in trouble.

"I don't know a couple of days? He spoke to me at the diner a few times and came by here just before Heather had her accident. He flashed some picture of a person I didn't recognize but as we talked, he described her. I knew this was a chance to get her out of our way." She looked up at him. "She isn't right for you."

"How do you know about the accident?" Thought of wrapping his fingers around her throat filled his mind. One little squeeze might make him feel better.

"I, ah, saw the video. It's been all over the news."

"I saw that video. They never showed her face on the

news. It was the version Al had that showed her face. So did he show it to you?"

"Oh." She didn't look at him. "Um, I guess. Look, he said she was wanted by the police. I knew she was bad for you, so I did my duty."

"Your duty?" It took all his concentration not to grab her by the throat. "You worked with her. She took over your tables when you didn't want to do them and still gave you the money. Did that seem like a malicious person? Did you ever ask why she was wanted?"

"No." Megan fidgeted, keeping her gaze downcast.

Something wasn't right. Her knowledge of the video bothered him, so he kept after her. "So how did you know about the video?"

"Like you said. The man showed it to me."

"Or did you take it?" It was the way she refused to look at him that had him asking the last question. It would make perfect sense. "What do you know, Megan?"

"He told me if we could separate you two, we could both get what we want. You'd be mine and Heather would be his. He gave me this weird little gadget." She pointed into the house. "Said if I waited for her to go by on her bike and aimed it at some rocks above the road, she'd take a spill."

Storm growled. "There were no rocks on the road when she had her accident."

"My aim wasn't that good. I hit the deer instead and poof, she was out in the road. Heather still took a spill. I thought everything would go according to plan." She shifted her weight against the door she clung to.

"What plan, Megan?"

"Al said she'd be sent to the hospital after getting banged up. I was to meet you in the emergency room and console you, but she never made it there. I watched her drive away with Bo then waited for hours near the emergency entrance after shooting that footage. She was supposed to show up. I found out later she stayed at Mike's instead and had you all to herself. Al called a day or two later and said there was a change of plans and he'd call me." She sighed. "Haven't heard from him since."

"You still have the thing he gave you?" He wanted to growl his frustration.

"Yes."

"Get it." His voice came out as a command.

"Why?" She looked frightened.

"Because if you don't, I'll call the police and tell them what you did. The man has kidnapped my wife. How do you think that would look on your record while you're still on parole?"

"Wife?" Megan paled at his words. "He never told me that. Just said he needed her for something."

"Yes, Megan, my wife. She came here to help me remember our life together and bring me home." He used his height to intimidate. "And I want the item he gave you. Now!"

She blanched and left the door to return a few minutes later with the object in her hand. Megan held it out. "Here. I haven't been able to get it to work on anything else."

"Thank you, Megan." He turned to go.

"I'm sorry."

Storm turned back.

"I didn't know he was going to kidnap her if things didn't work out for him. He said she was dangerous, that she needed to be locked up. I was only trying to protect you."

"You knew I didn't want to be with you, yet you persisted. I'm sorry, Megan. I'm not buying it. If he does something to harm Heather, I will be coming after you."

Storm returned to Bert's place and handed the device to him. "Ever seen it?"

"Sure. We have used these things to cultivate with." He turned it over in his hands a few times before he placed it on the table. "It's a farming tool. Plants, cultivates, removes debris in the way. That kind of thing. This is what he gave her?"

"Yes, it seems that Ialog found another purpose for it. He gave it to her to make a rockslide. Thank God Princess couldn't aim. Heather could have really been hurt if Megan knew what she was doing." Storm growled his frustration. "Why doesn't he give up?"

"He made Heather for a reason, and it seems he still wants to implement that plan. He never told any of us what he created her for. We all just assumed he wanted her as a companion in the beginning. It wasn't until he started manipulating DNA to get a certain sequence that we realized he had other plans."

"And you stopped him." Storm picked up the little handheld farm tool. "I know Heather and I wouldn't be here if it weren't for him, but you could have put an end to this a long time ago. How are we so important that you allowed him to cause all this trouble?"

"Because of my vision. We knew he would create you and Heather, but it would be thousands of years later. If we didn't put him in stasis, you two never would have been born."

"So, you don't think we would have been born without him?"

"You wouldn't be the people you are now, and you have to be just as you are to fulfill my vision."

"You keep saying we're the hope of the future, why?" Storm put down the tool.

"What have I told you before?"

"You smile at me and say I know. I'm now assuming you have told me in another timeline and just don't want to reveal the information too soon."

"Hmmm. That is the problem with time travel. It is hard to know what timeline is the right one to reveal information. Understand I am going by my vision. What I have seen. When Ialog was creating Heather the first time I saw that version in a dream. She was like Heather in certain ways but this one obeyed his every word. You ended up mated to another woman. Another off-worlder. As my vision continued, I saw your world die. The first Heather didn't care about the people or the planet.

"Then I had a second vision, again while I was sleeping. One with your Heather in it. It was so beautiful. She was surrounded by children. Hundreds of them. Teaching them some sort of exercise. Laughing as the children ran and gave her a group hug."

"That sounds like my mate. She always has time for the children that approach her."

"That was how my abilities came about. At first, I saw her in dreams. Bits and pieces of her life with you, before she met you, run-ins with Ialog. I started writing them down in a journal. Every time I have one, I put it in my journal."

"Then you are still having those visions." When Bert remained quiet, he knew he wouldn't get an answer so he decided to change the subject. "How long ago did you make those books for us?"

"Books?"

"Never mind." Maybe Bert hadn't made them yet, even though he and Heather had thought they were thousands of years old.

"You found them then?" Bert studied Storm.

"Yes. Two. One for Heather and one for me." Was Bert fishing for information?

"I see." He didn't say much more. He stood and walked to his office. He came back with two books in his hands. "Are these the two?"

Storm looked at them. The color and size were different from the ones he knew. "No. The ones we found came from the computer under the elder's chamber. What are these?"

"Ask me when you see me again. I promise I'll answer you then. Those other books I wrote just before we placed Ialog in the stasis chamber. One of my visions showed you two finding them. I just didn't know when. It's good to know you found them. Can I assume you are trying to control the abilities I have outlined for you?" He placed the new books on a nearby table but made sure they were out of Storm's reach.

"Yes. Although I wish you had spelled out what my abilities were in the book. It would have helped me adjust faster."

"Sorry. When I wrote that one, I hadn't actually seen your shifting ability. Only saw Heather's mental strength through the run-ins with Ialog." He crossed back to the table and sat down. "Now, how do you plan on getting Heather back?"

"I don't know. First, I need to know where she is." Storm focused his thoughts to Heather. *My heart, can you hear me?*

Yes. He didn't try to block my thoughts. Not sure if he doesn't think my mind has developed that much or if he knows it won't work anymore.

Has he said or done anything to make you think he broke the mindwipe?

I don't know what to think right now. If he has come from our future, we'll never get away from him.

He knew pushing her would only frustrate her. *You will figure it out, my heart. Do you know where you are?*

No clue, although it does seem familiar. I really haven't seen that much other than this small building I'm in.

Can you let me in? Let me get a whiff of where you are? I might recognize the area by scent. Storm felt the unique brush of Heather's consciousness against his as they switched minds. He settled into her body then blinked and looked around. Ialog was nowhere to be seen. Heather was strapped to a chair. He closed her eyes and inhaled deeply. He knew where he was. *You can come back, my heart.*

You know where I am?

Yes, and I'm coming to free you.

He looked at Bert and smiled. "You have a map of this area?"

"That was amazing. You two do that all the time?"

"Enough." Storm watched as Bert stared at him. "The map?"

"Right." Bert got up and went to his bookcase. It took him a few minutes, but he found what he was looking for and pulled it out. "It's a couple of years old but should still do the job."

Storm opened the atlas and flipped to the back to look at the state of Washington. He pointed to a small reserve. The same place where Ialog had her in the future. "I need all the data you can get. I need to know what type of technology this timeline would consider top of the line. It would also help to know what type of technology Ialog might have brought with him."

———

Bert gave Storm everything he had available. Anything he didn't have he put on a list for Storm. He'd have to get the rest on his own. Not wanting to change the timeline Bert remained at his place. Ialog didn't seem to know about any other ancients. If he learned about Burt inadvertently it could change things in their future. They might not have ever met Bert, and Heather wouldn't have had the means to bring him back. It opened up too many paradoxes they didn't want to deal with.

Cim sat in a pocket of his temporal suit, scanning for any anomalies as they traveled. Along with Cim, rested a hand-written note of things he needed to pick up to rescue his mate. Storm needed help getting everything on that list and he knew where to get it. He rode the bike to Mike's place, parking back by his house.

He climbed off the bike and pulled his helmet off. Turning to the parking lot, he rested his helmet back in the slot designed for it in the bike. The diner was jumping, which figured. It always seemed busy. He needed to speak to his friend without being seen.

Just as he tried to figure out a way to get his friend's attention discreetly, Mike came out the backdoor, wiping his hands on a towel. He raised a brow at Storm's temporal suit. "That's a new look for you."

"Not really. I've been wearing something like this for years." He smiled at his friend. "But I know what you mean."

"Did your memory come back?"

"Yes, but at a great cost." Storm needed his help. He hoped he would agree once he explained everything.

"Everything okay?"

"No. You remember that Homeland Security man who kept coming in? Al? Even though we didn't tell him Heather was here he figured out where she was and now has her. I need to get her back."

"I don't remember him showing us pictures of Heather.

Except for the diamond one and even then, it didn't really look like her. I just recognized the cat."

Storm knew better, but Heather could have used her mind to make people see someone else when shown a picture of her. She would protect herself in any way she could. "We didn't know her before so wouldn't have recognized her and I thought the last time we had done a good job pretending, but he must have seen through it."

Mike nodded. "So, what do you need?"

"I have a list." Storm handed him the sheet of paper with everything he needed to pull off the plan Bert and him set up. He just hoped it would work.

"This will take me a while." Mike checked over the list. "So do you remember everything now?"

"Yeah." Storm smiled as he crossed his arms over his chest. "She's my life, Mike, and we have been through a lot together, including children."

"She pretty much said the same thing about you." He walked across the worn dirt path to his house. "She called you her heart."

"Heather told you about us?"

"Yeah, but I didn't really give her a chance to act clueless. I could tell by the way she behaved around you there was something between you two. She did and said things that told me she knew you, yet she acted like she didn't. It didn't make sense."

"So, you confronted her."

"Had to. If she was here to try to take advantage of you, I was going to stop her. My Nancy would never forgive me if I didn't try to protect you after all you did for her."

"She would be very proud of you."

"And she would have loved Heather." He gave him a wistful smile as he climbed the stairs to his house. "Give me a few minutes and I'll see what I have on this list."

"Want me to help?" He stepped up two of the stairs.

"You can, but on one condition." Mike turned back to look at him.

"And what is that?"

"Let me come with you when you go to rescue her. I want to help."

"It would be too dangerous."

"Don't give me that. You need someone to work with you. There is no way you could pull this off on your own. I can see it in your eyes. You're so worried about her you just want to get there." Mike turned and headed inside. "You need someone with a level head."

"That sounds like something my wife would say."

"She is a very smart woman, after all, she did marry you."

Storm laughed. "There are times when she might disagree with you."

"All couples fight. That is part of being married." He pulled a few of the items Storm needed out of a closet. "It's how you make up that counts."

"Oh, we're very good at that."

Mike laughed. He studied the list for a second. "I'm not sure why you need batteries. Any particular size?"

"Nope. Just need about six of them."

Mike shrugged. "Some of this stuff doesn't make sense."

"Nevertheless, I need everything." He wasn't about to explain to Mike what he could build with the odd items or how it would stop Ialog from being able to travel back to this timeline ever again.

"We're going to have to go to the hardware store to get some of this stuff. I don't have magnets."

"That's fine. Give me what you do have, and I'll pick up the rest on my way."

"You're not going without me." Mike turned to glare at

him. "You're going to have to wait until I make sure I have enough coverage at the restaurant. You take off before I get back and I will hunt you down."

"I promise to wait for you, Mike." Storm wanted to laugh at his behavior. Like an overprotective brother.

Mike nodded. "I'll be as fast as I can."

Storm waited in the house and communicated with Heather. *Has he come back?*

Not yet. I'm not sure why he has disappeared. Be careful.

I'm at Mike's now. If he has gone back to the cabin to look for me, he won't find me.

If he's looking for you then he'll go to the diner to see if you're there once he knows you're not at your cabin.

I'll be ready. Heather?

Yes, my heart?

I love you.

My heart, you don't have to use such a human phrase.

But I want to. I now understand why you use it so much. I saw Mike with his wife before she died. They said it to each other every day and I saw it in action time after time. I knew I wanted what they had before I remembered I do with you.

I love you too, Storm. You are my heart.

He could feel her love for him fill his mind. It was beautiful.

Storm kept an eye on the window, more to watch for Mike's return, but was glad he was watching when Ialog showed up. Damn, Heather was right, he knew where to go. How? *You think he gave me some sort of implant so he would know where I was all the time?*

It is possible. Although he's never seen you as a threat, more of a nuisance.

Can you check?

She was quiet for a moment. *I can try.*

He felt her mind search his, it was a little different than

the way they communicated. It was like she was sliding all around him. Storm found it highly arousing.

Found it. Now we have to lead him away before I trick him and turn it off.

How do you want to do that?

Can you see any animals nearby? Something a wolf would chase? Once you put a few miles between you and Ialog I'll deactivate it.

But he'll know I can shift. Are you sure that is wise?

It's the only way. If you have other animals to chase, he might not think anything of it and believe the wolf, if he happens to see you, is just chasing its next meal. He shouldn't think you're the wolf unless you do something to give yourself away.

Storm went to the back of the house and found a family of deer nearby. Perfect.

———

Mike came back to his house to find it empty. He went out his back door and spotted Mountain Man's clothes in a neat pile near the steps. "Damn it."

"Worried about me?" asked Storm as he stepped out from behind a tree. He walked up and grabbed his garments.

"Decide to take a run?" He relaxed. Mike knew Storm well and had feared he had taken off without him. Seeing his clothes sitting there was a bit odd, but now he knew Storm decided to shift before he took off. His desire to bring Heather back was as strong as his desire to protect her, and Mike was happy to see he kept his promise to bring him with him.

"Needed to stretch my legs."

"Right." He waited until Storm dressed. "Your friend was in the restaurant."

"Asking for me?"

"Of course." He looked back at his house. "Is that why you took off? You knew he was here?"

"Yeah." Storm looked at the diner. "Did he leave?"

"Yeah, about ten minutes ago. I waited to make sure he was gone before I came back here."

"Then we should get going in case he decides to return."

———

They had everything on the list Bert gave Storm. The closer they got to where they believed Ialog took Heather the more uneasy Storm became. It was the compound Storm knew too well. This was the same place Ialog had taken Heather before. *Would* take Heather? Storm shook his head. He didn't need to worry about that right now. Although in the future, it was their past.

Mike stopped the truck at Storm's request. They gathered what they needed and headed toward the area where the compound would be.

No wonder Ialog was able to protect the borders with his advanced technology when Storm tried to rescue her in their timeline. He had set it up in the past before there were any rules against it. Knowing where the sentries started had him slowing his steps as he got close to them. Were they on? It would be best if he didn't take the chance.

"Mike, I need you to stay here." Storm opened the seal to his suit.

"You need me."

"This man has killed, and I don't trust him." He pulled his arms out then slid the suit down his legs. "If you try to cross here, I fear that could happen to you."

"What makes you think that?"

"Because he has used this compound in my past and had

his system set to kill anyone who tried to cross the parameter. I'm pretty sure he has already set that up as a safety precaution." Storm picked up the backpack that had his provisions and put it on. "He knows me a little too well. My wolf was able to slip through the last time. So I'm assuming he still has it set to allow wildlife in. You willing to take that chance?"

"I feel helpless out here."

"I'd rather you feel helpless and be alive than helpful and dead." Storm shifted. Mike adjusted the backpack he wore so it would sit right on his fur and Storm took off. Just like before, he paused when he hit the spot where he knew the sensors were. Making sure his shift would fool them, he trotted across the barrier. He sniffed the ground as he worked his way to the small building. Heather's scent was strong. It led him right to her. Ialog's was much weaker. Storm felt relief knowing he had beaten Ialog back to the compound. Now he had to get his mate out before the man returned.

He passed through a wooded area that he recognized. The pond was smaller, the trees surrounding them were still saplings, but he knew the spot. Memories of their intimacy here on the grass near the pond filled him. Such beautiful memories that made him hard for his mate and he was glad to have them back.

This was where he stopped long enough to shift back and slip the suit Heather had left for him back on. No need to let Ialog know he could shift if the man wasn't aware of it yet.

Storm wished he had his weapon. Going in defenseless went against his training. He inched toward the building. Unlike the large compound he had seen in the future there was only one building here. No one stood outside. There were no guards?

He reached the door and wondered if it was booby-trapped. There was only one way to find out. He pulled Cim out of a pocket in his suit. "Need your help, Cim. Can you detect any defensive mechanisms that might be guarding this place?"

"It is clear, Storm. I find nothing activated."

"Then Ialog has security set up."

"Yes, but only the outside system, he hasn't completed the system for this building yet. You should be safe to enter."

Pushing the door open, he paused. Nothing happened. Storm stepped in, moving cautiously toward his mate. Heather sat in a straight-back chair in the center of the room. That wasn't where she was when she allowed him to take over her body earlier. Ialog must have come back and moved her.

"My heart?" He moved to her side, kneeling down beside her he looked for restraints. "Ialog left you without any guards?"

He altered this thing on my neck again. I can't move or speak. With him believing you have no memory he didn't see a need to hire people to keep you away.

"I can't believe he underestimated me. That doesn't sound like him, but I can fix your lack of movement and speech." He pulled a weird contraption out of his backpack and pressed it against her neck. He watched as the indicator let him know when it freed Heather's motor reflexes. "Bert said this would deactivate the device on your neck."

"Crap."

"What? I free your voice box and the first thing you're going to say is crap?"

"He's coming. You have to hide."

ELEVEN

Storm looked around, but the small room was too sparse. There was a closet and he hoped there was enough room for his large frame. Just as he closed the door, Ialog walked into the room.

"Good of you to wait for me, my dear." He laughed as he pressed something on his wrist. "I forgot I made sure you couldn't scream for help. Is that better?"

"Let me go, Ialog."

The device on his wrist gave Ialog the ability to free parts of her when he wanted. Storm found that good to know. He just needed to find a way to get that away from him.

"Now, now, if you're going to start like that, I'll change the settings back."

"What is it about me that makes you want me so badly? Why won't you let me live my life the way I want to?"

"You can. Once I'm finished with what I need from you."

"I refuse to be a baby machine for you."

"Is that what you think I want from you?" He laughed again. "Don't be so crude."

"You want to make the perfect race."

"True, but not through you. Through your progeny. You see you will have the child that will be what I need to create the race I want. I just don't know which child it will be. So, in order to make sure you give birth to the right specimen I need to help you along."

"You plan on keeping me pregnant until you get the child? What if you're wrong?" Storm could hear the frustration in her voice. He peeked out the cracks in the door so he could see what was going on.

"I'm not. The computations have been run and the same answer keeps coming back."

"And how does Storm figure into this?"

"He doesn't. I have someone else in mind to father your children."

Storm wanted to know who. The thought of Ialog forcing her to be with another man had him seeing red.

"No one else will ever touch me."

"Heather. You don't need to worry about that. All I really need is your eggs." He moved about the room and out of Storm's limited view.

"You already tried that and learned only Storm's semen could inseminate my eggs."

He was surprised she offered that information, but Ialog took the bait and gave them enough to know he'd already had Sam's egg fertilized. So, what did he know? When was he from?

"True, but I have done more research and have found a way around that." Storm heard scraping. Was he getting ready to move Heather?

"You still need me to go along with all this and you should know my answer by now."

"I do, but I also know what will change your mind."

Storm heard another set of footsteps. These were smaller, with a shorter gate. He took a deep breath and felt ill. Sam.

Their daughter. Was he going to try to blackmail Heather with Sam?

"Have you two met? What am I saying, of course you have. You've had the twins, so you have already spent time with me at the compound I set up on Earth. The question is how did you get free?"

"What makes you think I escaped? You could have sent me back to stop you from making a mistake."

"True, but I'm sure I would have sent something to prove I sent you."

"Release me and I'll show you."

Storm grinned. That was his mate.

"Now, Heather, not in front of the child."

"So, you think using Sam as leverage will make me more compliant?" Storm could hear her anger. "Have you not learned from our previous encounters?"

"You do have a stubborn streak that surprises me, but I can work around that as well."

Storm heard him moving around. He crossed back into Storm's line of view.

"Sam, you have to get back to your lessons," Ialog said to their daughter.

"Yes, sir." Her voice sounded so young and innocent. Storm wanted to bang the door open and keep her from Ialog. His mate's hesitation kept him where he was. He trusted her, even as he questioned why she hadn't tried to stop Ialog.

Storm heard their daughter walk across the floor, her steps getting fainter as she exited the building. Did Ialog have a ship outside? It would explain how they were able to cross through the parameter without a scratch and how Sam came to be here.

"Now. You shall accompany us, Heather. I will release enough of your motor reflexes to get you on the ship."

"I'm not going with you, Ialog." The confidence in her voice made Storm smile.

"You don't really have a say."

"Yes, I do."

———

Heather waited until Sam was out of harm's way. Not knowing what Ialog would do to their daughter when she refused to go with him made her leery. She could feel Storm questioning her motives, but he let her handle this her way and she was grateful.

She focused on the remote, pulling it out of his grip easily and drawing it to her. Using her mind to press the right buttons she freed herself and stood. "There is nothing you can do that will make me go with you."

"I see your mind has expanded." He grinned with pride. He didn't seem too upset. Why? "But that is only the remote. The mainframe is on my ship, and you can't override that."

She didn't respond. What could she say to that? He thought his ship could control her. "So you have a ship that has a temporal drive?"

"Of course. You come along nicely I'll even think about bringing your mate along."

She felt Storm yelling in her head. He wanted her to run, but would it do any good? "You don't frighten me, Ialog. You know I'll never come along nicely. I will fight you with every breath. Why do you persist? Aren't you getting tired of the constant battle between us?"

He just smiled.

Heather knew she had to do something she had never tried before, but she didn't know if she had the energy to do it. *I need your help, my heart.*

What do you need from me?

Your strength and support. She focused her mind on Ialog. He had been in her mind, now she wanted to be in his. She needed to know the layout of the ship. See the control panel and temporal drive.

What are you planning?

Sending him home with no way to get back here.

I have a device that will stop his temporal drive from working. We just need to get it onto his ship.

Where is it?

Outside, hidden. I can show you in my mind.

The necklace she wore became warm again. Not as bad as before, but she could feel the entity inside helping her once more. Searching Ialog's memories, she found the information she needed to destroy the drive then pulled back out. It was her turn to smile.

The device Storm created was easy for her to lift and send onto the ship. Ialog still had the hatch open. Following the information her mate shared with her she placed it in a secluded spot, activating it.

Her focus then turned to Ialog's chest. Using a strong burst of thought she shoved him backward. When Storm realized what she was doing he helped by giving her as much of his mental power as she could take. Combining his with hers she made another short burst and got him out the door.

"What are you doing?" he shouted. The shocked look on his face made her feel good. He never thought she'd do something like this.

"Sending you back, Ialog." Heather kept a strong hold on Ialog so he couldn't escape as she walked to the doorway. The ship wasn't too far from the small building they were in. She kept using short bursts, pushing him back in the direction she wanted. He fought her, causing her to use more and more energy. Heather feared she'd run out before she could get him in the ship as she planned.

Her necklace heated up more. It felt like it was burning a hole in her chest as energy filled her mind. One last shove sent him flying into the ship. It took a little more energy to seal the door and reprogram the drive. She set it to send him and their daughter back to the time they left, making sure the added device was programmed properly so it would freeze the temporal drive and Ialog would be trapped in their timeline. The only way he'd be able to come back would be either to rebuild it or find another way to travel back. Heather would know right away. If he reappeared in front of her right after she sent him away, then he was able to repair it before she was able to use the prayer to stop him. If he didn't then what she did hopefully worked.

She dropped to the ground as the ship disappeared from sight.

Storm came out of the closet and crouched beside her. Touching her face, he checked to make sure she wasn't hurt. "My heart, are you okay?"

"Yeah." She touched the side of her head. The drain of pushing Ialog had her wanting to close her eyes and rest, but she knew there was no time for that. Taking a deep breath, she looked up at her mate and smiled.

"We need to get out of here before he can come back." He helped her to her feet and wrapped an arm around her waist. They headed toward the perimeter where Mike waited for them. They passed by the pond and Storm slowed them down. "Does this look familiar?"

"No." She spotted a few things she recognized. "Wait. Is this my sanctuary?"

Storm nodded. "I have some very fond memories of this place."

"We did have some wonderful times here, but I hated

this place and the way he kept me trapped." Heather looked around at the area. "Each time his schemes get more elaborate. I want him to stop."

"He only bothered us this time because of our time travel." Storm urged her to start walking again. "He is still powerless in our time because of that prayer my sister gave us."

"But how did he know we were back here? How did he know to look?"

"I wish I could answer that. Maybe Bert can." He paused for a moment. "May I ask you a question?"

Heather nodded.

"Why didn't you free Sam? You could have."

"I wanted to, but I would have changed our timeline. She was younger here than when I first met her. That told me Ialog hadn't captured me yet or if he had I had just become his guest. If I took Sam, I would have changed all of that. In our past, he knew my mind was powerful which is why he put that contraption on my forehead. It could have been because of what I just did. When I went to his compound this had already happened to him and he knew firsthand what I could do even though my mind hadn't gotten that strong when he took me." Heather's strength was coming back, and she was able to walk on her own. "Think about how much would have changed if I brought her home now, much younger than she was and over two years later?"

"She wouldn't have worked for Mason."

"She also wouldn't have met Skye, and we wouldn't have met Bert. My biggest concern right now is while I was his prisoner, I remember that he left me at that compound alone for several hours. Was he gone because he had found a way to come back here? Until we get back home, I will worry that he will try to stop us." She saw Mike in the distance. "Do we know if the sentry is set up?"

"Not really. I was in such a hurry to rescue you I shifted to be on the safe side. When I got to the building, I asked Cim if he had anything set up around the place and he confirmed that the perimeter was in place, but that was all." He couldn't ask Cim now. Not in front of Mike.

"So how am I supposed to cross?" She felt a warmth encompass her once again. Storm was talking, but she didn't catch what he said. Wrapped in the warmth, she felt a strange sensation when her viewpoint changed. She looked up at her mate. What just happened?

Storm looked at her in shock. "How did you do that?"

Heather found she couldn't talk. Did Ialog come back before they could get away? She looked down at her feet and found two white paws. She looked up at Storm in shock. White paws? Did the ancient she held in the necklace do this? The woman could shift. She saw her do it. Heather still felt like herself so knew the woman didn't take over her body so how did she do this?

"If you can hold that, try to cross through. Bert gave me something to use as well, but he did say it might cause you a little pain. You shouldn't feel anything as a wolf."

Heather nodded, walked back a few feet and ran for the perimeter. She passed through without any trouble. Storm had shifted and trotted through behind her. The moment she was on the other side she shifted back to her normal self.

Mike wrapped her in a big bear hug. "Glad to see you're okay."

"Thanks, Mike." She looked at Storm, who had shifted back and was pulling his uniform back on. She had changed back with her clothing on, so the ancient knew how to control that. Perhaps she could teach Storm how to do it as well. Fear that Ialog would just reappear in front of them had her shaking. "Can we go?"

They climbed into Mike's truck and headed back to the diner.

"Where's my bike?"

"At Mike's place. So are the helmets. You going to explain what happened back there?" Storm turned so he could look at her.

"I honestly don't know." She pulled the chain out from the back of her neck and showed him the locket. "I found this while I was at the cave. It seems to help me focus my energy, maybe it helped me borrow your ability to shift."

I know there is more to it than that.

And I will explain, but not in front of Mike. He already knows too much about us and that can be dangerous for him.

They rode the rest of the way to Mike's in silence. Heather rested her head on Storm's shoulder, meditating to recharge her mind. Those shoves took a lot out of her, and she was amazed she could move at all.

The bike and their helmets waited for them.

Heather gave a sigh of relief when she saw it.

"You were afraid it was gone?"

"Ialog had to know I came back on some sort of machine. If it had been taken, then I'd know he was back and trying a different tactic. He wouldn't have left us a way home." She walked up to the bike and flipped the switches to activate it. Reaching into the frame, she pulled out the second helmet and handed it to Storm.

"Neat trick," commented Mike.

"A friend of ours designed it." Heather looked at Mike. She hated racing off like this, but it had to be done. The sooner they were back in their timeline the better she would feel. "Thank you for all you've done, Mike. Taking Storm in when he had no one. I don't know how to repay you for that. Then allowing me to work for you when you knew nothing about me. Keeping our secrets. Being a good friend to us both."

"Mountain Man was there for me when I needed someone. I'm grateful for his friendship. I don't think I would have survived those first few months after Nancy's death." Mike hugged her. "Will I ever see you two again?"

"Honestly, I don't know." She looked at Storm and smiled. "This was a bit of an accident the first time. If we can come back, we will try."

"Take care of yourselves." He shook Storm's hand before pulling him in for a quick back pounding. Then he wrapped his arms around Heather, giving her a squeeze before he let go. "Get going. I know you need to get out of here before Al shows back up."

Heather knew she should wipe his mind so he wouldn't remember any of this, but she would also have to reach out to anyone they had touched while they were there. She didn't have the power to do it. Mike had kept Storm's secret and knew he would keep theirs. Ialog shouldn't be able to come back and cause trouble for Mike and she could make sure he was safe by making the Bert in this timeline aware.

"I'd like to leave a note for Bret. Do you have some paper and a pen?"

"Sure." Mike's brow crinkled a little, but he ran into the house to get what she needed.

"My heart?"

"I want to make sure Bert knows the secrets Mike has so he can help him if he needs it."

"You could remove the memories."

"I thought about that, but I'd have to push myself again to remove us from everyone we have had contact with. I'm not sure I can do that after using all my energy to push Ialog. Besides, Mike deserves better. You were there for him when his wife died. I don't know what removing you would do to him. I can't take that away."

Mike came back out and handed her paper, a pen, and an envelope. "I figured you don't want me to see what you're saying to Bret. Is he someone like you?"

Heather smiled. She didn't answer him as she wrote to Bert. Once she was done, she put it in the envelope and sealed it. "Can you mail it for me?"

"Sure." He looked at the envelope.

"Promise me you won't read it."

Mike sighed. "Okay."

Storm climbed on the bike and patted the front seat. He gave her a knowing smile before he put his helmet on. Heather grinned as she snapped hers into place. She slid in front of him and programmed the bike to head into the park.

She opened her mike. "You going to try to make me wreck again?"

"The last time was amazing." His hands slid around her waist. This time her suit was sealed so he couldn't just slip his hand inside. "It's nice to know you can't ignore my touch, even if we could have been harmed. I also learned that if you are otherwise occupied you can't stop me from taking advantage of arousing you. So many times you have stopped me because you needed more than foreplay. Now I know what to do to get my way."

"That is so evil."

"I have to level the playing field from time to time."

"You are incorrigible." She laughed. "We need to be far enough away where no one will be affected by the EMP."

"There is something I'd like to get from my cabin before we head back. Or do you think it isn't safe?"

"I don't think he's going to come back, but every minute we stay here keeps my nerves on edge." Heather steered the bike up the path to his cabin. It would be great to relax for a moment. She loved their time together there. Nothing to worry about. No family member interrupting them. Except Ialog. If he hadn't been there it would have been perfect. "What do you need?"

"The memory chip from my camera. I have some photos of you that I don't want to lose."

"They couldn't have been that good that you would want to bring them back."

"I have found I have an eye for beauty. Probably what attracted me to you in the first place. And some of these images rival anything I have of you."

"How did Bert decide to make you a photographer anyway?" She pulled up in front of his cabin.

"I have no clue." He climbed off the back. "I'm assuming he kept an eye on the timeline and knew what I would do before he met me. You coming in?"

"I know you too well, my heart." Heather shook her head. "If I go in with you, we might not come out for a while."

"Are we in a hurry to get back?" He pulled his helmet off and gave her a smile. That wonderfully bone-melting smile that made her want to do whatever he asked.

"I would feel safer at home. Seeing Ialog sort of shook me." Heather pulled off her helmet. Already the smile was making her forget her desire to leave. All she could remember was her desire for him.

"If he was here, we would know by now." He touched her face with soft fingers. "He can't stay away from you any more than I can."

"Bert did say if everything went right, we'd arrive within seconds of us leaving, so the children won't lose any time away from us that way, but I miss them." She found her feet moving toward the three steps that led to his cabin.

He grinned. "I promise to make it worth your while."

"You always do."

He took her hand and brought her inside. "The first thing that needs to go is your outfit."

"Shall I remove it?"

"You know better than that." He closed the door behind them. "That is my job."

"Yours needs to go too."

They undressed each other, caressing as they went. She loved the feel of his hands on her skin.

He lifted her in his arms and carried her up the stairs to his bed. Storm gently laid her on the bed before joining her. His mouth claimed hers as he touched all the right places to ignite the passion she had for him.

She felt her desire spike. "Storm."

"I love the scent you give off when you're aroused. It's intoxicating." He pressed his lips against her mark. "And the taste of you. I can't seem to get enough."

He drew the soft tissue of her mark into his mouth before his lips left a wet trail down to her breasts. When he drew a nipple into his mouth, she arched up against him. He slipped his arms under her to keep the angle that gave him complete access to her breasts and nibbled against the tip, making her squirm in his arms. Once Storm was finished with the one, he moved to the other. Heather found the hold he had her in kept her immobile, allowing him to take his time.

She needed more. Whether he read her thoughts or could smell her need, she wasn't sure, but he knew what she needed as one hand worked its way down to her mound, slipping into the folds and caressing her, heightening her want. The sucking motion on her breast paired with the gentle brush of his fingers against her core brought her swiftly to the brink.

"So close."

Storm kissed his way back up her body, sliding in deep just as she started to climax. Her body quaked and her release ebbed enough for him to bring her back from the edge as he set a fast pace. She clutched at him, her orgasm racing toward her once again. Heather met him thrust for thrust, wanting this so bad. A scream tore from her throat when it finally washed over her.

"That's my girl." Storm continued to pump into her. Her muscles tightened against him as her second orgasm started to build. He groaned as he slid in and out, her sheath exquisitely tight against him. His mouth found her mark, pushing her over the edge once more. Her world splintered around her, shattering reality for a moment. Euphoria filled her.

Storm continued to pound into her, his climax very close. She tilted her hips and she felt him shake as he soared through his. "Oh, my heart."

———

Storm touched her face tenderly. "More?"

"Now what kind of question is that?" Her words came out as a sigh.

He chuckled. When he first met her, she had been all business, no desire for intimacy. Now she was like him, could never get enough. "Not in a rush anymore, are you?"

"You have me trapped."

"Ha! You wouldn't leave if I was to move, and you know it." He started to nibble on her neck. "So you want to explain how you were able to shift?"

"I don't really know. You remember the white wolf who followed you around?" Heather sighed her response as desire started to fill her again. "I met her a few times. Once when you were there trying to protect me from her. She sort of befriended me. Watched her shift right in front of me. She knew Bert and Ialog so she has to be another ancient. I wanted to ask her, but she was worried about being detected in her human form."

"Another one?" He lifted his head and looked at her.

"I know it's like they are falling out of the woodwork all of a sudden." Heather wasn't sure if she was making any sense, but he wasn't fighting fair. His fingers continued to use feather-like caresses against her skin as she spoke. "She didn't say much, just told me Ialog trapped her here then gave me the necklace I showed you and entered it."

"She entered it? I don't see any necklace on you." He was right. It had sunk back into her skin. Heather reached behind her neck and slowly started to pull the chain and then medallion out. Storm wasn't sure if he liked the idea of it burying itself into her skin.

"You don't know anything about her and you're wearing it? How safe is that?" He hadn't stopped touching her, but his demeanor changed.

"I've had it on since the cave. She lent her power to me when I pushed your mind to free your memories, then when I pushed Ialog back into his ship and I'm assuming she lent her ability to me when I needed a way to cross the perimeters. If she wanted to harm us, she didn't need to do any of those things."

"And you think it is wise to take her back to our timeline?" He touched the medallion, still warm from being inside her.

"I don't think she can come out of the necklace without help now, or she would have done so already. The threat from Ialog is gone so I would assume she would have shown herself to you, especially if she wanted to convince you to bring her back to our timeline. Bert probably has to help her and if she is dangerous then he would make sure she stayed put so she can't cause any trouble."

"I'm not sure bringing her with us is a good idea."

She touched his face. "I'd like to give her the benefit of the doubt. She has helped me when I needed her, and I would feel awful if we were to leave her behind only to find out she is an ally and she needed our help."

"Must you wear it?" He still held the medallion and felt a calming warmth fill him.

"I think so. Besides your camera chip, it's the only thing we're bringing back that we didn't bring with us. Which reminds me, where is your uniform? The one you arrived in? That needs to go, too. We can't leave anything behind that could change the timeline we're from."

"Not sure I like the idea of her being inside you, but if you feel it is safe then we'll bring her forward with us." Storm laid the necklace back on her chest and watched as it sank beneath her skin once more. "My old uniform is in the closet. I'll get it before we leave. I have other things on my mind right now."

"Like being inside me? You don't like the idea of the necklace in my body, but you strive hard to fill me as often as possible." She tightened her muscles against him.

"Of course, but that is where I belong." He lowered his head to nibble on her mark once again. "And you can't deny that."

"Wouldn't dare." She turned her head so he could have better access. "You might try to cut me off."

"That would be detrimental to us both."

———

Bert watched as Heather faded from sight. If all went well, she should reappear at any moment. He smiled at the memory of meeting her for the first time. She was very straightforward with him yet revealed nothing. He had liked her instantly.

Storm had been a surprise. He knew the man was from the future because his temporal machine went crazy. He saw the timeline falling apart and he knew he had to do something quick. Grabbing a few items, he raced from his home to the site of the anomaly. Bert didn't expect it to be a man without his memories. When he met him, he didn't know who Storm was, but his physical features screamed Vespian. He found him in the hospital and the only thing Bert had on him was a blocker like the one Heather had in her body. Emergency was busy that day and an amnesia patient wasn't high on the treatment list so he was able to slip it into him before the doctors could run a lot of tests. He listed himself as an emergency contact and waited for the doctors to talk to him. He told them Storm was a nephew and he had heard about his situation on one of the police radios he loved to listen to and had realized his description sounded familiar.

The doctors couldn't find anything physically wrong with Storm, so he was released into Bert's care. Once he got Storm comfortable, he checked the timeline to see if the man was part of it. That's how he figured out he would be a photographer.

They spent several months in and out of the hospital, the doctors wanted to see why he had no memory and tried lots of things to free those memories. When he learned Al had been in the same timeline he wondered if the man had seen the same anomalies and by sheer luck, Bert got to Storm first. Al couldn't have known there were other ancients in this timeline. If he had he would have traveled back so he would be the first one to see Storm. He probably ran the same computations Bert did and saw the timeline hadn't changed so didn't think twice about how he got out of the hospital.

Bert took Storm under his wing and created a new life for him. In fact, helping Storm gave him his identity as well. They worked side by side for two years. It wasn't until Heather showed up that he realized Mountain Man was the catalyst. The mate of the woman he had been having visions of for years. He didn't remember what Storm looked like until Heather came looking for him.

It had to be some sort of protective thing in his mind. Storm was in so many of those visions he should have known who he was. Why there was a protective shield around his identity Bert didn't know, but it was probably for the best. He could have damaged everything if he had known the truth.

He hated what he had to put Heather and Storm through before they could return but knew Ialog could be quite resourceful. If he suspected Storm was getting help, he would have made sure he was the first person to find Storm. That would have changed everything.

The timeline couldn't be changed either. Heather had to try to get Storm's memory released. Ialog had to kidnap her once again. Nothing could change.

Storm had become his friend in the two years he was trapped in time, and he hated keeping him in the dark, but Bert did what was needed to protect them. But once he had given Storm the instructions to turn the damping device attached to Heather's neck off, Storm didn't come back and say something went wrong. They must have been successful.

The shimmering effect started one second after she winked out of sight. It took time, but he could make out the bike and two figures. Perfect. The stream that flowed through the chamber he programmed to receive them filled in as they slowly rejoined their proper timeline. He waited until they had solidified before telling them to stay put until he gave them the all-clear.

The first thing he did was run a scan on the timeline and was happy he found no abnormalities, then Bert did the same with them. He frowned when he got a blip from Heather and Storm. The scan showed a foreign object on them.

"Something wrong?" Storm asked, noticing his frown.

"I'm getting an odd reading from you two." He stepped close to the chamber so he could run the handheld scanner over Heather and located the source. "What are you wearing around your neck?"

"A necklace." She reached behind her and pulled the chain out of her skin. Once she had the whole thing free of her body, she held it out to Bert. "While I was back there, I ran into a woman who could shape-shift like Storm. She was a bit frantic when she gave me this so didn't really tell me much except Ialog trapped her back in the early twenty-first century and she was happy to know I knew you. Never got her name but I think she is an ancient. She is inside the necklace. I wasn't sure if I should bring her forward but couldn't leave her behind after all she did for me."

Bert recognized the necklace.

"And you, Storm? What did you bring forward?"

"A memory chip from my camera." He pulled it out and handed it over.

Making sure there was nothing else causing the odd readings, he had Heather drop the necklace into a special container as he allowed them to exit the time chamber next to his temporal computer. The memory chip he didn't worry about. He knew what it was the moment he saw it and assumed Storm wanted to keep the pictures he had taken of Heather.

"It can't be." He ran all the proper tests then touched the necklace with great reverence. He had wondered what happened to her. To know she was trapped in a timeline he had been in made him want to slap himself. He should have detected her. "What did she do for you, Heather?"

"She helped me defeat Ialog and bring back Storm's memory. I don't think I could have done it without her."

Placing the medallion on one of his computer surfaces, he ran a series of scans to find the trigger to open it. Once he found it, he picked the necklace up and pressed the proper sequence to release the woman he had called his mate. He smiled as the essence of the woman he had known all his life coalesced in front of him. "Dian!"

"Bert!" She touched her arms, waist and legs before she ran to hug him. "You figured it out. Thank goodness. I feared I'd be trapped in that thing forever."

"How did you end up inside that in the first place?" He brushed a piece of hair out of her face. She was finally back in his life and now he was no longer alone. Joy shot through him.

"Pure luck." She pointed to Heather and Storm. "I happened to be in the right place when the catalyst arrived. I saw you with him and how you set everything up to protect him until his mate showed up."

"Why didn't you let me know you were there?"

"I couldn't tell anyone. Ialog trapped me there. He would have learned you were there too and as far as I could tell he wasn't aware there were any other ancients other than he and I. It was the only way to keep you safe."

"How did you know Storm was the catalyst? I never guessed who he was until Heather arrived."

She looked at him oddly. "You showed me a picture of him."

Bert didn't remember a picture. He was finding there

was a lot he didn't remember.

"You don't remember do you?" She touched the side of his head. "You were the one chosen to follow the banned family to keep them safe. All of us were worried that your visions were too important for you to do that. Looking back, you were right to go."

"I'm not sure I understand." Memories that had been blocked began to fill his head.

"When it was time for you to go, I locked some of the information away to keep you safe. If you remembered everything it might have made you leave the family you were to protect too early. We knew the visions would keep coming and knew how important they were to the survival of all the worlds so I didn't want to block those but had to work with you so that when you had them you wouldn't question why you were having them. I even urged you to write them down like you did when you first started getting them. Our goal was to be sure they became a reality. It was your plan and I see it worked."

All kinds of data flooded his mind. It all made sense now.

"After you went with the banned family, we continued to search for the reason why we have our zero population. As time went on several of our people went out into space, following leads. The rest of us blended into the societies of different worlds. When the woman of your visions was born, I volunteered to be her guardian. I wanted to protect her for you. Ialog must have known what the elders were up to because he was on Earth when Heather was sent there, waiting for me. He used time against me, sending me back to Earth's early technology and trapping me where I couldn't help her."

"You were supposed to be there for me?" asked Heather.

"Yes, my child." She turned toward Heather. "My goal

was to show up as an aunt so I could raise you. Prepare you for the life you were born to live. It is Ialog's fault there was no one there to watch over you and I am sorry about that. Although from what I can see everything worked out the way it was supposed to." She smiled at Heather. "I never thought I would make it back until I saw Heather looking for her mate. I knew she would be the one to help me."

"I remember when you made this." Bert lifted up the necklace. "How did you know you would need to hide inside of it?"

"I didn't. When I created this, it was to help me continue to work without resting. I could rest part of my consciousness inside as I worked so I would never tire. I didn't know if it would hold me until I tried with Heather and then didn't know if I could be released until you were able to bring me out."

"I'm glad to have you back." He took her hand in his, lifted it to his mouth, and kissed the back.

"It's good to be back, but there is more." She touched his chest. "First I must ask, where is Ialog?"

"Heather erased his memory."

"Have you been keeping track of him?" She looked at Heather and Storm.

"Yes, why?" Heather didn't like this. She had done a good job of wiping his memory. What did this woman know?

"Because he wasn't working alone."

"What are you talking about?" asked Storm.

"Are you sure?" asked Bert. "They disappeared eons ago."

"Well, they're back. And they're coming."

THE END

Don't miss out on your next favorite book!

———

THANK YOU FOR READING

———

Did you enjoy this book?

We invite you to leave a review at your favorite book site, such as Goodreads, Amazon, Barnes & Noble, etc.

DID YOU KNOW THAT LEAVING A REVIEW...

- Helps other readers find books they may enjoy.
- Gives you a chance to let your voice be heard.
- Gives authors recognition for their hard work.
- Doesn't have to be long. A sentence or two about why you liked the book will do.

ABOUT THE AUTHOR

Writing for Barbara Donlon Bradley started innocently enough, like most she kept diaries, journals, and wrote an occasional letter but she also had a vivid imagination and wrote scenes and short stories adding characters to her favorite shows and comic books.

As time went on, she found the passion for writing to be a strong drive for her. Humor is also very strong in her life. No matter how hard she tries to write something deep and dark, it will never happen. That humor bleeds into her writing. Since she can't beat it, she has learned to use it to her advantage.

Now she lives in Tidewater Virginia with a cat who thinks he owns everything, her husband and daughter.

www.barbaradonlonbradley.com

ALSO BY BARBARA DONLON BRADLEY

Novels
Love Is…

A Portrait in Time

Love on the Run

Love's Quest Series
A Quest For Love

Magical Quest

Desire Series
Dominated by Desire

Passionate Desire

Animal Desire

Unwanted Desire

Hesitant Desire

Forgotten Desire